RAISED BY WOLVES

UNDERDOGS 8

Geonn Cannon

Supposed Crimes LLC • Matthews, North Carolina

www.supposedcrimes.com

This book is typeset in Goudy Old Style.

PROLOGUE

DALE FRYE was in the middle of a lovely dream involving Anne Hathaway and a motorcycle when "Wolf Like Me" by TV on the Radio broke through and brought her back into reality. She was reaching for the phone before she was even fully aware of what was happening. The light from the screen made her squeeze her eyes shut, and she jabbed the answer button without reading the screen. Only one person called at this time of night, and that person would be calling from a payphone or unknown number anyway.

"Anne Hathaway," she said. "On a bike. Tight jeans, leather jacket. She was about to toss me a helmet so I could climb on the back."

"Oh shit," Ariadne Willow said. "Should I let you go back to sleep?"

Dale was already sitting up. "No, I'd never get back to it. You have to owe me, though."

"Consider me indebted. I'm at a Shell station on Government Way. It's on the east side of Discovery Park."

She had pulled her jeans on over the underwear she'd worn to bed. "Damn, that's far."

"There's a bus stop nearby. I can..."

"No, it's not about that," Dale said. "Are you okay?"

Ari sighed, and Dale could hear the weariness creep into her voice. "I'm tired."

"I'm coming, puppy. I'll be there soon. I love you."

"I love you, too."

She put on a jacket over her sleep shirt and got a bottle of water out of the fridge since Ari was usually parched after a long run. When she left their basement apartment, she saw that the lights in the upstairs portion of the house were off, which meant their landlord/neighbor was asleep. She found the address of the Shell station where Ari was waiting, entered it into her GPS, and left her headlights off until she was out of the driveway so they wouldn't sweep across the house.

When she first started working with Ari, getting up in the middle of the night to retrieve her after a run had been a huge trial. At some point over the past decade, her body seemed to have adjusted to the new demands, and she found sleeping straight through until dawn to be almost impossible. She liked going out at night and exploring the city when most of its residents were fast asleep. It wasn't deserted by any stretch of the imagination; she'd grown up in Pennsylvania where she knew what a truly closed-down town looked like. But for a big city, Seattle did get relatively quiet once the clock ticked over to midnight.

Her route took her through downtown, its glass towers reflecting streetlights that glowed serenely in the darkness. The city was quiet and calm at night. Now that Ari's transformations didn't hurt her as badly as they used to, there was no real need for her to play chauffeur. But Dale enjoyed the drives so much by this point that she would miss them if she had to stop, so Ari still called her if the wolf took her too far away from home and she didn't feel like going all the way back on foot.

The shining part of the city gave way to a grungier, "under construction" stretch of urban sprawl. Trees huddled together on one side of the road while warehouses and partially-built parking garages stood alongside a jungle of cranes and other construction equipment. The road ahead of her emptied out, and for the moment it seemed like she was the only person awake in the entire world. She reached down and turned on the radio so she wouldn't get lulled into sleep.

Over the past few months, they'd gotten a taste of what a normal life would be like. While Ari was in prison, she took a drug that suppressed her ability to transform. At the time, it had been a lifesaver. The only downside was that they didn't have a way to flush it out of her system when she was released. So for six months, Ariadne was just a normal human being. No late night runs. No unexpected transformations.

It was nice to have Ari in bed with her every night, and she liked knowing that she could roll over at any point and reach out to her. But she knew losing the wolf weighed on Ari. Most nights, Ari laid awake and stared at the ceiling. On one of those nights, Dale had reached over and glanced up to see Ari had been watching her.

"Go back to sleep."

"Are you okay?"

"Mm-hmm." She had stroked Dale's arm. "I was thinking... I could get used to this. If you wanted me to. I could get my hands on some more of the drug. You could have a normal girlfriend. No wolf."

Dale had kissed Ari's throat. "Normal is not what I signed up for, Ariadne. And you need the wolf as much as I need you. And I need the wolf, too. It's part of you, puppy." She'd stretched up and kissed Ari's lips, and then put her head on Ari's chest. She'd gone back to sleep, and Ari had never mentioned it again.

Her ruminations had taken her all the way to the residential area of Magnolia, way out on the far western tip of the city. The wolf had gone for an epic run, covering seven or eight miles. Of course that was nothing compared to the hundred mile trek it had taken when the drug first wore off. At least this time she hadn't gone over any bridges. Dale tried to remember what was in their Discovery Park stash. It was so distant that they rarely refreshed it, so the clothes might have been out there for years.

The Shell station was a shining island in the darkness. She saw Ari waiting by the payphone, her shoulder against the ice machine, and her heart stuttered against her ribs. *There's my puppy.* Ari saw her coming and pushed away from the wall. She was wearing baggy sweatpants and a lime-green T-shirt.

Ari waved to the clerk through the glass and jogged to meet their car in the middle of the parking lot. A familiar scent swept into the car when Ari climbed into the passenger seat. It was pine needles and crushed leaves, wet fur, earth, and sweat.

"All good?" Dale asked.

"I scraped my hand a little when I had to jump a fence," Ari said, twisting her left hand to show Dale in the light coming in through the windshield. "No blood, but it stung a little."

"Poor puppy." Dale brought the hand to her mouth and kissed

it. "Do I owe the clerk any money?"

"No, there was a little cash in the duffel bag. We need to change that out, though. Everything smells like mildew." She pulled up the collar of her shirt, sniffed, and grunted. "I definitely need to take a shower when we get home."

Dale handed her the water bottle, and Ari made a sound of pure bliss as she cracked the top. She tilted it up and drank half the contents in one swallow.

"Thank you. I already had one that I bought from the store, but the wolf did not come here in a straight line."

"How far do you think you ran?"

Ari took another drink as she considered it. "I remember most of the run. How long was I gone?"

Dale looked at the clock and realized she'd never checked the time. "Well, it's almost half-past three now. The drive took me about twenty minutes. We were in bed by eleven, so you probably left around midnight?"

"I think it was about twelve-thirty." Ari was looking out the window, idly crunching the plastic bottle with her fingers. "I woke up and I could feel the wolf coming out. I barely made it to the door to let myself out. Then... yeah, ran around town. Up through Capitol Hill. Around Lake Union for a little while. When I got to Discovery Park, I kind of just let the wolf take control. Who knows how long she went crazy in there before I changed back."

"I've always wondered about that part," Dale said. "When you're the wolf, and she's in control, sometimes you 'wake up' and you're already human."

"And naked."

"Mm-hmm," Dale said. "So does the wolf decide it's time to change again? Or does she feel you pushing at the edges the way she pushes at yours? And I know, I know, it's not another entity, it's all you. But for the sake of my sleep-addled brain, let's simplify."

Ari chuckled. "Fair enough. And... I don't know. When I'm control, I kind of tell the wolf when it's time to change. I assume the same thing happens in the other direction. I'm just not privy to that mental conversation any more than she's aware of the talks I have with you."

"Do you think there will ever be a time when she decides to... not bring you back?"

"No," Ari said, without hesitation. "It wouldn't be possible, any more than if I decided to never let her out again."

"I know that," Dale said, "but you *did* suppress her for six months. What if she decides to even things out? Is there a chance some night you'd go for a run and she'd just keep going? You got all the way to Discovery Park tonight. The first time you transformed after the drug wore off, she ran almost all the way to Port Townsend. What if..." She flexed her fingers on the steering wheel. "What if she's trying to go far enough that I can't come get you?"

Ari considered the question for a long time. "How far would she have to go?" she finally asked.

"The moon, puppy. She'd have to take you to the moon."

Ari reached over and touched Dale's knee and left it there until they were almost home.

When they arrived, Dale turned the headlights off and rolled into the driveway, being respectful of the neighbors and landlady. They walked into the apartment together, and Ari immediately stripped out of her stash clothes as soon as they were through the door. Dale took them into the laundry room and added them to the bag holding the stash clothes Ari had worn the day before. There was enough to start a load, so she would take care of that before work.

Ari was still in the shower when Dale undressed and crawled back to bed. Some nights her feet required quite a bit of scrubbing, depending on how much mud she had to walk through to reach a stash. Dale had almost drifted back to sleep when the water shut off and Ari joined her. This time she brought a scent of shampoo and body wash, and Dale smiled as her partner crawled into bed and settled on top of her.

"Sleeping?" Ari whispered.

"Almost," Dale said.

Ari nibbled Dale's ear and slipped her arms around Dale's waist. Dale pressed her butt into Ari's hips, raising up enough to make room for a hand between her and the mattress.

"Still a little wolfy?"

"Is that okay?" Her tongue trailed the shell of Dale's ear.

"Mm-hmm. You have to pay for your ride home somehow..."

Ari chuckled and moved her hand lower. Dale spread her legs and Ari settled between them. Dale slipped her arms under the pillow and let Ari do what she wanted. She'd long ago decided they had four distinct styles in the bedroom: fooling around, making love, fucking, and rutting. The last one was more aggressive, and only happened after a transformation. It was Ari dominating, taking what she wanted from Dale, and Dale absolutely loved it. She smiled as Ari left her ear to focus on kissing, licking, and sucking her neck as her hand began to move inside Dale's underwear.

Dale pressed her cheek into the pillow, moaning and moving her hips to indicate "more" or "try something else." But at this point, she and Ari had been partners long enough that neither of them had to say much of anything. Dale knew this sort of sex was all about her pleasure, so she didn't try to reach for Ari or repay anything that was being done to her. Instead, she began to speak in a low murmur.

"I love that, puppy... don't stop... that feels so good, Ariadne." Ari responded by gently biting down on Dale's shoulder, making her groan and writhe. "Good girl, puppy..."

She felt the tremors in Ari's body and was pressed down into the mattress as Ari put all her weight down onto her. Her free hand moved up under Dale's T-shirt to her breast, and the biting teeth turned into softly brushing lips which traveled up her shoulder, to her neck, to the spot behind her ear that made Dale squirm and sigh when she came. Ari stayed on top of her, idly kissing her neck and shoulder before finally rolling to one side.

Dale repositioned herself and rested her head on Ari's chest. Ari reached up to brush Dale's hair with her fingers, and Dale kissed her collarbone. "Feeling human again, puppy?"

Ari chuckled, and Dale felt it against her cheek. "A hundred percent. How long until we have to wake up and go to work?"

"About two hours," Dale said, already close to sleep. "Maybe three."

"Perfect," Ari said.

Dale smiled. Hearing an exhausted Ari say that under her breath was the perfect thing to hear before passing out, so she finally let sleep take her.

The next few days were normal but, on Friday, Dale received another call that took her to Magnuson Park, a location which was so far away they'd never bothered to put stashes there. Ari found and raided a clothing donation bin, then used the phone of a security guard at a condominium complex to call for a ride. It was nearly six o'clock when they got home, and upstairs Neka was already awake and getting ready for work. Dale climbed into bed and was woken up moments later by Ari climbing on top of her.

Dale squirmed away from her. "Really? Ari, we have to be up in an hour."

"The wolf just wanted to run," Ari said.

"The wolf has been running the show a lot lately. And not just out in the streets. I think you've been letting the animal out a little too much in bed."

She felt Ari tense beside her. "I haven't..."

"No," Dale said. "But a couple of times it's been borderline. It's fine. If it wasn't fine, I would have said something, and you would have stopped. I know that."

Ari scooted away from her. "I'm sorry."

"You don't have anything to be sorry about. I like it when you get wild. But not every single time."

Ari remained silent so Dale rolled on top of her. Ari put her hands on Dale's shoulders to push her off, and Dale gripped her wrists and pinned both hands on the pillow above Ari's head. Their faces were lined up, and Dale stared into Ari's eyes. It was too dark to really see them clearly, but she imagined she could see glinting gold in the hazel. It was the color she associated with Ari's wolf form.

"You and the wolf don't seem to be talking to each other right now, so let me talk to both of you. Ariadne locked you up for a really long time, and that sucks, but she did it to keep you both safe. You're taking it out on her now, and it's unfair, because she would never have done it if she had a choice. Stop running her ragged. Be kind to her."

She bent down and kissed Ari, feeling the tension seep out of her body. She let go of Ari's arms, sliding her hands over her arms until they were on her shoulders. Ari brought her hands down and rested them on the back of Dale's head to hold the kiss.

When they parted, Ari bumped her forehead against Dale's and whispered, "Thank you. From both of us."

"There's just one of you, Ari," Dale said, "and I adore every bit of it. Let's get some sleep, okay?"

Ari nodded. Dale slipped back to her side of the bed, and Ari spooned against her from behind. She knew they were going to oversleep, since neither of them had bothered to set the alarm, but Dale decided work could start a little later than usual, just this once.

CHAPTER ONE

ARI LOOKED at the clock from her perch on the corner of Dale's desk. It was thirteen minutes past eleven, meaning the man with whom she had an appointment was almost fifteen minutes late. It had been a slow Monday morning so far, and it looked like her first real work of the week was a no-show.

"It's a standard societal rule," Ari said. "If you're this late to an appointment, you can't expect the person to be there when and if you finally show up. Especially if it's this close to lunchtime."

"No one told you to book a meeting this close to lunch," Dale said.

Ari rolled her eyes. "I offered earlier, but the guy said this was the only time he had free. Which means he's probably on *his* lunch break." She twisted to look at the door, as if the potential client had appeared in the fogged glass. "He probably stopped to eat somewhere on his way..."

Dale sighed. "Okay, I'm obviously not going to get anything done with you sitting here pouting like this. Would you like me to go get us something to eat?"

Ari's face brightened. "I'll take a Bandit from the Honey Hole."

"Ooh, I love it when you talk dirty to me."

Dale had just stood up when the door opened and a man stepped inside with an air of importance and impatience. He was looking at his phone and only glanced up to make sure he didn't run into anything before he reached Dale's desk.

"Hello," Dale said. "Can we~"

"Mark Hubbard, I have an eleven o'clock with Ari Willow."

Ari said, "You're a little late, Mr. Hubbard."

He grunted in response and twisted to look past Ari into the office. "Well, he ain't even here, so I guess it doesn't really matter, does it?"

Ari and Dale looked at each other. He looked up at them and gestured impatiently.

"Well? Do you expect him back soon?"

Dale started to answer, but Ari spoke first. "You're welcome to have a seat and wait for him."

Hubbard checked his watch and muttered, "Unbelievable," under his breath, but he went to the orange plastic chair and sat down.

Ari looked at Dale and said, "You can go ahead."

"You sure?"

"Yeah, go on."

Dale smiled and headed for the door. "I'll be back in a flash."

Ari took a seat behind Dale's desk. She minimized the window and found a game, which she clicked open and started to play. She glanced at Hubbard every now and then to gauge his irritation. He looked out the window behind her as if he would recognize "Mr. Willow" on the street, looked into the office as if he'd magically manifested there, and frequently checked his watch. He was a tall man, lanky and lean in the way that some high school football players end up. He had a very high forehead and a poor attempt at a combover to hide it.

"You'd think the guy would know to be in his office when he has an appointment."

"Yes, well, you know how it goes," Ari said.

"Maybe you could call him, see where he is."

Ari shook her head. "Me? No, I never call Ari."

Hubbard sighed and went back to poking at his phone. "What does a guy need with two secretaries if he's never even in the office?"

"That's an excellent question," Ari admitted.

Dale came back after twenty minutes with two sandwiches. "Are you messing up my computer?"

"I'm playing a game," Ari said.

"Just don't download anything."

Ari abandoned the keyboard to take and unwrap her sandwich. She had been smelling it since Dale came into the building, and she was starting to salivate. She gave up the seat so Dale could retake her throne, moving to sit on the windowsill. She thought for a moment it might be a little rude to eat in front of their client, but he hadn't given her any reason to care about that. She took a bite and watched him as she chewed.

Finally, he stood and approached the desk again. "Excuse me."

Dale looked up and wiped a bit of aioli from her bottom lip. "Yes?" she said, once she'd swallowed.

"Where is Mr. Willow?"

"There is no Mr. Willow," Ari said.

Hubbard stared at her. Finally, squinting, he said, "I beg your pardon?"

"There is no Mr. Willow," she repeated. "You have an appointment with Ariadne Willow. That's me. This is my agency."

He blinked at her. "What... Why the hell didn't you just *say* that in the first place?"

Ari shrugged. "You never asked. You came in here and asked about someone named Mr. Willow. I don't know who that is, but I guess there was a chance he would come in at some point."

Hubbard looked between Ari and Dale, his face growing red from anger and embarrassment. "You're the private investigator?"

"Yes, sir. If you'd like to step into my office, I'm almost finished with my meal..."

"Unbelievable," he said again. He spun and stormed out of the office. He slammed the door behind him when he left.

Dale laughed and leaned back in her chair. "I think you just lost a client."

"Something tells me I wouldn't want to take whatever case that guy was bringing." She bent down and kissed Dale's lips, bowing for a second longer kiss when she tasted the onions and peppers on Dale's breath. "Mmm, love that. Spicy."

"I'll get it for you next time."

"Please do." Ari took the rest of her sandwich into her office. "It's just Monday," she said over her shoulder. "The week is bound to start looking up after this."

Dale said, "Famous last words."

The first time Ari sat across the visitation table from Shae Segura, the inmate squinted at her and said, "You're doing this all wrong. Once they let you go, you never ever come back."

Ari said, "The way I see it, I owe you a debt. You helped me out when I was inside. Now that I'm out, it's my turn to help you."

Shae had been Ari's cellmate during her incarceration, and one of the people who helped her survive the ordeal. She was a con artist, a grifter, a thief who made a living by cheating other thieves at their own games. She came to Seattle to find out what happened to make her sister jump off a bridge, but the law caught up to her before she found any answers. When she discovered Ari was a private investigator, she assigned herself as Ari's right-hand woman in the hopes she would pick up the case when she was released. Ari knew she likely would have died without Shae's help, and she legitimately liked the other woman. She would have tried to find answers for her no matter what.

Unfortunately this visit required her to deliver bad news disguised as good news. Segura sensed Ari's mood as she crossed the room, and she braced herself as she settled into the other seat.

"How sad am I about to be?"

Ari pressed her lips together. "Last time I told you I was trying to track down some of the people Maria went to school with, to see if any of them knew something about why she did what she did. I finally found someone. Jessica Curry. She said Maria had a secret boyfriend for about six months before she died. She never said a name, but she saw a note signed with a W. Maria had a professor named Daniel Wines. He's married and, three years ago, he had a newborn daughter."

Segura said, "It couldn't have been Maria's."

"No, I'm pretty sure the baby came before the affair started. Knowing how men like that think, the baby may have been *why* the affair started. I went to talk to him and threatened to tell his wife everything. He said Maria wanted him to leave his wife. She was talking about marriage. He was more concerned with his career, so he ended things with her. That's when she stopped going to classes. She tried to get back together with him, but it didn't work. I could look into the possibility that he pushed her off the bridge, either physically or psychologically--"

"No," Shae said. She'd brought her hands up in front of her mouth. Her eyes were filled with tears. "No, Maria... Her heart was so big and so fragile. If she asked him to end his marriage, then she loved him enough to be completely broken when he rejected her. God, I hate that she ended this way. She was so smart, you know? She couldn't been anything. And she just ends like this."

Ari sat silently and let Segura cry. When the guard gave them a five-minute warning on visitation time, Segura held out her hand. Ari squeezed it.

"Debt paid, Ariadne."

"I wish it had a happier ending."

Segura shrugged. "No matter what story you found, it still ended with my sister dead. At least now I know why. It sucks that there's not really a bad guy to punish... although the professor..."

"Oh, yeah, someone might have sent his wife an email suggesting he was taking advantage of his students. As of last Thursday, the university put him on a leave of absence."

"That's something at least." She sniffled and wiped her cheeks again. "I have two years left in here. When I get out, I'm buying dinner for you and your lady."

Ari said, "It's a deal. And we can discuss bringing you on at Bitches until you find something more permanent."

Segura said, "I appreciate it. I appreciate everything." She looked at the guard and sighed. "Okay. Back inside."

"How's your new cellmate?" She lowered her voice. "Does she look the other way when CO Vogel comes by for a pillow fight?"

"No. Mel and I have had to get creative. It's fun, but it's a hassle. And on top of that, the new chick is grumpy and vaguely racist and always talks when I'm trying to read."

Ari said, "That was the first rule!"

"I know!" She shrugged and stood up. "But at least she doesn't try to change into a wolf in the middle of the night. That's a bonus."

Ari laughed and held up her fist. Segura bumped her own against it. "I'll still see you in a couple of weeks even though the case is closed, right?"

"Count on it."

The guard escorted Segura to the door, and Ari stood to leave through another exit. Segura was almost through the door when she turned back. "Yo! Hey, Willow!"

Ari stopped and looked back.

"Thank you," Segura said, her voice heavy with sincerity and emotion.

"You're welcome, Shae."

Segura nodded, and allowed the guard to lead her into the hallway.

Ari didn't have a high opinion of Anne Foster, a gut feeling that only cemented itself the longer the woman talked. The fact she was on time for her appointment was the only mark in her favor. She wanted to hire them for a surveillance job in the hopes of finding evidence that her husband was having an affair. It was Ari's least favorite kind of case, but beggars couldn't be choosers. She'd spent the week up to that point tracking down a deadbeat dad for late child support and acting as a mystery shopper for a local boutique.

Mrs. Foster had provided her husband's schedule, and Ari was skimming it as the woman finished explaining what she wanted. Ari was about to explain their rates when Foster said something that stopped her short.

"And I'd really like to have something by Monday if that's at all possible."

Ari said, "I plan to start work on the case as quickly as I can, but I can't promise results by any specific date. It depends on if your husband arranges a meeting with his mistress over the weekend or--"

Foster rolled her eyes. "I don't care what you have to do. And of course, if you actually have to *do* anything with him, you would be compensated for that."

Ari bristled. "Whoa, whoa. We don't do that sort of thing."

"What sort of thing? I want you to prove my husband is having an affair."

"By entrapping him?"

Foster shrugged. "If you have to."

Ari stood up and rounded the desk, ushering Mrs. Foster to the door. "I think there's been a misunderstanding. You called a private investigator. Prostitute is a little lower in the phone book." She opened the door and held her arm out. "I would wish you luck with another agency, but I really don't care if you succeed or not."

Foster left in a huff, shaking her head as she stormed through the waiting room and out through the main door. Ari sighed and leaned against the door frame, while Dale looked at her expectantly.

"Are prostitutes listed in the phone book?" Ari asked.

Dale's eyes widened. "Uh... I would be very surprised if they were."

"Oh well. I think it was a good line, anyway. She wanted to

hire me to sleep with her husband and use the evidence to prove infidelity."

"Pre-nup?" Dale asked.

"Most likely. I didn't ask for the details."

Dale sighed and folded her hands in front of her on the desk. "I have to say, there's some appeal to the situation. Not, you know, adultery. But in an established relationship. One person is at the bar, their significant other comes up and pretends to be a stranger, they flirt, they make up outrageous lies about who they really are, and it ends in wild sex in a hotel room." She shrugged. "It's a fantasy. But for a healthy relationship."

Ari said, "Is it *your* fantasy...?"

Dale pursed her lips and turned back to the computer without answering.

Ari grinned and pushed off the wall, sliding back into her office. "Okay... something to remember on your birthday."

"Our anniversary is closer," Dale called after her.

Ari laughed.

"Bitches Investigations, this is Dale. How can we help you?"

The woman on the other end of the line gave a breathy, closed-mouth laugh. "I was curious if you actually answered the phone with that name."

Dale decided she sounded more amused than offended or haughty. "It helps to keep away the wrong kind of clients."

"And what would constitute a 'wrong' client?"

"Men who don't believe a woman can be a private investigator."

"Ah, I believe we are in agreement on the definition, then. Are you the woman in question?"

Dale said, "No, I'm her assistant. Would you like to make an appointment to speak with the detective?"

Ari chose that moment to come into the office. Her clothes were wet, and her eyes were dark with violence she was restraining herself from dispensing on whoever had pissed her off.

"I would like to arrange a meeting, yes, but there are extenuating circumstances. Would she be willing to make a house call? I would, of course, pay her for the time."

Dale mouthed 'house call.' Ari shrugged and nodded distractedly as she went into her office to change clothes.

"That would be fine. What time would be good?"

When Ari returned a few minutes later in clean clothes, Dale had finished the call. She held up the notepad on which she'd written out the information.

"Vivian Burroughs. She wants to meet this afternoon at three."

"Where is this address, Capitol Hill...? Off Aloha?" Realization dawned. "Millionaire's Row? No. No more rich clients. We have a bad track record with them."

Dale said, "I know, puppy, I know. But this is just a client meeting. And she's paying you the usual hourly rate just to listen. You can turn down the case if you smell something rotten, but... look, I know we haven't had the best track record when it comes to rich clients, but we haven't had a good track record with *any* clients this week. At least the rich ones can pay their bill."

Ari sighed.

"You look sexy with your hair all wet and slicked back like that."

Ari narrowed her eyes at her. "Don't try to get all cute and flirty with me."

Dale folded her hands and rested her chin on them. She gazed adoringly at Ari.

"Fine," Ari sighed. "I'll go talk to her. But no promises."

"Thank you, puppy. Hey! How'd you get all wet?"

Ari grunted. "The things some people will do to avoid being served with a summons."

Dale laughed and turned to add the Burroughs meeting to the calendar.

CHAPTER TWO

MILLIONAIRE'S ROW was an unofficial neighborhood south of Volunteer Park, with some of the oldest houses in Seattle, and it certainly lived up to its name. Ari had grown up with money, but she felt uneasy even parking her car there. She was suddenly aware of every ding on the bumper and feared it might drip oil on the street and some Homeowners Association militia would swoop down and charge her for the cleanup.

The address Dale gave her was on an elevated plot of land with a stone retaining wall between it and the driveway. A handful of trees along the edge of the property provided a barrier to casual trespassing but didn't block the homeowner's view of the street. The house was an A-frame made of wood and stone, so dark and seemingly carved from stone that it blended in perfectly. She appreciated that it was a nice, simple home rather than an eyesore of metal and glass.

Ari went up the front walk to the covered porch, pausing on the steps to look at the windows to either side for signs she was being watched from within. None of the curtains twitched, so she continued to the door and rang the bell.

"I assume you're the private investigator."

Ari looked for the origin of the voice and saw a small camera mounted above the door. A speaker was built into the wall, so discreet it could barely be seen by anyone who wasn't looking for it. So she had been observed on her approach. She smiled into the lens and lifted her hand in a wave.

"Yes, ma'am. Ariadne Willow from Bitches Investigations."

"The door is unlocked, Miss Willow."

Ari went into the house. The front hall was comfortably warm and reminded her of a cozy mountain lodge. There was a bench next to the door under a canopy of coats and rainslickers hanging from hooks. She saw rooms to either side and another straight ahead, beyond the stairs, but only one of the rooms was open. Ari was already walking toward it when she heard the voice again.

"To your left, Miss Willow."

The living room was lovely but surprisingly spartan. A couch and a few armchairs huddled around the fireplace. Her hostess was seated at a desk with her back to the door, so she didn't see the brief look of surprise on Ari's face when she realized the woman was in a wheelchair. Ari glanced at the stairs and only now saw the lift mechanism. When she faced forward again, the woman had turned her chair around.

"Thank you for coming. As you can see, it's a bit difficult for me to get downtown."

"Of course. We're actually less than a mile from my office, so it wasn't an inconvenience. No traffic. I assume you're Vivian Burroughs."

"I am. It's a pleasure to make your acquaintance. Please..." She gestured at the foyer and Ari stepped aside so she could get by. "The reason I called you involves going to the second floor, and it takes me a bit longer than most people. So I thought we could begin the process while we're talking."

Ari said, "Makes sense. Do you need my help with anything?"

"No, dear, thank you. I've gotten quite good at it."

Ari waited while Vivian positioned her chair on the platform and pressed a button to begin her ascent. She was an older woman, older than Ari's mother but not elderly, with dark red hair which seemed natural instead of dyed. She wore a button-down white blouse and black slacks, and sat with her back straight and her hands resting lightly on the arms of the chair like a queen on a litter. Ari began to climb, measuring her steps to stay behind the chair.

"I admit, I'm worried that the job I hope to hire you for may not be in the purview of a private investigator. All I know about your job is what I gleaned from books."

"We have a pretty wide variety of jobs," Ari said. "It keeps things from getting dull."

Vivian smiled. "I'm sure it does. What do you know about the houses in this neighborhood?"

"They're as old as they are expensive. Not much beyond that."

"Simplistic, but accurate. This house was built in 1904. It's been modernized quite a bit over the years, as you can tell by the contraption I'm riding, but the bones of the house are the same. I've lived here forty years. I raised my children here. I have four, all grown. Preston, Evelyn, Eleanor, and Elizabeth. Taking the case will unfortunately mean you have to deal with them, however briefly."

"So noted," Ari said.

They arrived at the top of the stairs and Vivian gestured down the hall. "The first door on the left." Ari led the way with Vivian behind her. When they arrived, Vivian took a key from the pocket of her slacks. It looked like a cartoon key, long and thin, silver, with an ornate design at the top where Vivian pinched it. "This door is always left locked."

"Okay." Ari had to admit she was intrigued, in spite of herself.

Vivian leaned forward, unlocked the door, and pushed it open. She wheeled herself inside and Ari followed.

The room was a study. A rolltop desk stood against one wall, flanked on both sides by bookshelves. There were no windows, but the wall to the left of the desk was covered with dozens of paintings in a variety of sizes. Vivian positioned herself with her back to this display and Ari followed her gaze to a tapestry hanging on the opposite side of the room. Ari guessed it was about her height, and four feet from side to side. It was a swirl of blues and greens with a faded gold border.

"That's beautiful."

"Take a closer look."

Ari stepped around the wheelchair and examined the image. The blue on either side was layered like the scales of a dragon, whereas the green strip down the center was more featherlike. Once she realized the green shape wasn't uniform, she understood what she was looking at.

"This is Seattle."

"Very good, Miss Willow. Although technically it depicts the area where Seattle would eventually blossom. It's called Crossing-

Over Place. It was woven by a Duwamish artist in 1851, which means it is as old as the city itself."

Ari took a step back. "Holy shit."

"Holy shit indeed," Vivian said. "Do you have any idea what a collector would pay for this at auction?"

"Not a clue," Ari said without even bothering to think about it. She had no idea what something like this would be worth, and at auction? People to whom money was no object, worked up into a frenzy, trying to get something historic and unique? Any attempt to put a price on it made her head spin.

"Somebody once implied this tapestry is worth more than the house, but I think he was just being a bit ridiculous."

"I don't," Ari said. "This is art. People go nuts over art."

Vivian exhaled once, a sound that Ari took as a laugh. "Very astute, Miss Willow. And that brings us to the purpose of calling you."

Ari tore her gaze off the tapestry and saw Vivian was holding up the room key.

"Take it," Vivian said.

"I don't understand."

Vivian lowered the key to her lap. "I'm dying, Miss Willow. An inoperable brain tumor. The rest of my life has two distinct paths. Either I slowly become less of a person and more of a burden, or I begin endless medical treatments which will decimate my health and make me unable to enjoy the things which once gave me pleasure. Both those paths end with me dead. So I have decided to take the third choice, the utterly horrible option which no one dares speak out loud but is, in fact, the most reasonable course of action given the situation."

Ari didn't know what to say. "I'm sorry."

"I'm not! What the hell do I have to be sorry about? I've had love, I've lived a life with very little hardship..." She glanced down at her chair and seemed to anticipate the question Ari would never have dared to ask out loud. "This is not new. I learned to live with it so long ago that I barely think about it anymore. Compared to many others, my life has been ridiculously blessed. I have no interest in ending it withering away in a bed like some husk. I want to go out on my own terms and that is exactly what I intend to do."

"What does that have to do with me? I hope you don't think--"

"No, no. I wouldn't ask that of a stranger." She held up the key. "I want you to hold onto this. As I said before, I have four children. In a life with very few regrets, those four... they are disappointments, Miss Willow. I'm ashamed to say it, but it's the truth. When the time comes and the will is read, I know this tapestry will be contested more than any of my other assets. All of my children have asked for it at some point in their greedy lives and I'm certain my death would only redouble their efforts. They might even attempt to steal it before I pass on. That's why I would like you to have the key, the only key, to ensure that no one else has access to this room in the weeks leading up to my departure. When the time arrives, you will be contacted by the executor of my estate. You'll bring the key and the person I've chosen will be able to take their treasure."

She held up the key again. This time, Ari took it.

"This is a lot of trust to put in someone you don't even know." She realized the fallacy as soon as she said it out loud. "You didn't call the agency at random, did you?"

Vivian smiled. "One drawback from being wealthy is that one has to spend far too much time with lawyers. I was a client of GG&M. I was important enough that when I showed up to demand answers about why the firm which has handled my family's finances since my great-grandmother's day was suddenly collapsing, they couldn't turn me away. They tried to lie, of course. But finally I found someone who was willing to tell me about a young woman who uncovered evidence that Cecily Parrish and the name partners were involved in unsavory activity."

"Oh." Ari wasn't sure what else to say, but she was very aware of the fact that Vivian was between her and the only exit of this windowless room.

"You're worried that I'm upset," Vivian said. "On the contrary. I was disgusted when I found out what the firm had been up to. You cracked the egg and everything spilled out. The three partners are facing life in prison if they ever show their faces again, and Cecily Parrish has so many criminal charges against her, I'd be shocked if she ever sees sunlight again. I would have taken my business elsewhere even if you didn't destroy the firm, and that alone is enough for me to entrust you with this assignment."

"But that's not all you based it on."

Vivian shook her head. "I told you my children are, ah... let's call them 'spirited.' My daughter Elizabeth had a particularly wild streak about ten years ago, just after high school. She started running around with a young woman named Laura Gavin."

Ari actually gasped when she heard the name. "Oh," she said again.

"Laura and Elizabeth were bad influences on each other. Two poisons that only made the other more potent. Thankfully my name doesn't sell as many papers as Gavin, so we were spared the infamy, but we suffered the fallout just the same. One day, Laura wasn't coming around as much. And then she was discovered dead. I remember reading the news and being... very cold..." Her eyes drifted toward the floor. "I thought she had it coming. That she had brought it on herself. Then the news broke about her mother, and the whole story came to light. Laura had turned her life around, she was doing good work, making something of herself." She looked at Ari again. "That was also because of you."

Ari cleared her throat. "Laura deserved to be remembered as the person she'd become, not who she had once been."

Vivian said, "I imagined if it had been Elizabeth in the paper. If someone read about my girl's death and clucked their tongue and said 'well, it's her fault, she did this to herself.' I was disgusted with myself and it made me glad to know there was someone like you ensuring the truth was told. That's the main reason I trust you with the key. I believe you will do the right thing rather than the easy thing."

Ari held out her hand. "In that case, it would be my honor to take your case."

"Wonderful." She placed the key in Ari's hand. "I'll let you do the honors."

"Are you sure?" She looked at the desk, the shelves. "You won't be able to get anything out of here for... well, until..."

Vivian gave her a knowing smile. "For the rest of my life? I've read the books I care to read, and I've cleared the desk of anything I'm likely to need or want."

Ari was still hesitant. "If you think of anything, I'll come back and let you in."

"Deal."

They left the room. Ari locked the door and gave the knob a good shake just to make sure. It was definitely locked.

"Excellent." Vivian sounded legitimately relieved. "Now, if you would go downstairs to the room where we met, you'll find a check for your services on the desk. I'll join you as quickly as the contraption will allow me."

Ari felt strange going back downstairs without her host, but it would have been equally awkward to linger while she rode the lift down. She returned to the den and found the check, intending to only glance at the total before she slipped it into her pocket. The job required so little on her part that she was willing to accept pretty much whatever Vivian offered to pay, but she hadn't expected to see a number anything like this.

She returned to the foot of the stairs. Vivian was two-thirds of the way down, and Ari held up the check. "I can't accept this."

"Why not?"

"For babysitting a key? It's ridiculous."

Vivian said, "My research indicates five hundred dollars a day would be a low estimate for your services. I assume it will take me approximately two months to put my affairs in order. That comes out to twenty-eight thousand dollars. I rounded it up to thirty because I like round numbers, and I assume the extra money would mean more to you than it does to me." She arrived at the foot of the stairs and looked up at Ari. "I want you to take this job seriously, Miss Willow. I don't want any of my children to track you down and entice you to hand it over before the will has been read. That check is buying security and loyalty."

"You could have had both for a lot cheaper."

She shrugged. "You get what you pay for in this life, and this will likely be one of my last large expenditures. I feel like you're worth it."

"I'll do my best to live up to it, ma'am."

"Does that mean you're officially hired?" Ari held out her hand. Vivian shook it. "If all goes according to plan, we probably won't see each other again. It was a pleasure to meet you, Miss Willow."

"Ariadne. And the pleasure was all mine. You have my word that this key won't end up in the wrong hands."

She left the house with the key in her pants pocket, but she still reached down to feel the shape of it no less than three times before she got back to her car. She had the only key to a room with a priceless piece of art and thirty thousand dollars to ensure it remained safe for the next two months. She wanted it on her at all times. But no, what if it fell off while she was out? She couldn't risk losing it somewhere in the wilds of Seattle. She could hide it in the office, but then it could be stolen or the building could burn down or...

"Stop overthinking it," she scolded. She didn't need to find the perfect hiding place immediately. The key would be safe until she and Dale figured out what to do with it.

CHAPTER THREE

ARI AND Dale spent the next two days trying to find the best hiding place for the key. There was a safe in the office, of course, but Ari felt this particular item required something special. Her nightmare was that she would choose a fantastic hiding place and then forget where it was by the time Vivian Burroughs' attorney summoned her back to the house. Dale finally told her, "It doesn't have to be Fort Knox, it just has to be a spot that's secure. A place you can put your hands on it at a moment's notice."

In the end, Ari took a tip from Edgar Allan Poe and hid it in plain sight, on her keychain. It stuck out next to the more mundane keys for their apartment, office, and cars, but at least she would always know where it was.

Once that was taken care of, Ari reluctantly settled into the next part of the job: waiting for the call that Vivian had ended her life. It was morbid, and working on other cases helped keep her mind off of it. She was very mindful of the fact she was basically earning five hundred dollars a day just to keep a key in her pocket and tried not to feel like she was running a con.

A week into what Dale had taken to calling the 'death watch,' Ari had the afternoon free and offered to pick up lunch. She chose sandwiches from Michou and had the bad luck of arriving during the lunch rush. She leaned against the wall to wait for her order, focusing on her phone so the wolf wouldn't get too distracted. In addition to being in a deli, the restaurant was located in Pike Place Market, which meant there were thousands of wonderful smells just hanging on the wind for her over-sensitive nose to lock onto. Fish, fruit, flowers, it was all good, and she could almost feel the hairs standing up on the back of her neck.

The wolf had been behaving lately and things were slowly reverting back to how they'd been before she took the restricting drug. No more long jaunts to unknown parks, no rough sex with Dale, no barely-contained urges to transform and run. It seemed as if Dale's pep talk had gotten through to it. And that pep talk... having Dale roll her over in the middle of sex, pinning her down, holding her arms over her head, and telling her exactly how things were going to be? That was definitely something she could get used to.

"Order for A-Rodney?"

Ari smile-grimaced and put her phone away. "It's Ariadne."

She took the bag from the clerk and headed out. She was vaguely aware of someone saying, "Wait, hold on a minute," as she left, but she kept walking as it didn't seem to be directed at her. She was almost underneath the Public Market Center sign when she heard the man calling again. "Excuse me! Wait a minute, please. Ariadne? Ariadne Willow?"

She turned and saw a man she vaguely recognized from the deli hurrying to catch up with her. He looked to be in his late fifties, with short-cropped hair that retained enough color for her to know it had once been brown. He was a few inches taller than her and reed-thin. When he smiled, his eyes almost disappeared, which wasn't difficult since they were already overwhelmed by large black eyebrows. He chuckled and slowed to a trot when he saw she was waiting for her.

"Hi. Hello. Sorry." He held up a hand as he caught his breath. He spoke with a slight midwestern twang, more ranch hand than hick, and his smile was genuinely charming. "Sorry about that. I'm- I'm not usually the sort to chase after a woman on the street, but I overheard your name in the deli. It's such an unusual name I couldn't help but make the connection. Are you Ariadne Willow?"

"Do I know you?"

His smile widened and he laughed once, softly. "No, no, we've never met." He pointed a finger at her. "But I've heard of you."

Between him and Vivian Burroughs, it seemed as if she was gaining quite a reputation. "Are you interested in hiring me? Mister..."

"Hayden. Isaac Hayden." He offered his hand, realized Ari was holding a bag of food, and withdrew it. "I'm not looking for a private investigator, but I've been looking for you for a long time."

Ari glanced at the throng of tourists moving past them on either side, like they were stones in a stream. She reached into her pocket. "Maybe this isn't the best place for this conversation. Let me give you my card." She didn't particularly like the idea of this man being in her office, but it was better than standing here exposed.

"Please, I just need a minute of your time."

"Free consultation," Ari said, holding out the card. "Just call and we'll find a time."

Hayden looked at the card. "Bitches Investigations." He laughed again, a quiet chuckle. "That's good, I like that." He looked at her again and held her gaze. "*Canidae.*"

Ari was good at not reacting to that word. "Is that supposed to mean something to me?"

"Are you claiming it doesn't?"

She shrugged. "It doesn't ring a bell. Is it the name of a town?"

Hayden maintained his smile and wiped a hand over his face, scanning the crowd. "Okay. Okay, you can pretend like you don't know what I'm talking about. But do you also claim you don't recognize the name Jacob Keighley?"

She wasn't practiced at hearing that name, the name of the man who assaulted her mother and caused Ari to be born nine months later. She nodded and hoped her expression was neutral. "He's the, uh, sports equipment guy who went to prison a couple of years ago."

"You're not a good liar, Ariadne Willow. I know you're his daughter."

Ari tucked her card back into her pocket. "I changed my mind, Mr. Hayden. I don't think my agency will be accepting your business. Have a good day."

She turned her back on him and started to walk. He quickly caught up to her. "He didn't just go to jail. You and your mother were instrumental in his arrest and bringing his crimes to light. I also know that he was involved in an attempt to poison Seattle's food supply in an attempt to expose *canidae.*"

Ari was moving faster now, but he was keeping pace. She

didn't want to actually run, because that would only make him believe he was right.

"Miss Willow, please, will you stop walking? Please."

She sighed and stopped at the curb. Hayden was out of breath and looked desperate when he caught up to her.

"Have you ever heard of a man named Karl Magnusson?"

"No."

"He was a cryptozoologist, like me..."

Ari said, "So he hunted ghosts and Bigfoots?"

Hayden grimaced. "No. No, no. I mean, that... there are cryptozoologists who study those. It's a pseudoscience and I would be lying if I denied that. But Magnusson had a very specific area of study, one that I share. For years, I've been looking for proof, actual hard proof that *canidae* exist. I think I'm on the verge of a breakthrough. I believe Jacob Keighley was a member of a group who hunts *canidae*. I came to Seattle to investigate them and I started hearing your name in association with his arrest. I can't believe you just walked into the deli where I was having lunch."

"Look, you seem like a nice guy. And yes, my mother and I helped with Keighley's arrest. He's a very sick man. These *canidae* delusions fed into that. He was a bad man who did awful things to people because of those delusions. I've learned to avoid anyone who shares them. Have a nice day, Mr. Hayden."

She stepped around him.

"Ask your mother where her money comes from."

Ari looked back at him. "Excuse me?"

"Your mother. Money has never been an issue for her. Aren't you curious why that is?"

"Inheritance," Ari said, "not that it's any of your business."

Hayden said, "Ask her, Miss Willow. Can I give you my business card? Just in case you decide you want to talk with me again?"

"I find that incredibly unlikely."

She turned her back on him once more, half-expecting him to catch up with her again. She was prepared to resort to violence if necessary if he continued pursuing but, when she reached the parking lot and looked back, Hayden was nowhere to be seen among the crowd. She released the tension she hadn't realized was gathered in her shoulders and went to her car. She touched Vivian Burroughs' key just to reassure herself it was still there, and unlocked her car.

The entire encounter had unsettled her more than she cared to admit. First a strange man running up to her, then the shock of him saying the word '*canidae*,' and the final blow of asking about her mother's money. The truth was, she didn't really know where their money came from. It had just always been there, a constant. They lived in a nice house, they never worried about bills... and when Ari was in prison, her mother had paid the rent for their apartment and the office without blinking an eye. She knew their family had connections, she knew there were wolves in Europe who might be helping her out, but suddenly this stranger's question shouted across a crowded sidewalk had her questioning everything she thought she knew about her family's history.

She looked at the key, and then at the bag of sandwiches. Whatever the answers were, she had more than enough to keep her mind busy without digging up ancient history.

Isaac Hayden and his mysteries would have to wait for another day.

Ari told Dale about the strange encounter while they ate their sandwiches. Dale furrowed her brow as she listened.

"Do you think he's dangerous?" she asked.

"I don't know. He didn't seem like he wanted to hurt me. He just seemed..." She replayed the encounter in her mind. "He seemed like an excited professor."

Dale pursed her lips. "Hm. Well... have you considered just telling him he's right? You know, validate all those years of studying and looking for answers. You told Diana and Lucy."

Ari said, "That was different. They're our friends. We know we can trust them. We have no idea what Hayden would do with the information."

"Right. Remember Wayne Corbett?"

"I try not to," Ari said, pushing away thoughts of the man who had tranquilized her and threatened to kill her in the name of research. She started to change the subject, but then something clicked in her mind. "Shit, that's where I heard the name Magnusson before. Corbett brought him up. That was how he learned about *canidae* in the first place. There was a collection of essays or something on display in..." She tried to recall what he'd said, but at the time she was strapped to a table and drugged for whatever horrible examination Corbett had in mind for her.

Dale swiveled her chair around to face the computer. "I'll see what Google says. Is it Karl with a C or a K?"

"I don't know."

"One S or two in Magnusson?"

"Don't know."

Dale sighed and shook her head. "Useless."

"My uselessness is your job security."

Dale grinned and scanned the search results. "Looks like Magnusson's book is part of a private collection in Frankfurt."

"Kentucky?"

"Frank*furt*," Dale said, "Germany. You need an appointment and it takes months to be approved, and the guy who owns it is pretty strict about who he'll allow in."

Ari said, "It doesn't really matter since I'm not planning to be in Germany any time soon." She came around the desk to sit in the window behind Dale so she could see the screen. "Are there any pictures? Scans or screencaps?"

Dale shook her head. "It says on the reservation page that no photography will be allowed. I'll see if anyone who's seen the book has ever summarized it or talked online about what's in it." She typed again. "I can also see what I can find on Isaac Hayden. Might as well find out if he's someone you should run screaming from the next time he shows up."

"Are you sure you don't mind doing all this research?"

Dale shrugged as she wrote down the names of everyone involved. "We don't have any ongoing cases right now. And if someone hires you, I can always put this aside. It'll be a nice little hobby to keep me from getting bored. So..."

"So?"

"The last part. The thing about your mother's money. Where *does* it come from?"

Ari shrugged. "I was always told it was an inheritance. That's what she told me when I was a kid, and it just became the default answer. I never really felt the need to push for more details. But now that it's in my head, I can't help wondering."

"You could always just call her up and ask."

"Yeah." She shook her head slowly. "But the way Hayden brought it up makes me... Okay, what if there *is* something strange about where her money comes from? We're finally getting along for the first time since I was a teenager. When she came back into our lives, she was trying to make me dump you and she blew wolfsbane in my face to show me how dangerous it was. She's changed. We've both changed. And now I have this hand grenade and I'm threatening to walk into the house and pull the pin. I want to know more before I risk losing everything."

Dale said, "That makes sense. Wasn't there a guy... when Milo first showed up and you reunited with your mom, there was a guy there. Ben? Benjamin..."

"Benjamin Moss," Ari said. "He was a guy Mom knew who helped put that whole scheme together. I think he abandoned her when things went haywire."

Dale smiled. "I wonder how he feels now that we're still together and your mom is sleeping with Milo."

Ari grunted and shook her head. "No, uh-uh, if we're going to discuss that relationship at all, we're going to call it 'dating'."

"Okay," Dale said skeptically, turning back to the computer. "I lived with them while you were in prison, and calling what they do 'sleeping' is very, very inaccurate."

Ari threw a napkin at Dale's head.

Over the next few weeks, Ari took on new clients and closed ongoing investigations. Work kept them both busy, so Dale didn't make much progress on investigating Magnusson or Hayden. The mystery man also didn't make any further attempts to contact them, which Ari counted as a victory. Dale hoped he would just forget about the encounter, but she didn't think that was very likely.

One case took her to Bellingham to find a deadbeat dad who was behind on his child support checks. She decided to turn it into a mini-vacation by taking Dale along and staying the weekend. Ari wanted to let the wolf explore Whatcom Falls Park, but Dale wasn't keen on letting her run around an unfamiliar place on her own in the middle of the night.

"What if we go during the day?" she suggested. "That way I can keep an eye on you, and it's less likely you'll get hurt or scooped up by animal control."

"So you would be walking me? Like... with a leash?"

Dale winced. "Sorry. Is that demeaning? I didn't mean it like that..."

"I know," Ari said. "I think it would be okay, as long as it's you."

The park was fine, and the wolf handled being leashed better than Dale would have guessed. She was excited by all the new sights and scents to explore and ended up wearing herself out by the time they got back to the hotel. Ari transformed and fell exhausted, sweaty and naked, onto the bed. Dale undressed and stretched out next to her, watching Ari sleep. Sometimes she could see elements of the wolf in Ari's sleeping face. A twice of her eyebrows meant she was dreaming *canidae* dreams. Sometimes she whimpered or grunted while her toes and fingers twitched. It helped remind her that while Ari shifted shapes, she was always both sides of herself: woman and wolf, human and *canidae*.

When Ari woke up, they had dinner and drove back to Seattle. They were almost to the edge of the city when Ari's phone rang with an unknown number.

"Hello? This is Ariadne Willow." She listened. Dale glanced at her and saw her expression become sad. "So soon? I guess I expected... no, it's fine. Wednesday is fine, yes. What time? I'll be there. Thank you."

When she hung up, Dale said, "Is everything okay?"

"Technically." Ari twisted in the seat and pulled her keys out of her pocket. She held up the one she'd been safeguarding, almost as if confirming it was still there. "That was the executor of Vivian Burroughs' estate. She's... uh. It was tonight. She's gone."

"Oh, puppy. I'm sorry."

"I only met her the one time, but she seemed like a great lady."

They rode without saying anything for a mile or so, a moment of silence for their client.

"The memorial service is Wednesday morning. I don't have anything that day, do I?"

Dale said, "Nothing that can't be moved."

Ari said, "Thanks," under her breath.

They passed under a streetlight and it glistened off the gold of Vivian's key. She'd gotten so used to seeing it when Ari unlocked the office that its absence was going to be odd for a while. Of course now they could officially deposit the massive check Ari had gotten for keeping an eye on it, which would be very nice, and the "case" would officially be closed.

She reached over and found Ari reaching for her, and they squeezed each other's hand as Dale took them back into Seattle.

CHAPTER FOUR

WHEN ARI returned to Vivian's house on Wednesday, she expected the street to be packed with cars and the house to be obscured by a crowd of mourners who couldn't fit inside. Instead she arrived to find the house as quiet and still as it was on her last visit. She checked her phone on the way up the front walk to make sure she had the right time. Nothing would be more awkward than to be standing on the porch when the mourners arrived from the cemetery. She was right on time according to the arrangements she made with the executor, so she continued on and rang the doorbell.

It was answered by a man in his early thirties, dark hair, unshaven. He'd bothered to put on a suit, but the shirt was wrinkled and the knot in his tie was haphazard at best. Ari couldn't tell if it was from lack of respect or the tumbler in his hand, but either way her first impression was of someone who just didn't care. He stared hard at her, seemed to realize who she was, and ran his eyes down her body.

"Oh. You must be the tree lady. Something with a tree..."

"Willow. Ariadne Willow."

He closed one eye and pointed at her with the hand holding his glass. "That was it. Private investigator from Bitches Investigating."

"Investigations," she corrected.

"Mm. Do you prefer Dick or Bitch?" He laughed at his own joke and waved it off. "Sorry, sorry, I've been thinking of that ever since Mom told me she'd hired you." He took a drink and waved her in, already walking back into the house. "Come on in. There's drinks in the parlor."

Ari went inside and closed the door behind her. "You must be Preston," she said as she followed him into the room where she'd first met Vivian.

"I don't know if he must be, but he frequently is." This came from a brunette woman sitting on the couch, more poised and polished than Preston. She wore a black dress, her hair was up in a bun. She wasn't wearing makeup and her puffy eyes were a clue as to why she hadn't bothered. She stood and approached Ari, forcing a smile. "I'm Eleanor."

"Ari." They shook hands.

Another woman was standing against the wall between the window and the desk. She was also brunette, although it was shaded so dark it was almost black, and Ari could see a trace of Vivian's features in her face. Her arms were folded over her chest, and she was staring at Ari with a look she couldn't quite categorize. She wore a blazer and slacks, giving off exactly the kind of haughty mean girl energy Ari had once been helpless against.

"That's Elizabeth. She's a bit rude."

"Fuck you, Eleanor."

Eleanor blinked and swiveled her head back toward Ari. "Case in point."

"Our mother just died. Don't you think I'm *allowed* to be a little rude? Oo, can't wait to hear the will and find out how much of my mom's stuff I get to loot today. Let's all have a party!"

Preston, who had slumped in the corner of the couch, raised his glass. "Hear, hear!"

Eleanor went to him and took the glass away. "I think you've partied enough for all of us." To Ari, she said, "Mr. Dodd is running a little bit late. He had to retrieve our other sister."

"Big surprise," Preston muttered, and Eleanor shushed him. "Well, *we* all managed to show up on time. Even the detective is here. And once again we're all stuck waiting on Evelyn. What else is new?"

Elizabeth said, "You got somewhere to be?"

Preston sneered and slumped back against the couch.

Eleanor held her smile but Ari could see she something manic behind her eyes. She was desperate to keep everyone calm and civil. She cleared her throat.

"So, do you all live here in the city?"

"No," the sisters said at the same time, while Preston laughed. He said, "Evie and Ellie couldn't wait to get away as fast as possible. Eleanor here stuck around for college, but then she headed to Philadelphia for a 'fresh start.' I'm the only one who stayed."

Eleanor's smooth exterior cracked slightly. "So much easier to ask Mom for money in person than begging for a wire transfer." There was a hint in her voice indicating she might be on the verge of screaming.

"Yeah, yeah, I'm the leech. I forget, which one of you turned down Mom's offer of paying for your plane ticket and hotel so you could be here when she ended it. You?" He twisted to look at Elizabeth. "You? No? Okay, then." He stood up and snatched his glass back from his sister. He drained it and Eleanor rolled her eyes.

"Sorry," Eleanor said. "We must be giving you a horrible impression of us."

Elizabeth said, "I think it's a great impression. A *bad* impression would be wrong or misleading. This is pretty much pure Burroughs."

Eleanor went back to where she'd been sitting when Ari came in and sat down again. Silence fell. No one had offered her a seat, so Ari remained standing awkwardly in the doorway. Long enough passed that they heard the house settle, a quiet groaning above their heads, before Elizabeth's attention was drawn to something out the window.

"They're here."

The front door opened and a man entered, followed by yet another brunette woman. He wore a suit, she was in jeans and a button-down. Ari assumed the man was Timothy Dodd, the executor of Vivian's will. He glanced up and saw her, and made a quiet sound of relief.

"Ah, the private investigator. Miss Willow? Great, so glad you made it. That means we're all finally here."

He continued into the parlor, while the woman trailing behind him stopped next to Ari on the threshold of the room. Ari assumed she was Evelyn, the third and final Burroughs sister. When the woman looked at her, Ari felt a wave of déjà vu that made her look at Elizabeth and then back at Evelyn. Both of them seemed to recognize the double take and laughed in the same way - one quick "haha," a dip of the chin, and then a toss of the head to get the hair out of their eyes.

"I'm guessing Mom didn't tell you Ellie and I were twins."

Ari said, "No, it didn't really come up."

Evelyn nodded. "Well, it's good to meet you." She put her hands in her pockets and let her eyes travel over her siblings. "Hey Presto, I see you're all lubed up already."

"Don't call me Presto," he grumbled, but he reached out and put his glass down on the table. Eleanor reached out and put a coaster under it.

Timothy stood in front of the fireplace and cleared his throat. "Obviously this situation is a bit unorthodox. The official reading of Vivian Burroughs' will is going to take place at a later date when all the beneficiaries can be contacted. But I was asked to take care of this particular item as quickly as possible and in this manner."

"Mom always loved a show," Evelyn muttered so low that only Ari could hear it, although Elizabeth looked over as if she'd also heard.

"Miss Willow," Timothy said, "if you would present the key which has been entrusted to your care?"

Ari took the key from her pocket. It was a small gesture, but at the back of her mind she realized that simply holding it up had basically just earned her thirty grand. She stepped forward to place the key on the table, noticing that Preston scooted to the edge of the couch to stare at it. Even Eleanor stared from the corner of her eye, trying very hard to look like she wasn't looking.

"Excellent." He produced a folded piece of paper. "This is a note Miss Burroughs included with her Last Will and Testament, and she would like it to be read now." He cleared his throat.

"To my children, in regards to Crossing-Over Place. There has been a great amount of discussion around the tapestry in recent years, no doubt brought on by my ailing health. Each of you have expressed an interest in it, either privately or publicly. It's always been my belief that the fairest solution would be to sell the damned thing and split the money equally among you."

Elizabeth made a noise Ari couldn't interpret. Timothy continued.

"I've often been depressed by the thought that none of you seem to know the true meaning of the word priceless. You take it to mean the tapestry is worth whatever price you ask for it. The true meaning of 'priceless' is that no one can, and no one should, put a monetary value on something of such importance. Crossing-Over Place is art, it is history, and it should never be cheapened by having a price tag hanging around its throat like a noose."

Eleanor lowered her head and put a hand against her temple. "Oh no."

"Therefore," Timothy continued, "I have decided to donate Crossing-Over Place to the Burke Museum."

Preston got to his feet. "That is bullshit!"

Timothy didn't even look up. "Ariadne Willow, acting as my proxy, is to give the key to Mr. Timothy Dodd, who will take possession of the tapestry until the museum can be contacted~"

"Bullshit," Preston said again, this time grabbing the key off the table and storming out of the room. Evelyn stepped in front of him, but he pushed her out of the way and kept going.

Ari didn't hesitate. She stepped around Evelyn and grabbed the back of Preston's jacket. She bent her arm and twisted, throwing him off-balance and sending him reeling toward the wall. She stepped in closer, grabbed his arm, and shoved him against the wall hard enough that the sliding door shook. She held him in place with one hand and plucked the key from his grip with the other.

"I don't think the man was finished speaking," she said.

Elizabeth, who had remained against the wall, had taken a step forward during the scuffle. "Well, hello, Miss Willow," she said under her breath. Some of the judgement faded from her face, the haughty sneer replaced by true interest.

Ari ignored that and let Preston go. She took the key back to the table and held it out. "Mr. Dodd, maybe you want to take this."

"Actually, Miss Willow, since you were the one entrusted with it... and you've just proven how strong that loyalty is... I believe Miss Burroughs would prefer if *you* held onto it. The rest of the note simply says that I should prepare the tapestry for transport to the museum. If you wouldn't mind following me upstairs to unlock the door..."

Preston said, "Oh hell no. No, that thing really *is* priceless, and there's no way I'm letting these two strangers walk in there and walk away with it."

"It's what Mom wanted," Eleanor said softly.

"Screw that!"

Elizabeth said, "I'm afraid I have to agree with the brat." She took out her phone and held it out in front of her. "I'll go with them and document everything they do."

Preston scoffed. "So you can sneak it away from them?"

Evelyn said, "Did you miss the part where she's going to be literally recording everything?"

"Like I trust her."

The twins gave up the fight. Ari noticed that Eleanor seemed uncomfortable, but already assumed she wouldn't speak up and take sides against her siblings.

"Look, why don't we *all* just go upstairs together?" Ari suggested. "That way no one has to trust anyone, and you'll all get a chance to say goodbye to the tapestry before it goes to its new home. Does that work for everyone?"

"It's fine by me," Eleanor said quickly.

Timothy nodded. "Seems like a reasonable tactic, Miss Willow."

Ari said, "Okay then. Let's go, campers."

She led the way upstairs. She didn't look back to see who followed her first, but she knew the room emptied out behind her. The chair lift had already been taken out. She was surprised by how sad that made her. Hopefully Vivian had done it herself before she passed, because otherwise its loss was a crass move by a family she had quickly grown to dislike.

She led the witnesses to the door and slipped the key into the lock. She turned it, both felt and heard the latch click, and twisted the knob. It was strange to think that she was the last person to enter the room, given how long ago it seemed, and she instinctively turned her head to the left as she stepped inside. Preston pushed past her, and Eleanor stopped next to Ari and gaped with her.

The tapestry was gone.

CHAPTER FIVE

THERE WAS no denying its absence. The wall was completely bare without it, a patch of light brown between two stuffed bookshelves. The rest of the Burroughs family had entered the room, along with Timothy Dodd, and they all stared at the empty space as if that was the work of art.

Preston was the first to recover. He aimed a finger at Ari. "You! You broke in here and stole it."

"And then came back so I could escort you all to the scene of the crime?" Ari said.

That tripped him up, but only briefly. "As an excuse if we find your fingerprints anywhere in here!"

Ari held her hands up. "I haven't touched anything."

Evelyn said, "Don't be an idiot, Preston. It's far more likely one of us broke in here and stole the damn thing."

Ari agreed. Unfortunately the fact that they'd all entered the room together meant that they had contaminated any scent they might have left behind while stealing the tapestry. She took a deep breath anyway, just to see what she picked up, but there were far too many people around for her to sort through all of them. It was an interior room. No windows, but every wall was shared with another room in the house. Walls were good barricades, but they were far from impenetrable.

"The air ducts!" Eleanor said. "Maybe someone used the vents."

"It's not *Die Hard*," Ari said. But that only mattered to someone human-sized. She'd seen werecats, mermaids, all kinds of shifters. Maybe someone who could turn into a snake or a rat could fit into the vents. But once they were inside... She looked at the door. "Is there a way to unlock the room from the inside?"

"All you would have to do is flip the latch," Eleanor said. "But that would mean someone was in here when you and Mom locked it up."

Ari said, "Yeah. That doesn't seem likely."

Elizabeth and Evelyn were standing near each other, heads bowed close, arms crossed. It was disconcerting to see two women who looked so much alike and seemed identical in every way except fashion sense. Evelyn saw Ari watching them and returned her gaze without blinking. After a moment, she stepped away from her sister and nodded at Ari.

"How much do you charge?"

Preston spun on her. "What?"

Evelyn ignored him. "Is it like a retainer or, or a daily rate?"

Ari said, "Your mother paid me very well to watch the key. Actually, she paid me for eight weeks and it was only six, so technically I'm still on the clock."

Preston said, "If she's not the thief, then someone who works with her or her boyfriend or... or..."

"Mr. Burroughs, I've been working in this city for over a decade. I have a reputation. That's why your mother hired me, in fact. I promise you, I haven't built a life here just waiting for a payday to fall into my lap. I actually ran away from a life of easy money. I lived on the streets and built my agency from the ground up. I wouldn't throw that all away."

Eleanor said, "Not to mention the fact she's the obvious suspect. The key was in your possession the entire time? You're positive?"

Ari took a moment to think about it. "If it wasn't in my pocket, it was nearby. It was on the same keychain as my house and office keys."

"Someone could have broken into your house while you were asleep," Preston said, with less of the fire than he'd started with.

Evelyn and Ari both glared at him. Evelyn said, "Someone

broke into the house of a private detective without her noticing? I find that hard to believe." She looked at Ari again. "We'll hire you. Or keep you on retainer, or whatever you want to call it. Find out what happened here, find the tapestry, and bring it back. And if you go over the time you had left, we can…"

"No, however long it takes, you're paid in full. Your mother didn't hire me to just watch a key, she hired me to ensure the tapestry was safe." She gestured at the empty space on the wall. "I obviously failed. The case is open until I get it back where it belongs."

Timothy suggested the family go downstairs so Ari could look around without distraction. Preston gave a halfhearted protest, but Eleanor stopped him by pointing out Ari couldn't exactly slip the tapestry under her shirt and sneak out with it. Ari said they could use the time looking around downstairs to see if anything else had been taken.

Once they were gone, Ari stood in the center of the room. She closed her eyes and breathed deeply. She would get a better result if she transformed into the wolf, but she wasn't about to risk that with everyone downstairs. The perfume, cologne, and body odor of everyone who had just left swirled around in the otherwise stale air of the room.

She checked the rooms which shared walls with the study and didn't find any evidence of tunneling. She counted steps in the corridor and determined there was no missing space that could indicate a secret passageway. The ceiling of the study was unbroken save for the light fixture, so there was no need to check the attic since no one could have accessed the room from there anyway. She looked at the hinges on the door, even though they were on the inside, and confirmed there was no evidence they'd been knocked out so the door could be removed without being unlocked.

"What the hell?" she muttered under her breath. It seemed impossible to access the room without the key, and she knew it had been in her possession from the moment the door was locked. She tried to remember any instances where she and her keys were separated. Other than running as the wolf, there was nothing. Whenever she had pockets, the key was in one of them. Even when they went to Bellingham, Dale had used her key so it would be with them.

There was no way into the room without the key, and either

she or Dale had always been in possession of the key.

She went downstairs, where everyone had again gathered in the parlor. The twins were on one divan with Eleanor, and Preston sat on the other with a fresh glass of something amber. Elizabeth also had a drink now. Timothy was pacing, but he stopped and looked at her hopefully.

"Ah, the great detective returns," Preston said.

"Did you find anything?" Eleanor asked, ignoring him.

Ari said, "Nothing to indicate who took the tapestry or where it might be now. Is anything else missing down here?"

"We didn't find anything amiss," Timothy said.

"Of course, none of them have been in the house for months," Preston said, "so how would they know?"

Elizabeth raised a glass to her brother. "To the grand martyr!"

"Stop it!" Eleanor snapped, and the two went back to sulking.

Ari cleared her throat. "Earlier you said that your mother paid for you to stay hotels. Was there a reason you didn't just stay here? There are plenty of rooms upstairs."

Evelyn smirked. "We're not even staying at the same hotels. Mom wanted her last days to be peaceful. Having the four of us under the same roof would be, um, counterproductive."

"I suppose that makes sense," Ari muttered. "Okay. Was anyone else staying in the house, or was there anyone who might have come by after your mother passed away? Did she have any romantic partners or—"

Elizabeth and Preston both laughed. Preston said, "Mom didn't have 'romantic partners,' not since Dad. He died in the same accident that put her in the wheelchair. She was... angry and grieving and depressed. A few years later, Ellie suggested she should start dating again, and Mom told her she would never again put her heart through that."

Eleanor said, "She was also aware that some men might see her differently because of the chair, and other men might try to take advantage of her 'weakness' to get access to her wealth."

"Seems like a reasonable enough concern," Elizabeth said.

Eleanor shrugged.

Ari said, "Okay. I'm going to need access to footage from the security camera out front. If there's a camera in the backyard, I'll need that footage, too. Mr. Dodd, if I need to get back into the house..."

"Absolutely, Miss Willow, I'll see that it's arranged."

She looked at the siblings. "The will reading isn't for another few days. I don't know how long all of you planned to stay in Seattle, but it would be great if you could stick around a bit longer, just until we have all the answers. I'll also need a way to get in touch with all of you so we can talk."

Evelyn rolled her eyes.

Eleanor took out her phone and began tapping at the screen. "I think that can be arranged. I'm here until Saturday, so I can push that back to a later flight."

Elizabeth shrugged and said, "I'll be around."

Preston said, "I live here, so whatever."

"Fantastic."

She took out her wallet to give everyone a card, taking their cards in return. Preston had to put his information on the back of one of Ari's cards. She had no idea where she would even begin to look if someone in this room wasn't revealed as the thief, but her mood was lightened by the knowledge of one person who would be over the moon about this news.

Dale listened calmly to the recap when Ari got back to the office but, once she was finished, she leaned forward with a manic grin. "It's a locked room mystery!"

Ari glared across the desk, but she was clearly amused. "Try not to act so excited, Dale. If I don't solve this, the best case scenario is that we have to return thirty thousand dollars. Worst case scenario is that we get sued for the loss of something that has been described two different ways as 'priceless.' I don't think the agency can take a hit like that."

Dale's shoulders slumped and she fell back against her chair. "True. But on the bright side, I have all the confidence in the world in you and your abilities." Her smile slowly returned, as if it was too strong for her to hold back. "But come on, puppy! A real-life locked room mystery!"

Ari couldn't help but smile at Dale's excitement. "Okay, yeah, that is kind of cool."

"So do you have any leads yet?"

"The whole family," Ari said. "Any of them could have done it. Elizabeth is quiet and grumpy, Evelyn is flaky, Preston seems like an alcoholic, and Eleanor... well, Eleanor seems calm and reasonable, but you can never trust the quiet ones. They're always hiding something."

"Okay." Dale stood and went to their bulletin board. She skimmed to make sure everything she was about to erase was outdated before she swept an eraser across it all. "We have the suspects. Are we going to add you to the list?"

Ari said, "Hey!"

"Come on, Ari, you had the only key and you recently got out of prison. If it was anybody else, they would look at you first."

Ari grunted. "Okay, fine, I'm a suspect, too."

Dale wrote the names on the board. "The PI's secretary is sleeping with the prime suspect in the case. Boy, this is turning into quite a noir."

"I'm not going to call you a dame."

"Even if I ask you nicely?"

Ari grinned and stared at the names Dale had written. Eleanor. Evelyn. Elizabeth. Preston. Timothy. And, of course, her own name at the end of the list. She obviously didn't consider herself a suspect in the theft, but there was always the possibility someone had gotten access to the key without her knowing. She'd been the wolf fourteen times in the past six weeks. Assuming two hours for every transformation, that was twenty-eight hours she couldn't swear to knowing where the key was. That was enough for reasonable doubt.

Dale hooked a thumb toward the door. "I'll let you ponder this while I go through three days of security camera footage to see who went in the Burroughs house after Vivian's death."

"Have fun," Ari said.

"I always have fun with security camera footage," Dale said on her way out of Ari's office. "Better than Netflix."

Ari got up and went to the board. She'd gotten some more information from each family member before she left the house, and she transferred the notes from her phone to the board.

Eleanor. The eldest, lived in Philadelphia. She had explained what her job was, but all Ari was able to understand was that she did public relations for a company that did something with an app that was somehow tied to sports. She'd arrived in Seattle exactly one week ago.

Evelyn lived in Portland, where she worked as a bartender who was also a driver for food-delivery and rideshare apps. She drove up last Wednesday, the same day Eleanor arrived. They had both taken their mother to dinner at SkyCity, the restaurant at the top of the Space Needle.

Elizabeth, Evelyn's twin, hadn't shown up until Friday. She

lived in Spokane, where she was the sales manager for a winery. They went to the Chihuly Garden and Glass Museum, then met their sisters for dinner at Canlis.

And Preston, the baby of the family, lived in Seattle. He dropped by the house every few weeks to check up on their mother and see if there was anything that needed to be done around the house. Evelyn had interjected that this was just an excuse to "pick up his allowance," which Preston hadn't exactly denied. He worked in construction and fixed up cars for his neighbors, and "sometimes things get slow." He claimed his mother was always happy to help him out. They hadn't done anything special in her last week, but they had gone out to dinner at No Anchor two nights before Vivian died.

Vivian ended her life on Sunday night. She'd asked for privacy on the last day of her life, and her children had agreed. According to Timothy Dodd, Vivian left the house at six o'clock and went to a clinic where her physician helped her carry out her plans. Ari couldn't help but feel sad thinking about that. She knew it was Vivian's choice, and it was done to prevent months or years of pain and hardship, but it still hit her hard.

There had been times when her transformations were still causing her unbearable pain when she'd thought about it. She had known they were getting worse, that one day she might be stuck in one form or the other, and a part of her brain kept suicide as an option when that dark day arrived. She liked to think she would never have gone through with it, especially after she and Dale officially became a couple, but there were days when she remembered how much it had hurt...

Dale knocked on the door, bringing Ari out of her reverie. "Sorry to disturb your thinking."

"It's fine. What I was thinking was worth disturbing. Did you find something on the video?"

"Maybe. I wanted your opinion."

Ari followed her out to her desk. Dale sat down and angled the computer so Ari could see the screen. The security camera was angled to show the front walk and the space where someone who rang the doorbell would be standing. They could see the majority of the lawn and the street in front of the house. Streetlights glowed on the opposite sidewalk, but the Burroughs property was shrouded in darkness.

"This is Monday night, the night after... you know. According to the executor, no one was in the house that day."

"Yeah, the kids all did their own thing on Monday and Tuesday."

Dale said, "Okay. This is ten o'clock." She hit play and Ari watched the street. A car went by, but no pedestrians. "Did you see it?"

"What was I looking for?" Ari asked.

"I'll run it back." Dale reversed the tape to ten o'clock. At six minutes past the hour, she stopped it and pointed at the lawn. Ari almost asked what she was looking for when she saw it: a square of light on the grass. She moved closer to be sure she was actually seeing it.

"Is that...?"

"I'm guessing one of the second-floor rooms. Someone turned a light on."

Ari said, "The study where the tapestry was hanging doesn't have a window, so it couldn't have been that room." She pressed a hard kiss to Dale's temple. "Good eyes, baby."

"Happy I could help. I just wish I could tell you who was in the house. I went back four hours and ahead to noon. I didn't see anyone go inside."

"You did your job," Ari said. "Time for me to do mine."

CHAPTER SIX

THERE WERE five houses with a clear sightline of the Burroughs property. It stood on a corner, so it had two across-the-street neighbors. One house behind it shared a fence with the Burroughs' backyard, and an eight-foot wall stood between it and its neighbor. Ari didn't see cameras on every property but she still visited all five and asked if there was any footage she might be able to examine. Someone at two of the houses said yes and handed over the tapes immediately. One woman couldn't agree without asking her employer, and one man told her she would have to come back with a warrant.

The man who lived at the last house, the one which faced the side of the Burroughs home, looked like he should've been in high school. Pudgy, curly-haired, and with a smattering of patchy hair on his cheeks and chin, he answered the door wearing jeans and a Seahawks jersey. He was wearing a headset, the microphone of which he pushed away from his mouth as he looked at her empty hands.

"Where's the food?"

"Sorry, I'm not whoever you were expecting. My name is Ariadne Willow. I'm a private investigator. I was hoping I could take a look at your security footage from this past Monday."

He blinked at her. "Wait, holy shit, you're really a private eye?" He moved the microphone back down. "Guys, I'm out." He took off the headset and held out his other hand. "I'm Fitz Anstartz."

Ari couldn't help but laugh. "I'm sorry?"

"Had it legally changed. That's the name of my company. We make video games. Do you, uh, d-do you play? I could give you a tutorial."

"I'm just looking for the security footage, if you have any."

"Oh! Right, god, of course, come in."

She hesitated, but he was already hurrying down the front hallway. She stepped inside.

The house was nicer than she expected given his age. Polished hardwood floors, beautiful furniture, nice ambiance, and it didn't reek like 'young dude living alone.' She heard the sounds of a video game battle echoing down the hall and moved toward it. She found Fitz in a den with a TV so large she wondered if a football stadium somewhere was missing its Jumbotron. The screen switched to the menu of a game, then to a different menu screen. He glanced over his shoulder to make sure she was there before he spoke.

"What time do you need?"

"Uh, ten o'clock. PM. I only need the angle facing the Burroughs house."

He said, "Right... the... Burroughs..."

"On the east," she clarified, "across the street."

"Oh! Wheelchair lady!" He cringed. "Oh shit, I'm sorry. I didn't mean that the way it sounded. I just mean, we never talked or anything and she was in a wheelchair. She seemed nice. Not, like, you know, a mean old witch or anything like that."

"I understand," Ari said.

He accessed his security cameras and scrolled through looking for the right time stamp. "So what happened? Was there, like, a break-in or something?"

"I'm not sure," Ari said. "Miss Burroughs passed away on Sunday and we're trying to find something from the house that went missing."

"Aw, she died? Man, that sucks. Sorry to hear that."

Ari said, "Did she have many visitors?"

"No. I never really saw anyone over there. Not in a creepy way, though. She kept to herself. She didn't mind when my friends came over and had to park in front of her house."

"So no boyfriends?"

He looked confused. "She was old…" The doorbell rang. "Shit, that's probably my food. Here." He handed the control to her. "I'll be right back."

He was gone before she could protest. Ari looked at the control's jumble of buttons and pressed one, hoping she wasn't about to erase anything she might need.

The screen was massive, and the image was so clear that it felt like she was standing on the roof of Fitz's house looking down at the street. The time stamp said ten o'clock, and the video Dale had showed the light coming on at 10:06. She watched and, as they suspected, the window above the front door suddenly lit up. She continued the recording and watched for signs of anyone approaching from the side of the house. The backyard wasn't entirely enclosed, so someone could easily access the back door from the sidewalk.

Fitz came back with a large bag of delivery food. "Hey, you're not rich are you?"

"Nope," Ari said, eyes still locked on the screen.

"What's a good tip on a twenty dollar delivery? Like, someone once told me, tips are ten percent, but then that's twenty-two dollars, and who carries singles? A twenty is the smallest I have, so whatever, I just give them two. They always ask if I want change back, and I mean, how much should I even let them keep? Fifteen?"

"A fifteen dollar tip on a twenty dollar bill would be very, very generous." It seemed that even someone with no concept of money should be able to figure that out. "Always tip on the side of caution. There's no such thing as too much."

Fitz sat on the couch and began taking containers out of the bag. "Have you found what you're looking for?"

"I confirmed something," she said. "Now I'm just looking to see who leaves."

"Cool. Well… if you wanted to, like, hang out or whatever. I mean, I ordered a lot of food, if you wanted to have dinner."

Ari smiled and kept her eyes on the screen. "Sorry, Fitz, I have a girlfriend."

"Aw, that sucks. Well, I mean, it doesn't suck. I'm an ally. It's all great. My last girlfriend was bi."

"Cool," Ari said flatly.

The video showed a handful of cars, but it seemed as if the neighborhood wasn't particularly lively after ten o'clock. The time stamp rolled past eleven. The light on the second floor of the

Burroughs house went off, but no one had appeared.

"Maybe they spent the night," Fitz suggested.

"Yeah, maybe. Doesn't really help me, though…"

Fitz said, "Well, I mean, I can give you the files. I can put them on a thumb drive or email them to you. Of course I'd need your email for that…"

"Thumb drive is fine."

"Yeah, cool, I was gonna say, just as easy… uh, I'll go, uh… I'll be right back."

He got up and left the room. Ari continued to scroll through Monday night on the video. Maybe the light didn't mean anything. Maybe there was a lamp in the room with a timer that automatically turned itself on to deter thieves. She was about to turn it off when someone emerged from the shadows behind Vivian's house and moved toward the sidewalk.

Ari punched the pause button and moved closer to the screen. Four o'clock in the morning, six hours after the mystery light. Whoever it was, they were unfortunately empty-handed. She hadn't really expected them to be carrying the tapestry when they left but she was still disappointed.

"Hey, you found someone!" Fitz said, having returned.

"Let's hope they show us their face."

The intruder jogged across the street, still just a silhouette even with Fitz's high-definition cameras. The image was slightly distorted but it didn't look tall enough to be either of the twins, and the body was too broad in the hips and shoulders to be Eleanor. She supposed it could be Preston, but the probability was just as high that it was someone else. Whoever it was vanished off the side of the frame without giving her a hint about who it might be.

"That's a bummer," Fitz said. "Almost as bad as not finding anything at all, huh?"

"Yeah. Maybe he was less careful when he arrived." She looked and saw a thumb drive in Fitz's hand. "Is that the footage?"

"Oh. Yeah." He held it out to her. "I went ahead and gave you everything from Sunday morning until today. Just to cover all the bases, you know."

Ari said, "That's a huge help. Thank you."

"Always happy to help. And, uh, I don't have to worry about… like, you know, security? This isn't about a crime ring or anything like that, right?"

"No, nothing like that. Thank you for all your help, Mister…

uh... sorry, but your last name is ridiculous."

He laughed. "Yeah, but the app got me this house and made sure I never have to work again, so I figure I might as well wear it with pride, you know?"

"App?" Ari said, and then realized what he meant. "Fits and Starts. That was you?"

"That's me," he said. "I cooked up a way to help my friends increase their productivity, and the next thing I know, Apple is backing a dump truck full of money up to my dorm room. Is there a chance they're using it to turn their workforce into mindless drones? Sure. Do I feel bad about that...? I mean... well, they were being treated like worker bees anyway. At least with my app they get bathroom breaks, you know?"

"Right," Ari said. "Well, it just goes to show you, no one becomes a millionaire by worrying about what happens to the other guy."

"Exactly!" Fitz said, missing her point.

She held up the thumb drive. "Thank you for this. You've been a big help."

"Let me know if you need anything else! It was great to meet you. Let me walk you to the door."

"That's okay. Your food is getting cold."

He looked at the table. "Right. Okay. Well, hope to see you again, Miss Willow."

She smiled and said nothing as she walked past him.

Dealing with all these rich people was getting to her, and it was keeping Isaac Hayden's comment about her mother's wealth percolating at the back of her mind. Vivian Burroughs was old money. Fitz Anstartz was new money. But the Willows...? There had never really been much discussion about her extended family. She didn't know her grandparents, didn't have aunts or uncles, which meant there were no cousins to speak of. It was just her and her mother.

So how the hell had Gwyneth Willow end up the sole beneficiary of an inheritance so large there was still plenty of it left thirty-some years later? The more she thought about it, the less sense it made, and the more likely their relationship was going to change when she finally summoned the courage to ask.

Ari stopped by the office to save Fitz's security footage and get stills of the mystery man leaving the house. She and Dale scanned backwards from ten o'clock to see if they could get a better image of the man on his way into the house, but he never showed up. Either he'd spent a full day inside or he'd managed to slip by cameras he hadn't even known to avoid. Dumb luck was a detective's worst enemy. Dale was also looking into art and antique dealers who might be contacted about the tapestry. There was no point in stealing something priceless if there was no market for it.

It was close to dinnertime when she called Eleanor to set up a meeting. She'd chosen Eleanor because she seemed like the most likely to give a solid, unbiased account of the family history. Both twins seemed to have a chip on their shoulders and Preston... well, she would talk to him when there was no other option. Eleanor was still on Philly time and had already eaten dinner, so she told Ari she could go ahead and come by the hotel if it was convenient for her.

Eleanor had a suite at the Hotel Monaco, a place so fancy that Ari went home to change into something nicer before she went to the meeting. The outfit she'd been wearing was fine, but it wasn't Monaco-fine. The elevator was only accessible via keycard, but Eleanor had called down to the front desk and a helpful young man sent her up to the correct floor. Despite changing into her nicest clothes, she still felt a bit conspicuous as she waited to be let in.

"Miss Willow, hello," Eleanor said, opening the door and then immediately going back into the room. She had changed as well since that morning at her mother's house, now dressed in billowing white silk slacks and a blue blouse. Her hair was also down, and Ari thought the look suited her better.

Eleanor stood next to the coffee table and flipped her hands up. "Sorry."

"For...?"

"For... this." She gestured at the suite.

Ari looked around. She wondered if Eleanor was indicating an invisible mess. "What's wrong with it?"

"The extravagance. It's unnecessary. But Mom insisted on paying, and if I chose a cut-rate hotel it would look patronizing, and I would be making myself uncomfortable for no reason other than my own self-importance–"

She was rambling more than Fitz Anstartz, so Ari stopped her. "It's fine. You can afford to be comfortable, so there's no reason for you not to be."

Eleanor sighed. "Thank you for understanding. Please, have a seat."

They sat next to each other on the plush white couch. "I doubt you've found anything since this morning."

"Not a lot," Ari admitted, "but I did want to ask you a few questions."

"Of course, whatever I can do to help."

"Mr. Dodd said that no one had been in your mother's house since she left Sunday night." Eleanor nodded. "We found evidence that someone was there Monday night, just after ten o'clock."

Eleanor furrowed her brow, head tilted to the side. "That's not possible."

Ari showed her the screen grab on her phone. "This is the second floor window, where the light went on. It was only on for a couple of minutes before it went out again. Then, about six hours later, this person appeared." She swiped to the next picture. Eleanor leaned in to get a better look. "Whoever it is seemed to be coming from the backyard."

"Whoever it is, at least he doesn't seem to be carrying anything." She squinted again. "Is that a he? It looks like a man."

"It's hard to say. We went all the way back to Monday morning, but we never saw him go inside. There's a chance he had been there since Sunday night."

"The night Mom... passed. But then she would most likely have known he was there. Or... no, that's ridiculous."

Ari said, "Nothing is ridiculous on the first day of an investigation."

"This probably is. In neighborhoods like Mom's, there's a certain justifiable paranoia about opportunistic thieves. They're afraid people are stalking them on social media, waiting for a post that says they'll be out of town or at the theater. The house will be empty, and the thieves can strike. I thought perhaps whoever it is knew Mom was gone, but... no, not that quickly. She didn't die at home, so there wouldn't have been an ambulance at the house. The death notice didn't run until Tuesday morning." She smiled. "Mom sent it to the paper herself. She wanted to be sure it was worded perfectly."

Ari smiled, then thought of something herself. "The notice wasn't out yet, but someone had to have known she was gone. The funeral home..."

Eleanor was already reaching for her phone. "She was cremated... but yes, someone from the funeral home... here it is. Ibrahim & Hoffman." She read the number and Ari entered it into her phone. "Someone from there may have recognized her. My god, how ghoulish do you have to be...?"

"Pretty damn ghoulish," Ari said. "But I've seen all kinds of inhuman stuff in my job."

"Yes, I suppose you have. But whoever that is in the picture didn't take the tapestry. It's much too big."

"He might have come back with a friend. We're still going through the tape, so maybe we'll find out he came back on Tuesday. Of course, this is all assuming the tapestry was stolen after your mother passed away. We only know for sure that the tapestry was there six weeks ago, when Vivian showed it to me. That's a lot of tape to go through."

Eleanor said, "I suppose so... but I don't think you have to worry about that."

"Why not?"

"I'm..." She looked away, focusing on her fingers curled in her lap. "My sisters and I have only been in town for the past week. Preston was here, but he would never dare to do something like that when Mom was still alive. You're most likely on the right track, focusing on us in the investigation. We're the only ones with real motive."

"There was still a chance one of you could have gotten the tapestry legitimately. Unless someone knew what was in the will."

"Well, nobody knew she was going to do that, except for the lawyer. He probably got a hefty bonus for keeping his mouth shut. Mom hated us asking about who was getting what when she was gone."

"You talked about it a lot?"

Eleanor shrugged and tilted her head. "Mom told us what she planned to do. Once we got over the shock and the sadness, we had legitimate questions about what would happen after. We all assumed Preston would want the house, since he was still living in town, but everything else was up for grabs. I wanted the books. Evelyn needed furniture. Elizabeth basically wanted the entire kitchen gutted and transferred to her place."

"And the tapestry? Your mother said you seemed interested in it."

"Mm-hmm, I asked her which of us would get it. I'm sure we all brought it up at some point, but we didn't really think about it. You know how you have something hanging in your house for years and eventually, one day, you just stop seeing it? That's how it was with Crossing-Over Place. It was just part of the scenery. Part of me wanted it, but where do you hang something that big? If I'd gotten it, I also would have probably just donated it to the museum."

Ari said, "Would your siblings do the same?"

"Oh, they'd get rid of it, but they wouldn't donate it. They would want the biggest payday possible." She raised an eyebrow and tilted her head the opposite way. "Take that with a grain of salt, though. They'll probably say the same thing when my back is turned."

"Seems like there's a lot of bad blood in the family."

"God, how much time do you have?" Eleanor shook her head. "Every family has struggles, Miss Willow. When money isn't an issue, the struggle turns inward. We were our own worst enemies. Including Mom! I'm sure she seemed like a sweet, wonderful woman when you met, but she could be vicious when she wanted to be."

Ari said, "I don't doubt it."

"We're much better one-on-one. Dad was something of a calming influence on all of us. When he died, everything sort of imploded. Of course, Mom was also angry because that was when the wheelchair came into play. Losing your husband and your freedom at the same time... she took it hard. Who wouldn't, really."

"Right. And I guess I don't have to apologize since you basically just admitted you were a suspect, but where were you on Monday night?"

She smiled. "The same place I was Sunday and Tuesday. Downstairs at the bar, then up here to work on some projects I have going." Her face changed and she raised a finger. "No, that's wrong. On Monday, I went out for dinner. Tulio, just down the street. I was back in the hotel room well before ten, but I can try to find the receipt if you'd like."

"I don't think that'll be necessary right now. But don't throw it away."

"Noted."

"I'll let you get back to your evening. And I'd like to ask you to not discuss our conversation with your brother and sisters. It's better if I can bring it up without them knowing in advance."

Eleanor winked. "Noted. Standard detective stuff."

Ari had to laugh at that.

She showed herself out and called Dale while she was waiting for the elevator.

"Hey, puppy. Did you beat a confession out of Eleanor?"

"Yeah, my knuckles are all bloody and bruised. She's gonna think twice about crossing me again." She nodded to the older man who had stepped off the elevator just as she said the last part. He was still staring in shock as the doors closed on her. "Did you find anything on the tape?"

"I went all the way back to the moment Vivian left her house. And then I went back a little farther just to be sure. Whoever that was either spent a really long time inside, or somehow got around the camera. Maybe he approached from a different direction."

"Eleanor thought it was a 'he,' too."

"You don't think so?"

"I think I have more female suspects than male, so I was kind of hoping it was a woman. But I think you're right. It looks like a man."

"Maybe one of the sisters hired someone to stake the place out. Or, hey, maybe one of them is a gender shifter. We've met one of them before."

"Yeah," Ari said, but she didn't sound convinced. "Right now, I'm off the clock, and so are you. Home for dinner, or do you want to go out?"

"Going out means no dishes."

Ari said, "Out it is. I'll swing by and pick you up. I'll take you somewhere nice."

"But not so nice I have to go home and change clothes."

"Fair enough. Talk to you soon. I love you."

"I love you, too."

Ari hung up and stepped outside. The sun had gone down, and the city lit up to take its place. The night was just chilly enough that she didn't need a jacket. It was a beautiful night, and it was a good case. They'd been paid very well, and in advance, and the only person who died had done it by choice. Still, she couldn't help but feel sad. The Burroughs had obviously left a lot of things unsettled even knowing Vivian's end was near. She'd healed so many old wounds with her mother, she was terrified of reopening them, souring what they'd built.

She shook off the melancholy and walked back to her car. Her mood was nothing that couldn't be fixed by spending a night with the love of her life, who was waiting patiently for Ari to come get her.

CHAPTER SEVEN

ARI TOOK Dale to Sizzle Pie for dinner, where they shared half a pizza and took the rest home for lunch the next day. When they got home, Dale put the leftovers in the fridge only to turn around and have Ari pressing her against the counter. Ari could taste the orange-y, pine-y aftertaste of the IPA Dale had with dinner. Dale's surprised paralysis faded, and she brought her hands up to slide them under the untucked hem of Ari's shirt.

"This isn't the wolf," Ari said between kisses.

"Good," Dale said, sliding her lips over Ari's cheek. "I don't care... but good to know."

Ari had gotten Dale's shirt off and exposed one shoulder, bending to kiss the cool skin. Her breath warmed one spot, so her tongue guided her to another as Dale's hands stroked the skin on either side of Ari's spine.

"This is about... mortality. Thinking about... Vivian, and the choice she made. Just feeling good to be alive. You know?"

"I know." Dale's hands drifted lower and came back around to the catch of Ari's pants. "I get it. Really, I do. I just wish you'd stopped me from having that third slice of pizza..."

Ari smiled and pulled Dale to her. They ended up on the floor, where most of their clothes remained when they moved to the couch. Though they shifted positions several times, Ari was on top when they finally caught their breath. She put her head on the pillow next to Dale's head and pressed her face into the tangles of her hair. Dale held her hand flat and ran it over Ari's shoulder, down to close her fingers around the bicep and squeezed. Ari flexed.

"Strong puppy."

Ari moved her head down and nibbled on Dale's neck.

"Change for me."

"You're not supposed to ask your partner to change," Ari whispered, moving up to her earlobe. "You're supposed to accept them the way they are. God, I love the way you taste..."

Dale moaned. "You know what I meant. I can feel the wolf. Your muscles are twitching under the skin. She wants to run, too. She's got that mortality itch. She needs to run like you just did. Change. I want you to change while I'm holding you."

Ari lifted her head and kissed Dale's lips. "You sure?"

"Yeah."

Ari kissed her again, harder this time. While she could transform whenever she wanted, she couldn't control the process. Sometimes it felt like her whole body changed at once, and other times it was a slower tip-to-tail scenario. Tonight she wanted her face to go last, so she held the kiss with the belief that the longer she was using her mouth, the longer it would stay human. She felt Dale's foot on the back of her calf, and the length of her thigh against her hip. Ari rolled her hips forward and pressed herself between Dale's legs as her body squeezed in on itself, becoming more slender.

Her stomach rolled and twisted, and she itched as her skin became thicker. Hair sprouted on her back and shoulders. Dale squeezed her arm again and Ari could feel the muscles twitching now. Her fingers were like divining rods, twitching rapidly and curling into fists.

"Love you," Ari said.

"Love you."

Ari arched her back and closed her eyes. She pushed herself up, her lower body twisting because her legs were positioned wrong. They had been much longer when she lay down, and now it was awkward. She jumped off the couch and shook herself, head down and shoulders up. She stretched out and yawned. There was something... she'd been doing a... there was a smell. A girl. *Her* girl! She spun to look at the couch, where Dale was smiling down at her.

Dale, flushed skin, freckles, pink nipples, sweat on her breasts and arms and legs. Dale smiling. Ari yipped. Dale cupped the wolf's face with both hands and kissed her between the eyes.

"My beautiful wolf."

Ari licked Dale's face, which made her laugh, which made Ari happy. Dale smelled like sex but also like Ari, which Ari liked, very much. She licked Dale again, and Dale climbed off the couch. She wrapped a blanket around herself. She went to the door, she opened the door, and outside smells rushed in through the door. Ari stood up straighter and hurried forward, but she stopped next to Dale. She looked up, hopeful. She made a hopeful sound in her throat.

"I can't go with you. I'd get arrested if I went out like this." She tucked her hair behind her ears and crouched down. "I'm not *canidae*. But I'll be here if you need me to come find you, puppy. Always." She gave Ari's face another kiss, then jerked her head toward the door. "Go on. Get your wilds out."

Ari didn't have to be told again. She bounded out, up the stairs, and into the yard. She smelled the ground and tried to think. Where to go, where to go. Some places smelled like *fish* and some places smelled like *people* or *gasoline*. She didn't like that last one, but there were so many around. Sometimes there was food to eat and not all of it spoiled, some of it old, but a lot of it good. But her belly was full, full of pizza and pepperoni, which was very good. It was greasemeat and it was heavy in her belly. She was happy she'd done that when she was a person, it was a Nice Thing.

Then she remembered the person was working on something. The person had a problem. The person needed wolf. The wolf thought about that, thought about how many nights she'd gotten to run as long and as far as she wanted. The person was being nice to her, so she wanted to be nice to the person. She would help with the problem.

So she ran. She ran through the playground, and through a backyard, to the alley. She smelled where someone had barbequed and she smelled fresh trash that had just been thrown out. She got a little lost and ended up in a park, which she thought was great but tonight she had a mission. Her person was always going in long boring straight lines to get to places. It was so much better to cut across, to jump and climb and scurry. It took a little longer sometimes, but it was so worth the effort.

She eventually got where she needed to be: the Burroughs house, and its backyard with smelly weeds and grass that went *shuffle* under her paws as she moved through it. She stood on the sidewalk and looked around, smelled for familiar people, looked for watching watchers, but there was no one in the dark. So she went up to the house. It was big and dark. It felt empty. The back porch was long and curled around the side of the house. It was *very* dark up there but she could see big windows and heavy-looking doors. There was a swing on the porch with cushions that smelled vaguely like people and cigarettes. She smelled oil, from the wheelchair.

Wheelchair. She stopped, lifted her head. Thought.

There were steps on the front porch. Steps at the end of the walk which led down to street level. How did Vivian get in and out of the house? No ramps, where were the ramps? The wolf rounded the house and found a side entrance which, according to the person's memory, would lead into the kitchen. This door had a ramp down to the grass! But there was a retaining wall around the whole property. About two feet. Easy enough for a wolf to leap or a person to step up onto, but someone in a chair would need help to get to any car waiting at the curb.

There was a tape, video, pictures of Vivian leaving the house. Surely that would solve the mystery, but the wolf wanted to help and she was already here. She went around to the front of the house to look at the stairs themselves. She only had to sniff around a little bit to find the answer to her question. There were two long aluminum tracks attached to the top of the stairs, extending down to the walkway. They weren't permanently installed, so there was a good chance they just hadn't been in place when her person came to visit.

The wolf nudged the track with her nose. They were sturdy, stable, good. She felt bad. She wanted to solve a problem for her person, but this was a very small thing and something the person would have figured out on her own. She felt like a failure, which made her sad and disappointed. She went back to the side door and sniffed around the grass. The ground was hard and dry so no footprints. People had used this door recently, but that wasn't a big reveal either.

Frustrated. Irritated. The wolf paced.

Something clattered in the house.

She spun around, ears perked, breath held, fully alert. No lights anywhere in the house. There had been cars parked on the street, but they could have been for the neighbors. She moved toward the back of the house, stealthy now, low to the ground and keyed in to any sounds coming from within. Now she focused on the ground and smelled for signs of recent passage. Someone had passed through the backyard very recently. She could smell him now, and it was definitely a him. *The boy Burroughs. Jeremy or Justin or... Preston!* She was proud she remembered his name. She surveyed the yard. He came from the east, which was just barely outside the range of Fitz Whatever's security camera. The trees along the curb would have blocked him from view when he stepped onto the lawn and headed to the side door, which was on the opposite side of the house from Fitz's.

The wolf moved into the shadows and hunkered down. Waited. A rabbit! No, focus. No rabbits. She drew on the person's patience to keep herself from rushing off. This was Important. She watched the windows. Time passed. A stray cat got too close and, when it saw her, it turned to stone and arched its back. *Get out of here cat your lucky night cat, GO ON.* The cat zipped away. The wolf grunted and put her head back down.

Hours. But then! The side door opened. Out he came, dressed in a big coat and a hat. He was holding his left arm across his torso like he was pinning something against his body under the coat. He looked toward the street and then moved toward the backyard. He didn't see the wolf. She waited until he was in the street before she left her hiding spot and gave chase.

She heard her person in her head. *Hunt is okay. Kill is not.* She knew this, but sometimes it was good to remember. Sometimes she was a bit more of an animal. She'd never hurt anyone, but it only took one time before things could get very bad for both her and her person.

Hunting was fun even without the kill. She followed, she stayed out of sight, she sneaked, while he went west and west and west and west. The road was mostly straight with some curves, so it was easy for her to keep him in sight without hurrying or getting too close. Finally, he turned. He went south. The wolf hurried so she wouldn't lose him. She didn't know if there were side streets or he might go into a building. But when she reached the corner, there he was, still walking.

She had no idea how much distance they had covered. She was moving at a person's pace, which seemed plodding, but she guessed it was about half a mile. She also didn't know what time it was, but there were only a handful of people out and about. Delivery trucks mostly. They were fun to chase. She refrained. She had Work.

Finally, he stopped at a corner shop: brick, with outdoor seating. The front was all windows, all shiny and gold-yellow with light from inside. The wolf was cautious because it was close enough to dawn now, and she was near enough businesses that someone might spot her. But also the man she was following might spot her, and she didn't want that. There was a fence around the patio and she moved in close and looked through the window.

Preston Burroughs had taken a table near the front door. He unraveled a wire from his coat pocket, bent down to plug it into an outlet, and then plugged the other end into his phone. He was still wearing the dress shirt from that morning, but the tie was gone. He needed to shave. He took out a small backpack and, with a look over his shoulder to see if anyone was watching him, began to go through it. He never took anything out so she could see what it was, but she assumed it was pawnable items from his mother's house.

After he went through what he'd taken, Preston closed the bag and put it in the center of the table. Then he crossed his arms over it, put his head down, and pressed his face into the crook of his elbow. Sleeping at a table in a coffee shop. The wolf remembered that, remembered her person wandering at nighttime and finding places that didn't mind if she napped a little in their booths.

That thought reminded her of home, the bed she had, the woman waiting in it. Dale, her girl. She'd done what needed to be done. She stretched and went across the street. She was very close to the office and she knew the way home from there, could run it in her sleep. So off she went, down an alley, across a parking lot, through a fenced-in construction area.

Eventually she was back in the neighborhood, with all its familiar smells. Dawn was close, very close. Some of the houses she passed had signs of life behind the windows. People were making breakfast or getting kids up for school. The wolf cut into the backyard of her house and went down the stairs, pausing on the landing in front of their door. She lowered her head and closed her eyes.

First her right shoulder popped up and out, then the left, and her body unfolded with a quiet "crack." Her fur receded and her mouth stretched strangely as her jaw repositioned itself. She dropped one paw on the ground and finger unfolded, and she stretched one leg out behind her with a series of almost inaudible pops.

Ari stumbled when she stood, putting one hand against the

wall to steady herself. She blinked and looked at the door. The wolf had taken her all the way home for a change.

She let herself inside and walked on the balls of her feet to the bedroom. Dale was curled up on her side of the bed, dressed in a long T-shirt. Ari knelt down next to her and only then saw that Dale was holding her phone. Waiting for the call. Ari smiled and slipped the phone out of Dale's loose grip and twisted to put it on the charger. When it was plugged in, she cupped Dale's cheek.

"Hey, sweetie…"

Dale jerked. "Where are you… sorry… I went back to sleep." She blinked her eyes open and looked at Ari. Her expression went from confused to happy in the space of a breath. "Oh. Hey, puppy."

"Hey. I just wanted to let you know I was home. No pick-up tonight."

"Mm. Good. Thank you. Get in bed."

Ari almost protested that she was sweaty, but that had never bothered Dale before. Ari went around to her side of the bed and, checking to make sure her hands and feet weren't too dirty, got under the covers and spooned Dale from behind. She kissed Dale's hair and listened to her breathing. She knew the wolf had gone somewhere, done something, could sense there was something important stewing at the back of her brain, but if it was important, it would still be there when she woke up.

CHAPTER EIGHT

ARI PUT a tall cup of coffee down next to Preston's head, tapping the table with its edge just loud enough to wake him. He sat straight up and squinted at her, grunted, and looked around as if he expected a mob to have formed. Finally, as Ari took the seat across from him, he looked down at the coffee.

"What's this?"

"It tastes like marshmallows. My partner hates coffee, but she thinks this stuff is more like cocoa. It's really good. I got a cup myself." She lifted the cup as proof, then took a sip. "You look like you've had a rough morning."

Preston sniffed the coffee. "Not much of a coffee drinker."

"Beggars can't be choosers."

"I'm not a beggar," Preston snapped, just a little too fast.

Ari smiled. "It's just a saying. Although..." She looked him up and down. She was dressed in jeans, a T-shirt, and a button-down under a hoodie, and she felt like she was on the hipster side of shabby. Preston's homeless attire looked a bit more authentic. "Does the hotel where your mom put you up not have a laundry service?"

Preston sneered at her. "Aren't you supposed to be looking for our tapestry?"

"I'm doing that," she said. "But I need your help. Maybe you saw something when you were breaking in to loot your mother's house."

He stiffened and looked down at the bag he'd been using as a pillow. "I don't know what you're talking about."

"Come on, Presto, I'm a detective. The barista said you've been coming in here every day for the past week. You use their outlets and their wifi, then head out when the crowds come in. So what was it? You were worried about not getting enough in the will so after she passed, you decided to get in there and take whatever you could carry?"

He kept his hands on the backpack, leaning in and lowering his voice. "It isn't like that. I'm not stealing anything."

Ari poked the bag. He rolled his eyes and unzipped it, lifting the top so she could see inside. Jeans, T-shirts, toiletries.

"I'm sleeping there. I had a disagreement with my landlord and I've been locked out of my apartment for about a week. I was crashing with friends, but they were starting to get sick of me promising I would pay them back with interest once... you know..." He had the good grace to look ashamed. "Once I got some money that was coming in."

"Classy," Ari said.

"Hey, it's not like I'm grave robbing. Mom made her decision. And there's shit in that house I actually *could* pawn, you know. If I wanted to. But I'm not going to do that. I go there at night to do laundry. Cook food. Sleep a few hours in a comfortable bed. I mean, it's just a big house sitting there, gathering dust. Amenities paid up until the end of the month. So why not take advantage of it? I sneak in after dark and then leave before dawn just in case anyone comes sniffing around."

"I thought your mother offered to put you all up in hotels."

He laughed. "The girls, the *girls*, she offered to put the girls up in hotels. Because they had to come so far. Because they have lives out..." He growled and wiped a hand over his face. "Someone had to be here, all right? Who do you think changes the lights in that place? Who do you think helps fix the lift when it breaks and leaves her stranded on the second floor? I know they talk about me behind my back and talk about my 'allowance,' but I earn that money, okay?"

Ari shrugged. "If you say so. I'm only concerned about that tapestry."

He put his head down on the bag. "I have no idea what happened to that stupid thing, lady. I'm in that house six, maybe seven hours a night. I didn't even think about that room because we were barely ever allowed in it. That was Mom's study. It was where she went to read and, I don't know, get away from us bratty kids. The door could have been unlocked the entire time and I wouldn't have known it."

"Just between us, you never considered turning one of those old books into rent money?"

He returned her stare without blinking. "I don't like you, Tree."

She pushed out her bottom lip in a pout. "I think I'll get over it, though. I have no personal opinions about you, Preston. I'm not one of your sisters. Right now, all you are is a person who had access to the scene of the crime when nobody else did. You're the only one who went into the house between Sunday night and yesterday morning. If you're not the thief, then you're the person best suited to know who it might have been. Were there signs of anyone else being in the house this week?"

"I have no idea. Like I said, I was there to sleep, eat, and do laundry. I wasn't counting the silverware. Besides, we're not talking about some dumb knickknack. You saw the size of that thing. Taking it would be a big job. There's no way you could sneak it out even if you wanted to."

"Yeah..." Ari hated to admit he had a point. Sneaking laundry in the side door was one thing, but taking out a six-by-four tapestry, even rolled up, would be noticeable. "Do you think it's possible the tapestry was taken before your mother passed away?"

"She barely ever left the house."

"She left the house four times in the week before she died," Ari said. "She took you and your sisters all out to special goodbye events."

Preston flinched at that, which she filed away as odd. "Sure, I guess those times. But the only people who knew about that was us, and I guess if she made reservations. No one could have planned a complicated heist to happen in the few hours she was gone. But it's just as unlikely anyone could have gotten in there when she was still around to catch them."

Ari held her hands up. "Help me out then, Preston, because the tapestry *is* gone. We're sitting here talking about how completely impossible it would be to steal it when we both saw it with our own eyes. How do you explain that?"

He shook his head. "I can't. That's supposed to be your job."

"Right," she sighed. She stood up and dropped a twenty on the table between them. "Get breakfast. It's on your mom's tab."

He looked like he wanted to fling the money back at her, but he grabbed it and shoved it into his pocket with what might have been a mumbled thanks. She started to leave but had second thoughts.

"I lived on the street for a long time. I had a house I could've gone back to, I had family waiting to take me in. If I had swallowed my pride, I could have saved myself a lot of grief. I might not have turned out to be the same person I am now. But I'm just saying, some people don't have the option of turning their back on a lifeboat just because they don't like who the captain is."

Preston snorted and looked out the window.

"Just some friendly advice. I'll be in touch."

She walked outside and stood on the sidewalk to watch traffic pass, standing not far from where she'd crouched as the wolf just a few hours earlier. The mystery of how a light turned on Monday night was solved, but the answer only gave her more questions and further solidified the impossibility of the tapestry being stolen in the past few days. She would have to get more security footage, both from Vivian's front door camera and Fitz's, if he was still feeling generous. She would owe Dale something fancy for going through so much boring tape.

The only thing she knew for sure was that Crossing-Over Place had been there six weeks ago, and it was gone now. At some point in between, someone had gone into the house and walked out with it. All she had to do was figure out the "how."

It sounded so easy on paper...

Dale had spent the morning on the phone following up with a few art dealers who might know where and how a person might turn a priceless tapestry into a big paycheck. Everyone she called was aghast at the implication they might know anything about the art world's black market, but a bit of gentle prodding led to most of them confessing they might have heard something somewhere, once, through whispers and urban legend. Nothing and no one they had ever done business with, of course, absolutely not. But maybe she might try this person, that gallery...

The majority of the people she talked to were extremely excited when she mentioned the name Crossing-Over Place. Two of them forgot why she had called and asked if they could come over and see it. She left the agency's number with all of them and asked that they call if anyone showed up trying to sell the tapestry. She got the impression that at least a handful of them were more likely to make an offer on it before alerting the authorities, but she had to try.

She was just finishing up with one call when there was a knock on the office door. A man opened it and stuck his head inside, his bushy eyebrows raised in question. Dale smiled and held up her hand, making three motions in quick succession: hello, come in, I'll just be a minute. He nodded and came in, sticking his hands in his pockets and looking past her out the window as he waited. His hair was faded silver from brown, and she guessed his age to be late fifties or early sixties.

"Thank you very much, ma'am. Yes, when it's recovered, I'll be sure to let the owners know you're interested." Not that the museum would care very much, but she hadn't said there was hope of a sale. "Have a nice day." She hung up and turned her attention to the man. He wore a button-down shirt and khakis. The strap of a messenger bag cut across his chest. "Hi, how can we help you?"

"I was hoping to speak with the, ah, the detective. Ariadne Willow."

"She had an early meeting this morning, so she's not in yet. If you'd like to leave a message, I can have her get back to you after lunch."

He twisted his lips in disappointment. "That's too bad. I was really hoping I could talk with her." He looked at her again as if reassessing her. "You're Dale Frye, right?"

Warning bells rang at the back of Dale's head, but they were quiet enough for her to push past them. "That's right. I didn't catch your name."

"Rude of me. I'm sorry. I'm Isaac Hayden."

Dale leaned back in her chair. "Oh, I see. Mr. Hayden. You're the one who thinks Ari is a werewolf?" She chuckled through the last word. "I hope you don't think you're being creative. We named our agency Bitches. Some people go a little too far with it. Are you here to call me a werewolf, too? Because Ari and I have talked about it, and we decided I would be a werefox." She gestured at her hair. "You know, because redhead."

Isaac chuckled. It was an honest laugh, almost charming, and he pulled out one of the chairs so he could sit down.

"You're funny, Miss Frye. Can I call you Dale?"

"Nah."

He nodded without missing a beat. "Okay, Miss Frye. I've done a lot of research i-into hunters and *canidae*. The evidence is out there for whoever bothers to look for it. There's..." He laughed and shook his head. "There's a second species living in the world which has been around as long as civilization. You can't hide something like that forever. Especially not now, in the age where every minute of every day is being chronicled somewhere. I assume I'm being recorded right now, either by a security camera or a microphone on your computer."

He wasn't, but Dale was disappointed she hadn't thought of it.

"There have always been wolves in the woods," he said. His tone indicated he was reciting something. "Beware."

"Ominous," Dale said. "There have been stories about monsters in the woods forever. Fairy tales about things lurking in the dark to keep children from wandering off and getting killed by the real dangers. Bears and actual wolves and just falling off a damn cliff. But now that the world is a lot smaller, people still want the myths to be real because... well, the real world is a mess. And believing in something fantastic makes that a little easier to take."

Isaac was still smiling. "I came to Seattle because I was following a group of hunters who relocated here a few years ago. I found out they were looking to rekindle something called wolf manoth."

"Wolf mammoth?" Dale said.

"You're clever, I'll give you that much. Wolf manoth. It was a yearly event where hunters would kill as many *canidae* as they could find. It almost happened here, in Seattle. I wanted to find out why it failed. I learned the name Ariadne Willow. She was a peacemaker. I hadn't even started to look for her when she wandered into the deli where I was having lunch. Do you think that's just a coincidence?"

"No. That deli has excellent sandwiches. They attract all kinds of species."

His smile had faded, but Dale still didn't think he was threatening her. He just seemed passionate. He scooted forward to the edge of his chair and poked a finger down on the desk.

"Okay, then, about six months ago. The Howl Around the Sound."

Dale raised an eyebrow. "The what?"

"A regular weekday afternoon when suddenly, out of nowhere, came the sound of howling."

"My neighbor's dog does that every time a fire truck goes by."

All the humor had faded from his expression. "Not like this. This was as if every dog in the Seattle city limits began howling. All at once. As if on cue. People heard it all across the city. There are videos all over YouTube, from the Space Needle, to Pioneer Square, from Fremont. The one on the ferry is particularly eerie, because the howls were amplified by all the water. You didn't hear it?"

"Of course I heard it. I was downtown. It didn't last very long. Everyone around just kind of looked at each other, and we checked out phones to make sure it wasn't some terrorism bullshit, and then we went about our day."

He wiped a hand over his face, clearly frustrated. "Okay. Well... I'm obviously not going to make you crack. I'll never play poker with you, Miss Frye." He opened his messenger bag and pulled out a small, thin book. It had a cracked leather cover and was held closed by a strip of rawhide around its width and wrapped around a button on the front. He placed it on the desk in front of her. "Maybe this will help open your eyes."

She leaned forward to read the gold leaf lettering on the front. Her poker face may have been good, but she still couldn't hide her surprise when she saw the title: *Canidae in the Modern World*, with Karl Magnusson's name underneath it in a smaller font.

"You recognize this, don't you?"

"You mentioned it to Ari when you ran into her a few weeks ago," Dale said. "I looked it up online. This should be in Frankfurt."

Isaac didn't blink. "It *should be* published, so the world can make up their own mind. But that's never going to happen." He took it back and returned it to his bag, taking out a compact book that looked as if he had bound it himself. He put it where the book had been resting. "That's a copy of the book. I'll leave it here for you and Miss Willow to peruse." He stood up and went to the door. "I have to ask one thing, Miss Frye. Has Ariadne asked her mother about their wealth yet?"

"That's personal business, Mr. Hayden."

"Okay," he said, nodding. "Okay, I was just curious. Happy reading."

He left, and Dale allowed herself a quick shudder. The man had been charming and personable, but there was still something about him that rubbed her the wrong way. She looked down at the book he'd left and thumbed it open. She thought he had just photocopied the book, but it seemed as if he actually transcribed it and printed it out. She couldn't tell if that was dedication or madness.

Whatever it was, she definitely didn't want to play poker with him, either.

CHAPTER NINE

ARI LISTENED as Dale recounted the conversation she'd just had with Isaac Hayden. The phone rang just as she was about to step into the Zoo Tavern and she walked back to the corner to take the call. Dale didn't sound overly concerned, but Ari felt as if she could run the two miles back to the office, pick up Isaac Hayden's scent, and track him down to wherever he was in the city to make sure he knew that Dale was off limits in whatever game he was playing.

"I'm in Eastlake," Ari said when Dale finished. "I can be there in ten minutes."

"What? No, why? Honestly, it was only unnerving in how charming the guy was. Well, that and the fact he had the book."

Ari said, "The book of essays?"

"Mm-hmm. You need an appointment to even look at it, and they don't allow you to take pictures even if you're lucky enough to get in. But this guy has the actual book...? Something really fishy there. I used the website to send a message to the owners, but they haven't responded yet. I think it's like nine hours later there, so I'm not worried. Yet."

"Well, I am. I really don't like the idea of Hayden just dropping in like that."

Dale said, "I appreciate how you feel. But you're working, right?"

Ari worked her jaw and looked down the steeply-sloped street toward Lake Union in the distance. "Yeah," she finally admitted. "I was about to meet up with one of the twins."

"And your girlfriend is tough enough to fight her own battles, right?"

That actually got a smile out of her. "And some of mine, too."

"Right. I'm fine. I only told you because I knew you'd go ballistic if I waited until you got back to the office. Go be a brilliant detective, puppy. I'll look over these essays and see if there's anything worth mentioning."

"Fine. I'll see you soon. Love you."

"I love you."

Ari put the phone back in her pocket and took a deep breath to calm her still-jangling nerves before she went into the tavern. The door was propped open by a cinder block and she smelled the pervasive reek of cigarette smoke even before she was over the threshold. The Zoo was a dive bar and proud of it, rude and crude to anyone too "boojee" to appreciate their finely crafted aesthetic. Ari was familiar with the place from her days of living on the street. She was surprised that anyone from the Burroughs family knew the place existed, and even more shocked that Elizabeth hadn't been thrown out for wearing shoes that cost more than the bartender paid in rent.

It was a good place to get out of the weather and play some games. Skee-Ball, darts, ping-pong, and, at the back of the room where Elizabeth Burroughs was holding court, pool tables. It was clear why the clientele was tolerating her presence: she looked like a music video come to life. Her jeans were painted-on, her button-down shirt was sleeveless, and her hair was down. Ari took a moment to appreciate her form as she bent over to take another shot, knowing Dale wouldn't mind her ogling as long as she shared the details later. A few patrons were watching her without being obvious, and the bartender was wiping down a spot which already looked like it would shine when he finally left it alone. Still given all the attention on her, she seemed to be playing alone.

Ari approached and watched Elizabeth line up her shot, though her attention wasn't exactly on the cue. "You're not the family member I expected to find hanging out in a dive bar on a Thursday afternoon."

Elizabeth looked over her shoulder and flipped her hair out of her face, gauging whether Ari had been checking her out. She smiled when she determined she was.

"But I'm also not the least likely. Right?"

"Yeah, it's pretty hard to imagine Eleanor in here."

Elizabeth laughed. "God." She straightened and wrapped both hands around her cue. "Let's get this out of the way. I don't have, or want, that stupid tapestry. In fact, I'm the one who suggested to Evelyn that we keep you on the case to find out who does have it. I don't want to color your investigation but I can save you the trouble and tell you it's Preston."

Ari said, "Not a lot of love lost between you girls and your brother, huh?"

"Not really." She jerked her head toward the table. "Do you play?"

"Not in years."

"Then we'll keep it low-stakes. Penny per ball. I'll rack 'em up, you break. If we're going to talk, we might as well play."

Ari retrieved a cue and chalked it as she walked back to the table. "Your mother claimed all of you asked about the tapestry in the past few weeks."

"Sure, I asked. I wanted her to admit she was going to leave it to Preston, ensuring he would never do a day of work for the rest of his life. Same as it ever was. I was holding her accountable for enabling his laziness. I never actually gave a damn about it."

"So why aren't you interested in a priceless treasure?"

"Because I have a great job, a house I love, and money in the bank. My boss will never fire me because I know the place better than he does, and wine won't go out of style until the zombie apocalypse, when my bank account won't mean jack shit anyway."

Ari lined up her shot and broke, sinking two balls with a nice clean strike that would let her take her choice of two more easy shots.

"Not in years, huh?" Elizabeth said, clearly impressed that she'd been hustled.

"Yeah, people stopped wanting to play me for some reason."

Elizabeth laughed and moved back to lean against the wall as Ari took another shot. "That's the good thing about pool. Even when you're losing, you get to enjoy the view."

"Heh," Ari said. "Guess I can't complain since you caught me checking you out, too."

"Fair's fair," Elizabeth said. "But let's change the stakes. Loser buys dinner."

Ari sank her third ball and straightened. "Can my girlfriend come?"

Elizabeth shrugged. "Sure."

"Are you trying to throw me off my game?"

"Trying to get laid, Miss Willow. What's the point of a vacation if you spend every night in your own hotel room?"

Ari laughed. "Well, sadly, I don't think it's in the cards."

Elizabeth clucked her tongue and shrugged. "Oh well. I can still enjoy the view, right?"

"Sure. Dale's not overly possessive."

"Lucky girl." She sighed as Ari sunk another ball. "Okay, so. What do you need to know from me? How can I help?"

"Do you know how someone could have gotten the tapestry out of the house without being seen?"

Elizabeth took a drink of her beer as she pondered the question. "Are we putting aside the fact it was in a locked room and you had the only key?"

"Yeah, we can worry about that once we've figured out how the thing was carried away. Basically I need to know if the house has any exits that aren't readily visible."

"There's a side door~"

"Off the kitchen," Ari said. "I saw it."

Elizabeth hmmed and angled her eyes toward the ceiling. "That's what I used to sneak out back in the day. If there were any secret passages, I would've known about them." She grinned and leaned forward. "Have you considered... the supernatural?"

Ari smiled. "What?"

"You know, curses. Mom told you Crossing-Over Place was made by a Duwamish artist back before Seattle existed, right? Well. That's because we don't really know the artist's name. We also don't know the original provenance, which means the thing was probably stolen from the artist's home by whoever was raiding the villages that day. Maybe the thing was cursed."

"I don't think that's it."

"Ah, a skeptic. You're a detective. You must know there's more to the world than meets the eye."

"Yeah," Ari said. "Sure. But there's a limit. I don't think a ghost walked in and took the tapestry down off the wall."

Elizabeth pointed her bottle at Ari. "When you've eliminated the impossible, whatever is left... that's Sherlock Holmes. He's, like, your patron saint."

"I could take him or leave him." She sank the last ball. "How about you play one and tell me about your family."

Elizabeth grunted and moved to rack up another game. "That'll take a lot longer than one game. And it's really not a great story. Lots of dumb little vignettes involving people who are completely different despite sharing blood and DNA. Have you talked to Eleanor yet?" Ari nodded. "Yeah, she's a fine little stress ball, isn't she? Spending money she didn't earn makes her twitch. I suppose that means she's your least-likely suspect. She would never steal even if she was down to her last dime."

"Would you?"

"Hell yes. I like to be comfortable and I like to survive. If I was desperate for money, I wouldn't hesitate. But like I said, that's not likely to happen any time soon. But Eleanor didn't like spending money she *did* have. She refused to go to private school. Mom said she might as well, since she could afford it, but no, Eleanor insisted. The rest of us went to Fusion Academy, and Eleanor went to Garfield. Go Bulldogs. We were paying forty grand a year and we were the ones going to school under the freeway."

Ari couldn't help herself. "Forty grand a year...?"

"Each," Elizabeth said.

"Damn. All that money, just for school."

Elizabeth said, "And Eleanor ended up smarter than all of us. Better job, too. She's explained what she does to me three different times, and I still don't understand it. Something to do with an app. That stuff is all magic to me. Grapes, though. I understand grapes."

"You're a manager at a winery in... Spokane... right?" Elizabeth nodded and took a shot. "Eleanor is in Philly, Evelyn is in Portland. Any reason all three of you girls went so far when you flew the coop?"

"I can't speak to them. Well, a little for Evie, I guess. But for me, it was anonymity. We weren't really famous here, but certain people knew the name Burroughs. People who would have been in the position to hire me. I didn't want that. I wanted my name to mean something because it was mine, not because I was the latest rung on a ladder."

"Sure," Ari said. "I understand that."

"It's the same reason Preston never went too far. The name was like an umbrella to him. He might stick his neck out a little, but as soon as a drop of rain hits him, he ducks back underneath where it's safe. I have no idea what the poor kid is going to do now."

Ari considered telling her, but she didn't know if it was necessary or her place to make that revelation.

"Cards on the table, you want me to tell you which one of us stole the tapestry? Honest answer, no bias or bad blood, I have to say none of us. You want to know if there's some secret way out of the house? Not that I know of, and I spent the better part of high school looking for one. I really wish I could be more help to you."

"I guess you have," Ari said. "Like you said, eliminate the impossible. So it's not one of the four prime suspects and even if it was, you couldn't have gotten it out of the house without being seen."

Elizabeth said, "You keep saying the thief wasn't seen. But Mom only had the one security camera over the front door. They could have just gone out the back."

Ari shook her head. "I have another angle. The guy across the street to the west had a camera showing almost all of your mother's property. Front and side yards."

"Fitz Anstartz?"

"You know him?"

Elizabeth rolled her eyes. "Yeah, I know him. I bet he was really eager to show you the tapes, right?"

Ari felt a sense of dread creeping in. "Yeah..."

"He was the same way two years ago when a delivery driver claimed he slipped on the front porch. Mom's camera didn't catch the right angle, so the insurance company called everyone in the area. They found Fitz, who had the perfect angle on the house and might have picked up everything. He turned in a tape with the right time stamp, and there was no delivery truck, no driver, no slip."

"That's great," Ari said, sensing a trap.

"Except Mom confirmed the driver was there at the time he said. She signed for the package."

"Why would Fitz lie?"

"He wanted to be the hero. He wanted to swoop in with a piece of damning evidence. 'Billionaire App Genius Assists In Fraud Case.' He later admitted he hadn't even checked the footage before handing it over. It turns out the camera only records when it senses movement, and half the time it doesn't even switch on. It misses cars, but it picks up wind blowing through trees and shit like that. I bet you or your assistant were watching it on fast-forward...?"

"Well, yeah..."

"Watch the counter. You'll notice some days have eighteen hours of footage, others have twelve or nineteen. I'm sorry, but you're not looking for a ghost. You're looking for someone who happened to get in and out of the house during a glitch."

Ari sighed. "More dumb luck. Fantastic. At least you wound up being helpful after all, just not in the way I would have hoped."

"Sorry about that."

"It's not your fault." She sighed. "Like I said, it helps to know there were windows where the thief could have gotten in and out. I should probably let Dale know about that." She put her cue down on the table. "Thanks for the game. Nice to know I still have the skills if I ever do want to hustle someone."

"You're free to hustle me any time, Detective."

Ari grinned and headed for the door.

"Mom..." Elizabeth's voice cracked. Ari was surprised by the emotion in that one word. She turned and saw Elizabeth rallying her emotions to continue what she was about to say. She was looking down at the pool table, her fingers steepled on the eight-ball. She twisted her lips. "Mom, um, told me you... you... knew Laura Gavin."

"Yeah. We only met briefly, but yeah, I knew her."

Elizabeth looked at her. Her brow was furrowed, like the effort to hold back her emotions was almost too much. "You did right by her. She was never a bad person. She... just let life... get ahold of her, you know? I didn't... I never knew she had cleaned herself up. Thank you."

"I'm glad I could bring the truth out."

"You know that I'm not just thanking you for Laura, right? If things had gone differently back then, if I hadn't..."

"I understand," Ari said. "Your mom felt the same way, just so you know. About the 'what if.'"

"Really?"

Ari nodded. "We'll talk again soon."

"Okay. I hope you find some better answers."

"Me too."

She turned and headed out. She couldn't help but feel they'd taken a massive step backward. She thought they had narrowed their window of opportunity down to something manageable. Now their all-seeing eye had selective blindness, and couldn't be trusted. They had been lucky it picked up Preston sneaking out on Monday night, although it explained why there hadn't been anything from Tuesday and why they hadn't seen him arrive. Anyone could have come to the house at any time and walked right out the front door with Crossing-Over Place under their arm. They were right back where they had started, except now she had all but eliminated three of her four prime suspects, and the last one standing didn't seem like a good candidate.

So where the hell did she go from there?

Chapter Ten

DALE WAS annoyed by the revelation about Fitz's security footage, but she still considered going through the tapes time well spent. They still had Vivian's front door camera, which at least eliminated anyone coming or going through the front door, which meant they weren't exactly at square one, no matter how it might feel. She finished scanning through Fitz's video and made sure to take note of the time. Sure enough, according to what he had recorded, there was only five hours and thirty-two minutes of sunlight on Tuesday. She checked online and saw that left just over three hours unaccounted for when the tapestry could have gone missing.

She kept the video running and pulled out the copy of Magnusson's essays. If she faced the monitor, she would pick up movement on the screen in her peripheral vision and go back to check on what it was. Multitasking at it finest. By the time Ari returned to the office, Dale had read three essays and slowed down the video to watch two dogwalkers, a grocery delivery girl, and a mailman. She even paused and zoomed in on the mailman to make sure his bag wasn't large enough to hold the tapestry, but he was cleared.

"Are you okay?" Ari asked as soon as she was through the door.

"I'm fine. I told you, the guy was calm and quiet. He was debating, not fighting."

Ari said, "I don't care. Sometimes the quiet ones are more dangerous." She nodded at the computer. "Anything?"

"I pretty much confirmed there are gaps in Fitz's footage. A lot of it is there, but it's like Swiss cheese. Not useless but also not definitive."

"Sorry I have you going through it all."

"It's part of the job. It's like a stakeout, except I have the benefit of fast-forwarding through the really dull parts."

Ari said, "And pausing to go to the bathroom."

"A *definite* plus." She held up the essays. "Plus I've been going through these. They're strange and fascinating."

Ari lowered herself into the seat Isaac Hayden had taken. "Want to summarize?"

"Well," Dale flipped back to the first essay. "They were all written between 1920 and 1933. Magnusson was a cryptozoologist, which means he was basically a monster hunter. Loch Ness Monster, witches, vampires..."

"Werewolves."

Dale nodded. "Ghosts and goblins and alternate realities. You name it, he was sure it existed and proof was out there waiting to be found. He spent his entire adult life trying to convince people he was right. The first essay mentions his 'previous volumes,' so there are probably other collections out there that he tried to get published but no one believed it."

"I would publish it as fiction. Then, once it's out there, bombshell, it's all based on the truth! You might find people who believe you."

"Or bad *canidae* who would kill you for spreading their secret."

Ari shrugged. "All I'm saying is JK Rowling knows more about magic than she admits."

Dale laughed and held up the pages. "May I continue with my book report?"

"Yes, yes, sorry. Go on."

"The first essay is the basics of what he knows. A lot of it is accurate, as far as I know. Is it passed down through the mother?"

Ari said, "I don't know. Seems reasonable, considering my situation. But I don't think anyone has ever studied it. For obvious reasons."

"Well, it looks like someone did," Dale said. "Inherited

through the mother, first change happens at the onset of puberty, voluntary transformations but with what he calls a 'window of necessity.'" She cleared her throat and read from the page. "*The wolf and the human are a shared entity, with neither one dominant over the other. A wolf cannot show preference for its human form, and the reverse is true as well. Too much time spent in one form will compel a transformation. These grueling, involuntary shifts are what I believe led to the myth of uncontrollable man-to-wolf shifts following a moon cycle.*"

"The guy did his research," Ari said.

"Do you think he knew a wolf?"

"He must have," Ari said. "The real question is if that wolf knew Magnusson was writing the essays and planned to publish them."

Dale said, "Well, let's say someday I wrote down everything I knew about you. How would you feel if I published something like that?"

"Betrayed," Ari said.

"Exactly. *Canidae* have kept themselves hidden for a reason. You were hunted to near-extinction a thousand years ago. I doubt the current climate would be much more accepting."

Ari grunted. "God, can you imagine? Not just a whole different species, but we look like anyone else. 'Ten Signs That Your Neighbor Is a Werewolf' articles all over the internet."

"Human Pride Facebook groups. I would never do that to you. So I can't imagine whoever Magnusson used for his study was a willing subject. I can do a little more research, but... I was also thinking maybe we could use another perspective on it. An older wolf's perspective. And maybe a European wolf..."

"Have anyone in mind?" Ari asked sarcastically.

"Hey, isn't your mother still dating a wolf from somewhere around Europe?"

Ari smiled. "As a matter of fact, she is. Is my girlfriend trying to get me to tell Mom about Isaac Hayden's arrival in the city?"

"As a matter of fact, she is. It doesn't have to be a big thing. Just ask them over for dinner. We're overdue for that anyway. Have you even seen her since you got the wolf back?"

"No. I think Milo got her wolf back recently, too."

"Yeah, it would've only taken a couple of months for her arm to heal."

Ari sighed. "I'll call her and see when they're free."

Dale nodded. "Good. How did things go with the Burroughs

twin, besides crashing our belief in the helpfulness of Fitz Anstartz?"

"It went great. So far she's my favorite member of the family. I beat her at pool. She asked if we were up for a threesome. It was a fun conversation."

Dale sat up straighter. "Hey, Miss Bury-the-Lede. What was that about a threesome?"

"We were a little flirtatious. She asked me out, I told her I was with you, she said that wasn't a deal breaker." She shrugged. "I told her no."

"Why? Not that I'm disagreeing. Although never say never. But why did you shoot it down so quickly?"

"Because she asked without knowing anything about you. She was only interested in me, and you would have been... I don't know, extra. An afterthought. I didn't appreciate that."

"Aw, puppy." Dale got up and came around the desk, setting herself on Ari's lap. She bent down to kiss her, one hand on the back of Ari's head. "I appreciate that. And just for the record," she lowered her voice and leaned in close to Ari's ear. "I'm not completely averse to the idea. In principle."

Ari slipped an arm around Dale's waist. "Yeah?"

Dale grinned and kissed Ari again before getting off her lap. "Just something to keep in mind. I'm not saying run out there and grab the first hot babe you see on the street, but... you know. Some day."

"Noted," Ari said.

"So what's the plan for tonight?"

Ari groaned and rolled her head back on her shoulders. "I guess I'll head back over to the Burroughs house and see if I can find any evidence of a thief. Preston kind of screws that up, though, because now I have to wonder if anything I find is from the thief or from him squatting there the past few nights."

"He's kind of a blessing in disguise, though. Right? At least you know the thief didn't strike during those hours."

Ari shrugged. "I'm not willing to go that far. But I guess it does clear up some potential theft times. But here's what I don't get. Preston said he hasn't stolen anything. I'm willing to believe that until I have evidence otherwise. But why wouldn't the tapestry thief take anything else? Why would you break into a house like that and focus on one thing in one room?"

"Maybe they didn't," Dale said. "The kids haven't been in the house for a long time, except for Preston. Would any of them really notice if some trinket was missing?"

"I think Preston would," Ari said, "but at this point, who's to say? We can't even trust videotape in this case. Hey, go through those essays again. If Magnusson proved ghosts exists, we'll just pin it on one of them. Thief was invisible and walked through walls. Case closed."

Dale smiled. "Werewolf versus ghost. That was my favorite Scooby-Doo."

Ari stood and leaned across the desk to kiss Dale. "I'll go over to the Burroughs house now. I'll call the lawyer to see if he can let me in. If not, I'll see if I can use Preston's method, see how easy it can be done by a non-family member."

"Good luck, mutt."

Ari flinched, her shoulders hunching. "Oof, no. Sorry, babe, not... no. I don't like that."

"Oh, okay. Sorry. Don't get arrested, puppy."

"Much better. Okay, see you soon."

Ari took her jacket and left. Dale started the video again and focused on the now-familiar street corner outside the Burroughs property.

"Show yourself, ghost," she muttered, resting her chin on her hand as she watched the day scroll by. She had been watching at double-speed, but now she'd slowed down to look for seams where recording stopped and started. They might not be able to see the thief, but she could at least try to see if she could find the windows of opportunity.

Timothy Dodd, the executor, was more than happy to let Ari into the house, and happened to be free when she called. She arrived before he did and took the opportunity to walk the property. She'd seen it from the wolf's point of view, but it never hurt to let the human side take a look as well. There were no obvious signs of passage, which didn't mean anything because she also wasn't seeing evidence of Preston going in and out every night. The ground was too hard and dry for people to leave footprints.

She heard the car pull up out front and went to meet Timothy on the walkway. He was in a suit and tie, but he had the relaxed air of someone on his way home from work rather than on a break. He smiled politely when he saw her.

"Miss Willow. Judging by the tone of your call, I assume you haven't made any breakthroughs on the case."

"Unfortunately not," she said. "I'm hoping today could shed a little light on the situation."

He held up the keys. "Let us hope."

"Lead the way," she said, stepping aside to let him pass her.

When they reached the porch, he bent over the latch and looked back at her. "I have to admit, I have mixed feelings about your involvement in this situation."

"Oh?"

Timothy pushed the door open and Ari followed him inside. Already the house felt abandoned, left behind, as if it had a spirit which knew its owner had passed on so it felt free to hibernate.

"Naturally," Timothy said, "the firm is grateful to have a private investigator involved given how things turned out the other morning. But initially, I was a bit annoyed when Vivian told me she planned to give you the key for safekeeping. I thought it meant she didn't fully trust me. Granted, I've only been working with her for about six months, but holding the key should have been my job. But then she told me why she had chosen you, and it made a lot of sense. People say you were responsible for GG&M crumbling. Not many fans of Cecily Parrish in our offices. Thanks for that."

"Oh. You're welcome."

He stood at the foot of the stairs and looked into the parlor, then twisted at the waist to look toward the kitchen. "Okay, well. You're the detective so I assume you'll need the run of the house. I'll try to stay out of your way down here and you just let me know when you're ready to leave."

"Will do. Thanks, Mr. Dodd."

He went into the parlor and Ari headed upstairs. She let herself into the study and looked at the empty space on the wall. Just a few weeks ago she had stood there and stared at Crossing-Over Place. She could have touched it. Now it was gone, just gone, and she had no idea where it was or how it had been taken. She had a lot riding on the answer to those questions.

Last time she'd been in the room, Vivian Burroughs had also been alive. Ari didn't understand that absence, either. Yes, she'd thought of suicide in a vague way, but how could someone just wake up and think, "Today, this is my final day, my last morning"? Vivian had not only known, she'd planned. She'd brought her children back into the fold to say their final goodbyes. She tied up her loose ends. In a way, that was the ideal ending.

The room felt smaller this time. She walked the perimeter,

letting her hand skim along the shelves. She'd already established there weren't any secret passages because there was no space for them anywhere. The floor was solid. The ceiling had no cracks or breaks. The door was as impenetrable as a prison cell. Without the key, no one was getting in or out.

She dropped her hand from the shelf and wiped it against her thigh. Looked down. Looked at her hand. Looked at the shelf. She ran her hand along the edge again, and her fingers came back clean. She reached higher, to the top shelf, and looked again. Her fingers were clean, which meant the shelf had been dusted, a shelf much higher than a woman in a wheelchair could reach.

"Mr. Dodd!" she called. "Did Vivian have a maid?"

"She had a woman who came in once a month," Timothy called up from the ground floor.

Ari went to the door of the study and tried not to get her hopes up as she called, "Might she have had a key to this room?"

CHAPTER ELEVEN

THE HOUSEKEEPER was a woman named Florence Warner. Ari got her number from the Rolodex in Vivian's downstairs office. Yes, she had a key to all the rooms in the house. Yes, she had been there to clean a week before Vivian passed away (and oh, wasn't that just such a sad thing). No, she hadn't kept any of the keys. She'd turned them in when she left because it was the last time she would be needed at the house. She'd left the right next to the Rolodex, a few feet from where Ari was standing.

"What did it look like?" Ari asked, not seeing any keys at all on the desktop. She assumed it was a ring with multiple keys. She opened one of the drawers.

"It was a long skinny key. With one tooth. Right on the end."

Ari frowned. "One tooth...? It opened every door in the house? Like a skeleton key."

"Oh my goodness, yes. That's what she said it was called. I couldn't remember and thought she'd called it a bone key, but it was obviously made of metal so I didn't know why it would have that name."

"And you left it here, in the office on the first floor. That was... when?"

"A week ago tomorrow. I remember because Vivian offered me

a glass of tea so we could have one final conversation." Her voice broke. "I still can't believe she's gone. She was such a lovely person." She sniffled. "I'm sorry, I won't blubber in your ear."

Ari smiled. "It's okay. It seemed as though Vivian inspired blubbering. I only met her the one time and I still feel like I lost a friend."

"She was like that."

Not according to her kids...

Ari thanked her, and Florence wished her luck in finding the key. Its absence from the desk didn't mean anything, but now she had a new lead. There was a second key out there, a skeleton key, one Vivian might not have even remembered existed, and it had been in the house in the days after she died. The door had just been blasted off their locked room mystery and the entire theft seemed a lot less impossible than it had that morning.

She searched the rest of the house for the skeleton key, but this time not finding what she was searching for was a good thing. If it wasn't in the house, someone must have taken it, and that person would have had access to the crime scene. It didn't get her any closer to figuring out who the thief might be, but at least she was chipping away at the impossibility of the theft.

The key was left on Friday. That meant all the kids had access to it, but Preston was the most likely culprit. He had to be getting in and out of the house somehow, and she got the impression he wasn't exactly careful about where he left his keys. She would have to track him down again and have another conversation.

She searched the house again looking for anything out of place or any glaring absences. A looted house usually had tell-tale signs: brackets were speakers had once hung, empty display stands, voids where there had once been a viper's nest of wires. Unfortunately, Vivian seemed to be a near-Luddite. Ari found a stereo and a laptop, and the television was upstairs in a small room off the den which seemed to be as pristine and untouched as a museum display. She found a phone charger in the TV room, but hadn't seen any indication of the device which went with it.

"Mr. Dodd!" Her voice echoed off the walls, bouncing down the stairs. "Did Vivian have a cell phone?"

"Much to her chagrin," he called back, his voice small having traveled from the other side of the house. "She didn't seem to care much for it."

Ari had a hunch the phone had found its way into Preston's

pocket, but she would confirm that when she asked him about the key. She stood in the hallway and looked down the hall to the bedrooms. She took a moment to brace herself for the invasion of privacy, then walked to the nearest door. She'd given these rooms a cursory look the day before, when the theft was first discovered, but she wanted to take her time and give them a second glance.

The air in the room was too cold to be stale. It was a typical girl's room, another museum display, likely untouched since its resident headed off to greener pastures. The bookshelf was full of books about dragons, King Arthur, Robin Hood. The window over the bed looked out onto the front lawn. There were no obvious signs about whose room it was, so it could have belonged to any of the girls until she went across the hall and saw two beds in it.

"Oldest Eleanor got her own room, the twins had to share," Ari said. "I guess that makes sense."

One bed was against the wall directly across from the door, with the other on the far wall. A floor-to-ceiling bookshelf separated the room into two distinct halves, although the desk in the corner was set up so they could work next to each other. One sister seemed to like birds and the other liked whales judging by how they'd chosen to decorate their sides of the room. The wallpaper was dark blue, as was the rug, and the curtains were heavy enough to block out the light even though the setting sun was currently aimed straight at it.

She left the rooms and went to the other side of the house. Preston's room was right next to the master bedroom. She wondered if that was a conscious choice on Vivian's part. Her baby, her only boy, kept close by while the girls were put at the other end of the house. She opened the door and saw the first evidence of a room in use. Preston was apparently sleeping in his own bed, and a bag of clothes was standing open near the door. The room also reeked in a way that the others hadn't. Someone had spent hours in this room, and very recently, and the wolf could smell it in every stitch of fabric.

Ari scanned the room carefully. The bookshelves had as many model airplanes as books. A basketball hoop was hooked over the top of the closet door, and she saw a tennis racket propped up in the far corner. The girls' rooms had looked like... well, like rooms where kids had grown up. Preston's seemed more like a movie set for a Boy's Room. It was hard to believe anyone had actually lived here. The models were the only personal touch, but she couldn't imagine the man she'd met putting them together and displaying them so proudly.

She wanted to give this room more than a cursory once-over, since someone had been staying in it. Elizabeth claimed she was the one who knew every potential escape route, but Ari suspected a teenage boy would have had a few secret exits of his own. There was also a possibility he had taken the tapestry and stashed it somewhere in his room where he could retrieve it later when the heat died down.

Ari got onto the floor and peered under the bed. Other than three pairs of shoes lined up under the opposite side, the space under the mattress was littered with fast food bags and empty cans of energy drinks. Preston was very clearly a boy used to having a maid clean up after him. She went to the wardrobe and opened it to find rows of empty hangers. She even pushed on the back to make sure it wasn't a doorway to another dimension.

"Miss Willow?" Timothy sounded like he was at the top of the stairs.

"In here."

He appeared in the doorway. "It's getting a little late. Do you think you'll be much longer?"

"I just want to check Vivian's room." He stepped aside and followed her to the room at the end of the hall. He waited outside when she went in.

It was magnificent. There was an actual four-poster bed with curtains opened to reveal a sprawling mattress with a nest of pillows against the headboard. There was a reading area next to a window seat which looked out over the backyard. She went to the bed and crouched down to look underneath. Nothing. This room looked even faker than Preston's, but she could understand that. Vivian had known the end was coming and would have removed anything she didn't want people to find after she was gone.

"Have you scheduled the reading of the will?"

"Yes, ma'am," Timothy said, "it will be Saturday at noon. I'm hopeful this situation will be settled by then."

Ari said, "Who gets the house?"

He stared at her, brow furrowed. "I'm not..."

She cut him off with a wave of her hand. "If one of the kids is involved, they might know the house is theirs. Vivian might have told them during the one-on-one dinners they had together last week. A house like this isn't just something you dump on one of your kids, especially if they live in another state. Vivian was practical. She would have tested the waters to be sure the recipient actually wanted it before putting it in the will. If they knew, and if they suspected the tapestry wasn't part of the deal, they only had to hide it somewhere in the house and wait until they took ownership. So... who gets the house?"

"Preston. He is not aware. Vivian offered it to Eleanor but, as you said, she wasn't interested in the hassle. So Vivian decided to leave it to the person who needed it the most." He stopped, but Ari could tell he wanted to say more. She let the silence grow until he continued. "I don't think she's doing him any favors. A person with Mr. Burroughs' income will never be able to maintain a home like this."

"He could sell it. Use the money to get something more fitting."

"Houses like this don't sell in economies like this. Even for Seattle, the price tag would be exorbitant."

Ari shrugged. "Like you said, this is Seattle. Someone is sitting on a billion dollars and they're looking for a summer home."

Timothy said, "You could be right." His tone suggested he believed otherwise, but wasn't interested in continuing the argument.

Ari looked at the bed and went to the window seat. She climbed up onto the cushions and stretched so she could see on top of the canopy.

"What on Earth are you doing?"

"Just checking," she said. "If I really was Sherlock Holmes, that's probably where it would've been hidden and I'd look like a genius."

Timothy said, "Aha."

Being near the window revealed to her just how late it was getting. She jumped down and said, "You've been a real trooper, Mr. Dodd. I don't think I'm going to make more progress tonight anyway, so we might as well go. Can I call you if I need to get back in?"

He thought for a moment and then took the keys out of his pocket, holding them out to her. "Miss Burroughs trusted you with a key to the most valuable thing in the house. I believe she would trust you with these as well."

"Thank you. I won't give you a reason to regret this."

"Saying things like that makes me anxious," he said as he

turned his back on her and headed down the stairs.

Ari smiled and looked around the upstairs before following him. She hadn't picked up on any scents other than Preston's. But she had some very intriguing puzzle pieces. Gaps in the security footage. A missing key which would allow someone access to the entire house. Those two facts would go a long way to figuring out the whole mystery.

She thanked Timothy again, secured the front door, and headed for her car. The streetlights, veiled by tree branches in this neighborhood, switched on above her. Their light was broken up by spider web branches and dark leaves. Ari had just unlocked the car when her phone rang. A quick glance at the screen revealed her mother's smiling face. She let it ring until she got into the car and closed the door.

"Hey, mom. Dale and I were just talking about you."

"Yes, I know," Gwen said. "She called to ask when Milo and I would be free for dinner. It just so happens that we're free tonight, and I have a fridge full of food I can turn into a meal with very little effort. Dale told me you've been interviewing people all day. Did you bother to stop for food at any point?"

"I had a little lunch," Ari said, but her stomach betrayed her by growling. Fortunately, Gwen didn't seem to hear it. "I was about to call Dale and ask what her plans were for dinner. I can swing by, pick her up, and be at your place in about... two hours?"

"That would be plenty of time. I've missed you, Ariadne."

Ari said, "I've missed you, too."

"Is everything... the wolf, Dale phoned to let me know it was back, but how is everything..."

"Everything is fine," Ari said. "I promise. We'll see you soon."

Gwen said, "I look forward to it."

Ari hung up and pinched the bridge of her nose. She was annoyed at and grateful to Dale in equal measure. Going to dinner meant they would, at some point, have to discuss Isaac Hayden. She very much did not want to do that, so she would have kept putting it off. It was better to get it over with as quickly as possible. But accepting it logically didn't mean she had to be happy about it.

She also wasn't entirely comfortable with her mother's relationship with Milo. It was her mother's first relationship with a woman - *that you know of*, said an inner voice before Ari could shush it - and Milo was Ari's age. Gwen was dating a woman who could be her daughter, and that was weird, no matter how many times Dale showed her pictures of Sarah Paulson and Holland Taylor.

It was strange, but it was something that would only get better by spending time with them. She started the car and pulled away from the curb, hoping that some of the food Gwen had in the fridge was her famous goulash. After running around Seattle all day, she was definitely craving some meat.

CHAPTER TWELVE

IT OCCASIONALLY crossed Dale's mind, though the thought rarely lingered, that she and Ari were different species. She didn't know if Isaac Hayden was to blame for it popping up now, but she was very aware of the fact she was the only human sitting at Gwyneth Willow's dinner table that night. Gwen and Milo were dressed casually - a blouse and leggings for the former, sweater and jeans for the latter - and both were barefoot. Ari shared details of some recent cases while Gwen finished cooking, and Milo filled them in on how the members of her pack were doing.

"It must be hard being away from them," Ari said. "Not that I would know, of course."

Milo snorted. "You've got a pack, Ariadne. Me, your mama, that pretty lady sitting next to you. You know exactly what it's like to be separated from your pack because it happened to you a couple months ago." She looked at Gwen. "Not that I'm comparing life with you to a prison sentence."

Gwen smiled. "Nice save, Millicent." She put her hand on Milo's leg under the table and her smile changed, becoming more sly. "Tell them where you were today."

"Oh, they don't want to hear about that..."

Ari said, "Am I going to need earplugs?"

Milo said, "Get your mind out of the gutter. I was, um... okay, look, I'm used to working two jobs and running around all day delivering shit. I don't know what to do with myself here. I can't get a job here. So I've been volunteering at the Beacon Women's Shelter."

Dale sat up straighter, impressed. "Wow! Is it a homeless shelter, or..."

"That," Milo said, "but also helps women who are just getting out of prison and don't have a girlfriend or a mom or a wolf pack to help get back on their feet. I thought about how tough it would've been if Ari didn't have all of us watching out for her."

"Wow," Ari said. "I took that for granted."

"Excellent. Because I was only working there to make you feel like shit. Mission accomplished!"

Ari laughed. "And you gave up the moral high ground, just like that."

"Damn. Well, back to the salt mines tomorrow, I guess. But if you really want to even the scales, they always need more help over the holidays."

"We'll be there," Ari said, glancing at Dale to get a quick nod to confirm she was onboard as well.

Dale kept quiet and watched the three other women, the three wolves, the family she had become part of through Ariadne. It was amazing to see them joke with each other like this considering how they'd all come together. Gwen, malevolent and cruel, had grown into a gentle and loving woman who genuinely regretted her past actions. But even the worst things she had done - exposing Ari to a dangerous medical procedure to make her a full-blooded wolf, and engaging Milo's services in an attempt to destroy their relationship - had led to happiness for everyone involved.

When they finished eating, Dale pushed back her seat and reached for Gwen's plate. "Ari and I will take care of-"

"No," Ari said, "Mom and I can do that."

Dale looked at her and caught the meaning behind her tone. She raised an eyebrow, asking if Ari was sure, and Ari dipped her chin once: yep.

"Okay," Dale said, "then Milo and I can have drinks in the living room and she can tell me more about the shelter."

Milo said, "Or I can take her out to the garage and show her my new bike. I'd also really love to hear about this tapestry thing you and Ari are working on. I love a locked room mystery."

"Me too!" Dale said. "Maybe you can pick up on something we missed." She watched as Ari and her mother gathered the dishes and disappeared into the kitchen. Hopefully Gwen would have a simple answer, and the conversation would be nothing but a long-overdue chat. She couldn't help worrying, but for now there was nothing she could do to help. She picked up her drink and followed Milo to the garage entrance. "Okay, the tapestry is called Crossing-Over Place..."

"You need to work on your subtlety, Ariadne." Gwen joined Ari at the sink and turned on the tap. "What's going on?"

"Maybe nothing. It's just something that's come up during a case. Not even really a case, just something that's going on..."

"You're also bad at stalling."

Ari sighed. "Does the name Isaac Hayden mean anything to you?"

Gwen thought for a moment before shaking her head. "I don't think so. Should it?"

"Maybe not. How about Karl Magnusson?"

"That one sounds familiar. Karl Magnusson..." She searched her memory. "Is it someone famous?"

"In certain circles," Ari said. "Magnusson wrote a book of essays about *canidae* back in the thirties..."

Gwen nodded. "Right, right, yes. I remember now. He was a cryptozoologist who hunted all kinds of mythical creatures. *Canidae* was just one species of many. I think he was most focused on us, though. The essays got a lot of chatter back in the day, but as far as I know, it's never been published. The only copy is essentially under lock and key in... ah..."

"Germany."

"Right. What brought that up?'

Ari said, "Dale has a copy."

Gwen looked at her. "That's not possible."

"That's where Isaac Hayden comes in. Apparently he's also a crypto... zoo... keeper, and he's trying to pick up where Karl left off. He was following the hunters, which led him to wolf manoth, which led him to Seattle. And we ran into each other in a deli."

"He just happened to run into you?"

Ari shrugged. "It would seem so, yeah. I've been having a lot of weird luck lately. Anyway, he had the book and gave Dale a copy of the essays."

"That isn't..." Gwen looked at the sink and turned off the tap. "If he has the book, then he stole it. And its owners aren't the type who would just give it over to the first person who threatened them. I need to talk to some people... I think I know someone in Paris."

"I appreciate the help. But that isn't really why I wanted to talk with you." She looked over her shoulder and saw Dale and Milo had returned from the garage and were loitering in the living room. This really was her pack, the family she'd finally found after years of being on her own. She was terrified she was about to blow it up, but she had to know. "The new guy. Hayden. When we spoke, he mentioned you. He... mentioned your money."

Gwen tilted her head to the side, not understanding. "What about my money?"

"Where does it come from?"

"It was an inheritance."

Something about the way she said it struck Ari wrong. She knew it was a lie, and Gwen wasn't even trying to sell it. Ari stared at her until Gwen looked away and resumed washing dishes.

"That might have worked on me when I was a kid," Ari said, "but I need more now. Inheritance from where? Your parents? I don't know anything about your family. The money is just... there. Don't get me wrong. I'm grateful you had it when I was in prison. You kept me from losing everything. But the fact this guy brought it up... I have to know."

Gwen looked into the soapy water. "You deserve to know. But not now."

"Milo deserves to know, too. And Dale will know as soon as I do."

"It's not about keeping it from them. It's about *how* I tell you. Do you remember the Arboretum, the spot I used to wait for you when you first started transforming?"

A wave of memories washed over her. A young girl just going through puberty, crashing through the underbrush and falling at her mother's feet. Exhausted, gasping for air, hauled back onto her feet. A firm hand gripping her jaw and forcing her eyes up. *Again*, Gwen demanded. Ari remembered whimpering and wanting to refuse, but she couldn't. She could still feel the hot irons of pain pressing into her joints as she became the wolf for another agonizing run.

She pushed the memories away. "Yeah. I remember it."

"Meet me there tonight at one-thirty. Come as the wolf. I'll have clothes for you there."

"What's going on?" Ari asked.

"I'll tell you everything tonight, I promise. Just meet me there."

Ari sighed and accepted she wasn't going to get a straight answer, so she nodded. She and her mother finished the dishes in silence, the unanswered question hanging between them. Ari couldn't tell if Gwen was angry at her or just trying to get her story straight. Either way, the mood of the evening had been effectively ruined.

When everything had been rinsed and put away, Ari went into the living room and touched Dale's shoulder. "Ready?"

"Yeah. Everything...?"

"I'll tell you in the car." She smiled at Milo. "Thanks for dinner... Millicent."

Milo flipped her off, but with a genuinely affectionate smile. She jerked her chin toward the kitchen. "Is she gonna be pissed at you tonight?"

"I don't know. I'm glad you'll be here for her, either way."

"Okay. Have a good night."

Ari took Dale's hand, leading her outside. Dale pressed tight against her, bumping her hip against Ari's. "She wants me to meet her tonight at a place where we used to run. She promised she'll tell me everything then."

"That doesn't sound good."

"No," Ari admitted, "it really doesn't."

The Arboretum was three miles from home, but it was even farther for Gwen. Still, when Ari arrived a few minutes before one, she was already there and waiting. She was still in wolf form, but transformed once she saw Ari approaching. Moments after her arrival, they were standing naked in front of a large boulder, both panting and covered in sweat. Wolves didn't much care about nudity around each other, especially when it came to family or pack members, but she still accepted the V-neck and sweatpants her mother handed her and pulled them on quickly.

"I stayed up wondering what possible reason you could have for insisting on this," Ari said. "Were you afraid I was wearing a wire at dinner?"

Gwen chuckled. "Such a detective. No, Ariadne. Nothing like that. I simply wanted you to be in the right frame of mind. I wanted to be certain the wolf was right under your skin when you heard what I'm going to say." She sat down on the boulder and patted the stone next to her. "Sit."

Ari complied.

"I think a lot about when you were younger. I made a lot of decisions without much thinking. I didn't have the luxury of planning. I was assaulted by men who saw me as less than human, and they left me with a daughter. A blessing and a miracle, but one which I was in no way prepared for. Sometimes I would look down at you in your crib and I would think about how... I didn't want you... but now that you were here, I would do anything for you. I knew you would do great things, Ariadne, but I had no idea how many people you would save or how many people would owe their peace of mind to you."

Ari shifted uncomfortably. "You're freaking me out."

"I know. I'm sorry. But I was thinking about the nights we ran out here. The nights when I made you hurt. I know you must have hated me for it, but I couldn't see another way. It killed me when I saw your face after a transformation. Knowing it was because of me. The things I'd done to you. I only wanted to give you a good life."

"The money, Mom," Ari said.

Gwen sighed. "I was in college when I was attacked. I was learning computers. It was in the very young days of the internet, when it was modems in garages screeching at each other. It seemed like sorcery back then, even though by today's standards it looks like monkeys chattering in trees. But I was good at it. I could see things no one else thought of. I found ways of moving through this new virtual world. If I'd stayed on that track, I could have been Bill Gates. But things changed. I dropped out of school because you were my future. You were all that mattered. But how could I give you what you needed flipping burgers? I was a college dropout who couldn't afford diapers, let alone a babysitter. So I came up with an idea. It was a joke. But then I kept thinking about it.

"Have you ever noticed that hunters tend to be rich? CEOs, captains of industry, tycoons. Whereas *canidae* are still poor. We're working class. We live paycheck to paycheck. Part of that is our nature. We want to stay close to the ground with one foot always in the woods. We could rise, but there's always a hunter in the way. Their bloodlines go back as far as ours, and the roots of their family tree are full of kings and gentry."

Ari said, "Mom..."

Gwen held up a hand, asking for patience. "I made a program.

I tracked down several hunters and got access to their bank accounts through a back door. I added a virus which took a fraction of their deposits and routed it to my own. I spent the first few months waiting to be arrested or the accounts to be locked down, but they never were. I never took enough that they would notice." She laughed. "You would be astonished at how much you can take without a rich person noticing."

Ari muttered, "This is the plot of *Office Space*."

"*Superman III*, actually," Gwen said. "I actually got the idea from an episode of *MASH* where Radar tried to mail a Jeep home by doing it one piece at a time. I figured if I took a few hundred dollars from this hunter, and maybe a thousand from this one, I could take care of my girl and give her the life she deserved."

"You stole... everything."

"I stole from people who would only have used the money to fund a genocide against us. I stole from the people who made me into their enemy by changing my life completely."

Ari stood up, arms wrapped around herself. "I really wish you would stop talking about me like I was some virus you contracted."

"Try to put yourself in my position, Ari. Picture yourself suddenly pregnant, with a child who desperately needs you, a child you have no plan for. I was terrified. I did the only thing that made sense."

"Stealing from rich people and putting me through a medical procedure that could have killed me."

"I won't apologize for making you into the person you are. I know you wouldn't change a thing, either. I'm not saying what I did was right, and I don't expect you to forgive or even really understand. But I was just a girl who had been victimized by very powerful people whose sole purpose in life was to see me dead. The only regret I have is that it took so long to figure out why transforming hurt you. I'll be forever grateful to Dale for figuring that out."

Ari kept her back to Gwen, eyes on the ground. "I don't want any more of your money. Not a dime. And I'm going to pay back everything you spent on the office and rent when I was in jail."

"I'll refuse--"

"I don't *care*," Ari yelled, finally spinning to face her. "Is there anything else, Gwyneth? Anything... any other fucking horrible thing you've done for my own good that I should know about? Did you send those kids after me so I'd meet Dale?"

Gwen kept her eyes on the ground. "No. There's nothing else. You've heard all my confessions, Ariadne. Now I guess you just have to decide if you can live with them."

"I think you're the one who is going to have to live with them," Ari said quietly.

"What does that mean?"

"I mean Isaac Hayden is in Seattle because he was following a thread left by hunters. He asked me about your money. I don't know where exactly his loyalty is, but I would be very worried that he knows what you did. The hunters may not have started wolf manoth, but they're still around. They're probably going to be pretty pissed off if he spills the beans."

Gwen looked away as she processed that. Ari also turned away, stripping off the borrowed shirt and letting the sweatpants fall to the ground by her feet. By the time Gwen looked at her again, the woman was gone and replaced by a large brown wolf.

"Ari, wait... Ariadne!"

Ari didn't bother looking back. She just shook out her fur, put her head down, and ran.

CHAPTER THIRTEEN

DALE HAD stayed up so she could hear all the details about Gwen's revelation. Ari was still so angry when she arrived home that her hands were shaking, and Dale was worried the pain was starting to come back. They sat facing each other on their bed as Ari explained what she'd been told. Halfway through the story, it had become clear that Dale wasn't sharing her anger, but she kept silent until Ari was done talking.

"Please don't take this the wrong way, puppy, but I think you're overreacting."

"She's a thief. Everything we had, everything she's given to us over the years..."

Dale nodded. "I know. Morally, yes, it's wrong. But..." She looked down at Ari's hands. "I don't really see much of a choice for her. She was scared and alone. All she wanted was to take care of this new life she found herself responsible for. You may not agree with what she did, I'm not sure I do, either. But her motives were pure. And what she did made you into the woman you are. It made you the woman who stopped wolf manoth, which means they basically funded their own downfall. I don't know. I think that's kind of... poetic justice."

"She still lied."

"Yeah. And you should be angry at her for that. But Ariadne..." She took both of Ari's hands in hers. "I saw what happened to you when Gwen came back into your life. I saw what it meant to forgive her and the weight it took off your shoulders. It changed her, too. Don't let this pull you back to where you were before. Be mad at her, but talk to her about it. Don't run."

Ari kept her eyes down. Dale reached up and tucked Ari's hair behind one ear, resting her hand on Ari's cheek.

"Puppy?"

"I think I want to marry you."

Dale sat up straighter. "What?"

"I know we said it was just a stupid piece of paper, but it's not. It's more than that, it means more. You're my girlfriend, my partner, my pack, you're everything to me, Dale, so why shouldn't you be my wife? And I want to be yours. I need you to be my rock when stuff like this happens. I know you'll always be here for me, and I'll always have your back, and... at some point, it just becomes silly that I can't call you my wife. You're my favorite person and I want to be bound to you in every possible way."

Dale had no idea what to think and, a moment later, she couldn't see because of the tears flooding her eyes. Ari reached up and brushed away the drops that had fallen free, and Dale turned her head to kiss the palm.

"We don't have to change our names or do the rings. I mean..." She touched Dale's wrist, the bracelet made of Ari's hair braided around a few strands of the wolf's fur. "Between this and the collar, we have the only symbols we need. It doesn't even have to be a big ceremony..."

"Puppy, you don't have to keep selling it. I want to marry you. I want to marry you more than anything. But ask me properly."

Ari repositioned herself so she was on her knees and scooted forward. She cupped Dale's face with both hands.

"Dale Frye, will you marry me?"

Dale grinned and stretched to kiss her. Their lips met as she said, "Yes, Ariadne Willow." They kissed to seal their engagement, and Dale squeezed her partner, her fiancée, and moved her head to Ari's shoulder. She was crying again. "I know we've been together for almost a decade now," she said, "and you've always made it clear how you feel about me. I never wanted to be someone's wife. And for a long time, I didn't think I *could* be someone's wife. So... hearing it... and hearing it from *you*..."

Ari stroked her hair. "Probably the same way I felt about saying it." She moved her lips to Dale's ear and lowered her voice even further. "For some reason I was still terrified you might say no."

Dale laughed and sat up. She kissed Ari's chin and the corners of her mouth. "Never. You're my puppy. Forever."

Ari smiled and kissed Dale, lowering her to the mattress. Dale hugged her tightly. She was well aware that Ari had changed the subject away from Gwen, but she also knew her argument had worked. Ari's anger was diminished, and she knew whatever was going to happen between her and her mother wouldn't be another relationship-ending battle. That was good enough to let her fall asleep, arms still wrapped tightly around the woman she loved.

The phone was ringing. Ari was aware of that only after taking note of Dale spooning her from behind, the sound of water in the pipes from Neka taking a shower upstairs, and sunlight streaming into the bedroom door from the front room. The ringtone faded and then started again, rising in volume until Ari worked her arm out from under the blankets and reached for it. Dale protested the move by sliding one hand down to Ari's stomach, lifting one leg to hook it over her hip, snuggling closer to her.

Ari vaguely recognized the number, but it wasn't assigned to any contacts. She apologetically patted Dale's hip and answered the call. "This is Ariadne Willow."

"I'm started to feel neglected."

"Excuse me?"

"You've talked to my sisters and brother, but completely ignored me."

Ari's brain slowly woke up. "Evelyn Burroughs. Right. I, uh, didn't intend..."

"I'm just teasing you, Miss Willow. I'm not even sure I have any information that can help you. But I wanted to make sure you knew I was available today. I'm driving back to Portland tomorrow so I can cover a shift at the bar but I plan to be back tomorrow night."

"Okay, that sounds great. I'd like to meet you for lunch today just to see what we can find out." Dale gave up on snuggling and rolled away, burying her face in the pillow. Ari pushed the blankets toward her and sat up, putting her feet on the floor. "There's a place near my office called Harry's Fine Foods. It's on Bellevue."

Evelyn said, "I'll find it. Say noon?"

"Noon is fine," Ari said. "I'll see you then."

Dale's voice was muffled by the pillow. "Don't make dates with other women while your fiancée is spooning you. It's tacky."

Ari hung up, put the phone back on the charger, then pounced on top of Dale with a primal yell, prompting a horrified scream from her prey.

This is my fiancée, Dale. Ari was seated on the booth side of a table near the door of Harry's, a bodega-turned-restaurant in Capitol Hill. She had arrived first so she spent the time sipping a tea and toying with the napkins. *This is Dale, my fiancée.* She couldn't decide which she liked more. She also didn't know what would happen once they evolved from that to... wife? Partner? She already called Dale her partner, and wife sounded archaic to her ears. It wasn't as bad as calling someone her 'spouse,' though she knew there were people who did that.

She was excited and scared by the prospect of marrying Dale. It wouldn't change anything, but it felt monumental at the same time. The words had come naturally when she said them. Now she couldn't believe they'd actually come out of her mouth. She was grateful to whatever had possessed her in that moment. A wedding, marriage, forever connected to Dale in life and in work. There was nothing in that to scare her, and just the thought made her eager to get on with it.

Her eye was drawn to the door when Evelyn stepped inside. She was in cargo pants and a leather jacket, which was unzipped over at least two shirts that Ari could see. She paused on the threshold and took off her sunglasses, scanning until she spotted Ari. She made her way over and pulled out the seat across from Ari.

"Miss Willow?"

"Ari, please."

Evelyn nodded as she sat. It was strange to see her after talking, and flirting, with someone who looked almost exactly like her the previous afternoon. Evelyn's hair was shorter and styled differently, wavier, and it better complimented the strong line of her jaw. She took off her sunglasses and put them on the table, then folded her hands on her lap and sat up straight.

"You're playing 'spot the six differences,' aren't you?"

Ari winced. "Sorry about that. Hazards of being a detective."

Evelyn shrugged. "We're both used to it. But enough about that... I want to help however I can. It pisses me off to think someone broke into Mom's house and took the tapestry."

"Were you hoping to get it in the will?"

"God no," she said. "What would I do, hang it in my studio apartment? Try to sell it? One, I don't have room and I don't need the stress of having something that valuable in my home. Someone might spill a drink on it, or the sun would fade it, the apartment would burn down, someone would break in... no. And I also don't want to bother selling it. I tried selling my car a few years ago and that was a *nightmare*. I imagine a historically-important tapestry would be an even bigger headache than a '95 Saab. I didn't even want to go to the reveal, but Dodd said he couldn't read the note unless we were all present."

"You came all the way to Seattle but planned to skip out on the actual bequeathing?"

Evelyn said, "I came all the way to Seattle to say goodbye to my mother and see my family. I haven't seen Eleanor in three years." She paused and looked away. "And I only said I didn't want the tapestry. There's still the will reading. There were other things in the house I wanted."

"Want to expand on that?"

"Not really," Evelyn said. "Not unless I have to. I want to make sure you know what you're dealing with. Crossing-Over Place wasn't some prize we were all hoping to win. Things got a little heated in the moment, but none of us would have been happy with our names being read. I asked Mom about it because I was terrified she was going to leave it up to us. She said she had plans for it. I didn't care what those plans were as long as I wasn't responsible."

"So none of you wanted the tapestry, but all four of you made a point to ask about it."

"If we wanted money, we could have had it. She could have had four Prestons running around with their hands out. Growing up with money can either make you spoiled or make you desperate to *earn* what you have. I don't want to be rich. I'm working three jobs right now. Actually..." She took out her phone and showed Ari an app. "I'm working right now. If someone dings for a food delivery, I can pick it up even though I don't live here. I've already made about a hundred bucks on this vacation."

Ari said, "Like you said, Preston isn't quite the same way."

Evelyn rolled her eyes and put the phone back in her pocket. "Preston has always taken the easy way out. You saw how he reacted when he found out the tapestry was being donated. He'd been counting on that money. He's the one most likely to steal it, but also the only person who expected it to still be there when you opened the door. He's the one who ran upstairs. He's the one who started pointing fingers. I think he fully expected Mom to leave it to him. One last boost to the bank account."

"He might be desperate. He's homeless."

Evelyn barely reacted to that, but Ari could see it was new information. "What? No, he's not."

"He's been breaking into the house every night, sleeping in his old room."

Evelyn wiped a hand over her face. "Jesus. I mean, I knew he... I went to his apartment to ask him point-blank if he'd taken it, but the landlord said he'd been evicted. It's not the first time it's happened, but I assumed he was staying with a friend. Sleeping in the old house... there's something creepy about that, don't you think...? I can't believe he's actually breaking in."

"Maybe he doesn't have to break in." Ari acted like the thought just occurred to her. "Is there, like, some kind of skeleton key Preston might be used to get in and out of the house?"

"We all used to have one for the exterior doors. Mom didn't like the idea of us getting locked out, so she made sure we were safe."

"But those keys wouldn't open all the inner doors?"

Evelyn shook her head. "No, there were other special keys for that. All of our bedrooms used to have their own locks, but Mom changed them when we moved out. I know what you're getting it, and if Mom told you the only key to the study was in your pocket, then that's the truth."

"What about the housekeeper?"

"She..." Evelyn raised an eyebrow. "Hm. That's interesting. Have you already contacted her?"

Ari nodded. "She had a key, but she left it at the house last Friday. It's gone missing."

"We were all in town by then, so it could have been taken by any of us. Or it was the housekeeper and she's lying about leaving the key, or it could have been Mr. Dodd." She laughed and shook her head. "I'm starting to regret having you stay on the case. For your sake, I mean. I'm starting to think this will turn into one of those urban legends. The priceless tapestry which vanished from a locked room and was never seen again. I wish we hadn't gotten you tangled up in it."

"Technically your mother got me tangled up in it. I just didn't take the opportunity to cut the tangles when I could have. If anyone is having regrets, it should be me. But I'm determined to solve this one."

"You sound confident."

Ari smiled. "Oh, yeah. I'm pretty good at mysteries. I have clues, I have a small pool of suspects, and I've spent the past two days eliminating the impossible. I think it's just a matter of time before I find the thread that leads to the only possible solution."

CHAPTER FOURTEEN

"YOU CAME to Seattle last Wednesday, a week before the disappearance was revealed. You and Eleanor took your mother to lunch at SkyCity?" Evelyn nodded. "Elizabeth and Preston both got solo meals to say goodbye. Was sharing your meal with Eleanor planned, or did you just happen to get into town at the same time?"

Evelyn waited for the waiter to walk away, having delivered her drink, before she answered. "Eleanor was already at the house when I showed up to let Mom know I was in town. Eleanor is the one who invited me to come with them. I thought it seemed a little rude to tag along on their personal time, but she insisted. I'm used to being treated as a package deal, it's just that I'm usually tied to Elizabeth. It was a nice change of pace."

"What did you talk about?"

Evelyn furrowed her brow. "Oh, boring stuff. Family history, things we wanted to get off our chest. Mom wanted to tell us she was proud of us all." She stirred her straw around the ice cubes in her glass and took a moment to compose herself. "You know how it is, probably. A loved one passes away, you want to make sure you say things you won't get another chance to say."

Ari nodded. "But no one got carried away? No one was overly emotional?"

"Not at our dinner. Eleanor was distracted by work, of course. I was anxious because one meal at that damn restaurant could buy me groceries for a week, but hey. Mom was paying and she chose the venue, so what the hell. I think Elizabeth's meal with her was a bit more contentious."

"Is that a twin thing? You could sense she was emotional?"

Evelyn gave Ari a good-natured glare. "No, because their heart-to-heart happened at Chihuly and then they met us at Canlis. Ellie put on a good front, but she polished off an entire bottle of wine by herself. Usually she has one glass with dinner. I sort of got the feeling she planned to have some more when she got back to her hotel."

"Your mother didn't mention anything?"

"Nope. She was all smiles. It was me, Ellie, Eleanor, and Mom at the dinner. Ellie joined in the conversation. She wasn't sulking. I only noticed the wine because... well, twin thing. It might not mean anything though. Mom and Ellie... let's just say Ellie wasn't Mom's favorite, and the feeling was mutual."

"Elizabeth didn't mention anything about her final conversation with Vivian when we talked. She *did* tell me that Preston was the one who took the tapestry."

Evelyn chuckled. "Yeah, they've never been fans of each other. Ellie thinks that Preston takes advantage of Mom. *Took* advantage of Mom... Even before that, when we were kids, Mom favored him. We were all Daddy's girls and Preston was Mom's favorite." She pursed her lips. "I'm not sure how much of this I should tell you. It's not really relevant to the tapestry. But it might help you understand why Elizabeth was so quick to point her finger at him."

"Everything you tell me is confidential. I'm good at forgetting things that aren't important to the case."

Evelyn took another moment, obviously still reluctant to give up her secret. Finally she sighed. "When Preston was seventeen, Mom caught him with a girl in his room. I don't know the exact details, thank God, but I know enough to be sure they weren't just studying. Eleanor claims there was full nudity involved. Mom gave him a slap on the wrist. Grounded for a month, no TV, no car privileges."

"Seems reasonable, I guess."

"Sure," Evelyn said. "Unless you're Elizabeth, who had been caught a year earlier kissing her study buddy in our room. They were just making out, but Mom went ballistic. Elizabeth was confined to the house from the minute she got home from school to the second she left again. Her phone was taken away. Her car was taken away. I overheard her talking to Dad about boarding school, but he talked her out of it. That lasted for the rest of the school year."

Ari said, "That sounds awful."

"It could have been worse," Evelyn said. "I was pissed off enough by it that I went out and got my hair cut just like Ellie's. If there was something she needed to do out of the house, we switched clothes and she went out while I sulked around upstairs slamming doors. It took Mom a few months to catch on, but when she did, she almost grounded me for aiding and abetting. Dad talked her out of that, too."

"Why was the response so different? Please don't tell me it's just because Elizabeth was with a girl."

"Ellie made the same argument when Preston escaped the same treatment. Mom denied it. She said she'd seen how Ellie and I conspired to get around the punishment so it was pointless to try it again on Preston. 'I won't become a warden in my own home.' Meanwhile, when she found out Ellie and I were swapping places, she started examining our faces every time we left the house. It was like having airport security stationed at your front door."

"Your own mother couldn't tell you apart?"

"To be fair to her, we were *trying* to trick her. Same makeup, same hair, swapping clothes. With the right makeup, Eleanor might even have been able to pass for one of us. Anyway, she said there was no point to go through all of that again. Mind you, this was just a year later. Ellie's prison sentence was basically just ending. And here was a new offender getting off with basically a warning. Ellie and Preston's relationship never really recovered from that."

"I can imagine. So you and your mother never had a final conversation?"

"I didn't need one. I didn't have anything to tell her, she didn't have anything to tell me. We had a perfectly neutral relationship. We loved each other. I miss her. I'm sad she's gone, but I love that she went out on her own terms. That's how I'd want to do it if I'm ever in the same position."

Ari nodded. "Wait, you and your sisters had lunch with Vivian on Friday?" Evelyn nodded. "That's the day her housekeeper left the skeleton key at the house. If you were all at Canlis, Preston could have gotten into the house and grabbed the key. He would have known he was about to be evicted and the house would be empty after Sunday."

"But how would he know the key would be there?"

"He may have just gotten lucky. Trust me, luck has been working very strangely in this case."

She thanked Evelyn for her time and paid for their drinks. On her way out of the restaurant she saw that she'd missed a text from Dale. She got into her car and watched Evelyn walking away as she returned the call.

"Go to your mother's," Dale said as soon as she picked up.

"What happened?"

"Nothing yet," Dale said, "but the longer you wait, the bigger the conversation has to be. Get out in front of it. You don't have to apologize, but let her know you aren't going to run away again. She's already lost you once. She's probably terrified it will happen again."

Ari pressed her lips together. She wanted to argue, get angry, refuse, but she knew that was just the childish part of her brain rebelling.

"You can't order me around just because we're engaged now."

"Sure I can," Dale said cheerfully. "But only because I could order you around before, and it carries over into the engagement."

Ari fought a laugh. "It's a good thing you know all these relationship rules. I haven't even heard of half of them."

"That's what I'm here for."

Ari's original plan was to call Elizabeth and see if she could find out what happened with Vivian at the Chihuly exhibit, but Dale was right. She needed to set things right with her own mother. Or at least as right as they could be, for the time being.

Traffic meant that it took her over half an hour to reach her mother's house, and she spent the entire trip rehearsing what she was going to say. She hadn't come up with anything that sounded remotely worthy by the time she parked at the curb, but she walked up the driveway regardless, hoping that whatever came from her heart would be good enough. She knocked on the door and took a step back, knowing it would be inappropriate to just walk in after the way they'd let things.

The door opened just enough for Milo to press her shoulder against the jamb. "She doesn't want to talk with you right now."

"Yeah, I don't really want to talk to her, either. But Dale thinks I should, and when Dale suggests something, she usually knows what she's talking about."

Milo nodded. Some of her defensiveness faded, and she looked past Ari at the street. "I thought Gwen should talk to you, too. We stayed up talking about it all night, and she only just went to bed. She was pretty bloody pissed last night, so while I'm trying to stay neutral, I'm not about to put my head on her chopping block."

"Smart. You have to side with her, I get it." She sighed. "Look, it's probably best we don't see each other right now. But let her know I'm not going anywhere. I'm mad but this isn't something I'm going to destroy our relationship over. I did it once before and she might be afraid I'll do it again."

"She'll be relieved to hear that. Dinner was good last night, though. Domestic. I liked it. When things settle down, we should do it again."

Ari said, "I think I can make that promise."

"Thanks for coming by. It'll mean a lot to her. Eventually."

"Yeah," Ari laughed, "I know the feeling. Take care of her for me, Milo."

"Always, pup."

She was back in her car and driving up Lake Washington Boulevard when her phone rang. She put it on the hands-free hook and answered on speaker.

"This is Ariadne Willow."

"Evie just called," Elizabeth said without preamble. "She said she told you about my relationship with our mother and everything that happened. I think you need to know the whole story."

Ari said, "I'm more than willing to hear it. Where are you? I can come to you right now."

Elizabeth was staying at the W, which was around the corner from where Eleanor was staying at the Hotel Monaco. Ari wondered if they could see each other's rooms out their windows. Elizabeth also had a suite on a high floor, indicating their mother hadn't played favorites with the girls. She remembered Evelyn was at the Executive Hotel Pacific, which was on the same block. Vivian might not have trusted them under the same roof, but she apparently wanted to keep them close to each other.

Ari knocked, and Elizabeth answered the door in a plush white robe. Her hair was a mess, loose tangles on the sides and held by a clip on top. She held up one hand before Ari could say anything.

"This isn't a seduction, despite how I acted at the pool hall yesterday. This is a hangover and sleeping until about forty-five minutes ago."

"If this could be confused for your seduction look, I feel bad for your sex life."

Elizabeth laughed and motioned Ari in. She went into the bathroom and pointed at the sitting area on the other side of the bed. "Have a seat. I'm going to finish putting myself together."

Ari went to the window and looked out. The Hotel Monaco was indeed visible, but she couldn't remember which direction Eleanor's room faced.

"How much did Evie tell you?" Elizabeth called from the bathroom.

"The girl in your room, your mother freaking out and putting you on house arrest. Then Preston pulling the same stunt, only worse, and getting a fraction of the punishment."

Elizabeth said, "I was kissing my study partner. Preston was naked on top of a girl from school and had her half-naked as well."

"Evelyn was under the impression it was because you were kissing a girl."

"She's right. Mom told me on Friday. That's what our conversation was about." She came out of the bathroom in a lace top and slacks. Her hair had been tamed and pulled back. Now this, Ari thought, was a seduction look. "She told me that she was harsher on me than she was on Preston because it was a girl. She told me she didn't want me to be gay. She thought a strict punishment would scare me into not being a lesbian anymore."

Ari thought back to her brief meeting with Vivian. "That's awful. I know I barely knew her, but I thought my radar for homophobia was better than that. Normally I can sniff people like that out."

"Oh, she would have been fine with *you* being gay. She didn't hate gay people in general. Just in the family. Do you want to know what we talked about at Chihuly? How sad she was that the family line would end with us. How at least Preston, Ellie, and Eleanor were doing their best but I wasn't even trying to continue the family line."

Elizabeth sat on the foot of the bed and looked at her reflection in the television.

"My mother flew me out here and put me up in this hotel so she could tell me, in no uncertain terms, about how disappointed she was in me for being gay."

Ari didn't know how to respond to that. She didn't think there *was* a proper response. So she walked over to the bed and put her hand on Elizabeth's shoulder. Elizabeth tensed, turned her head away, and then Ari felt a shudder, and then Elizabeth began to cry.

CHAPTER FIFTEEN

AFTER ELIZABETH composed herself, she went into the bathroom to splash some water on her face. She was dabbing at her cheeks with the towel when she came back, smiling bashfully.

"Have you ever actually done that? Splashed cold water on your face?"

"Sure," Ari said. "I kept seeing it in movies and wanted to know if it really worked. It feels kind of good."

Elizabeth laughed and sat on the bed again. Ari remained standing, leaning against the entertainment center.

"I want you to understand Mom isn't a bad or hateful person. She wasn't even cruel when she said it. She was just telling me to clear the air. Letting me know. I let *her* know that some things are better left unsaid. Sometimes a deathbed confession can just be silence."

Ari said, "Did she do the same thing to your sisters or Preston?"

"If she did, they didn't mention it. Just like I didn't mention this to them. I know Eleanor invited Evelyn to come along to their dinner. She may have been trying to prevent a conversation like mine." She sniffled and tucked her hair behind her ears. "I don't know what any of this has to do with the tapestry."

"To be honest, neither do I. Right now I'm just trying to bury myself with information and hoping I can find a motive for someone to have taken it. But the more I learn, the less I believe any of you actually wanted the damn thing."

Elizabeth said, "That's accurate, I think. You have to understand, it's been in our family for years. It was just part of the scenery. We knew it was worth a lot, but none of us really thought of it as a priceless piece of art until Mom told us about this whole crazy situation with you holding the key."

"It was all a bit dramatic, wasn't it?" Ari said. "Summoning everyone to the house and then revealing it was going to charity. She spent a lot of money on that little stunt. Hiring me, bringing you and your sisters to town. I doubt this room was cheap, and you've been here for a week. How much of that did Vivian pay for?"

"All of it."

Ari furrowed her brow. "What?"

"I have the room until Wednesday." She shrugged. "I figured she was just covering her bases if any of us fought over the will, or it took us longer than expected to go through the house and get what we wanted. Maybe it was just in case we got into a fight over something. Not that there's anything in the house I'd want enough to fight over."

"That's a lot of money for a 'just in case,'" Ari said. "She knew when she was going to end her life, and she knew when the will was going to be read. So why would she pay for so many extra days?" She remembered her own paycheck. "She paid me for two extra weeks..."

Elizabeth said, "What do you mean?"

"When she wrote out the check, she said it was to retain my services for eight weeks. It was the end of the sixth week when I got the call about her passing."

"So she wanted us all to be here for a week after we found out she was giving Crossing-Over Place to the museum, and she also knew you would still be working the case afterward. Do..." She made a face. "Do you think she knew the tapestry was missing?"

Ari said, "I'm really starting to wonder..."

"Anecdotal evidence suggests canidae society is matriarchal. The ability to transform is passed along by the mother, who is then charged with the young wolf's training. The father's responsibility is protection of the pack and the hunting. While the male may seem to be powerful, he is noise and

bluster and only acts at the command of his bitch."

Dale glanced up from the essay as Ari came into the office. The security footage was still scrolling on her laptop screen - Vivian's on the left, Fitz's on the right - and she was watching it from her periphery while she read. She rubbed her eyes and reached for a bottle of aspirin she kept in her bottom drawer.

"Hey, puppy."

Ari put down her bag and leaned across the desk to kiss Dale hello. "Everything okay?" she asked, nodding at the bottle.

"Yeah. Headache. Eye strain. Lots of reading and blurry videos to watch."

"Are you finding anything interesting, at least?"

"On the tapes or in the essays?"

"Either."

Dale sighed. "Not really. Magnusson really likes referring to female *canidae* as bitches."

"Well, it's accurate." Ari went into her office to hang up her jacket, then returned. "We can't complain too much because it's the name of our agency."

"Maybe it's because a man is using it."

Ari shrugged. "That does make a difference."

"How about you?" Dale said. "Anything on the tapestry?"

"Possibly. There's evidence Vivian planned to keep the kids in town for an extra week. She paid for all their hotel rooms until next Wednesday."

Dale said, "Maybe she just overestimated, the way she did with our payment. Maybe she wanted to be sure there was enough time for everything to be settled."

"I considered that. But it feels calculated. And at least it's something to grab onto, which is more than I can say about most of this case." She looked at the screens. "Anything here?"

"Nope. Typical suburban life, but with much higher property taxes."

Ari held out her hand. "Do you have the markers for the dry erase board?"

Dale found them in the drawer. Ari took black, red, and blue and went into her office. Dale paused the tapes and followed her in, sitting on the couch with her knees drawn up to her chest. Ari propped the board up against the wall and began to draw an overhead view of the Burroughs house. She was almost done when Dale tilted her head.

"Which way is north?"

Ari tapped the left side of the board. "Here."

"Why not put it at the top?"

"Because... I... the neighborhood... when I drove up to the house..." She waved her hands. "This way is north because that's how I've already drawn the map, okay?"

"Okay!"

"Can I finish?"

"Who's stopping you?"

Ari glared at her, sighed heavily, and went back to drawing. When she finished, she put down the black marker and drew a red cone stretching out from the front porch. Then she traded red for blue and made another cone, this one stretching from Fitz's property. It covered most of the western side of Vivian's property, with only a portion of the backyard out of range. It obviously couldn't see anything on the opposite side of the house. When she was finished, she stepped back and examined the finished product.

"Fitz's information is suspect, at best, but we do have occasional views of the house during the week since Vivian passed away. It's Swiss cheese, but it's better than being totally blind. Someone got into the house at some point during the past six weeks. They got into the study - how doesn't matter right now, but we know there was another key in play, so we can assume whoever it was used it. They took down the tapestry, rolled it up or put it in a carrying case, or transported it somehow. It had to be heavy..."

Dale said, "Do you know the exact dimensions?"

"No."

She got up and went to Ari's computer. "I can look it up. Something that old and historic has to be chronicled somewhere on the internet." She typed a bit, clicked and backed up. "Here we go, Crossing-Over Place. It's six feet by four feet... wow, so even rolled up, it would be about as long as carrying a body. I think we're looking at two people. Yes, someone could have carried it out of there by themselves, but not easily."

Ari twisted her lips and stared at the map. "There's a very small window where they couldn't be seen. And whoever it was, even if they knew about the camera over the front door, they wouldn't have known to avoid Fitz's camera, too."

"Didn't you tell me Elizabeth knew about them?"

"Right. Shit."

Dale got up and went to stand behind Ari. She put her hands

on Ari's shoulders and began a gentle massage, working the tension out with her fingers and thumbs. Ari grunted and slumped slightly.

"I miss massaging you," Dale said.

"Don't stop on my account," Ari said.

Dale kneaded harder and leaned in close to Ari's ear. "You're going to figure this out, puppy. Because you're the best detective in the Pacific Northwest. You've solved so many cases other people couldn't figure out. You took down Cecily Parrish. You stopped a war. You can figure this out because you are Ariadne Willow."

"Thank you, Dale."

"Whenever you need it, baby." She kissed Ari's cheek and let her hands slide down Ari's back. "This is just another case. And there are very low stakes. No one died. No one is trying to kill you."

"Yet."

Dale pinched Ari's side. "Knock on wood, Ariadne, now."

Ari reached out and rapped her knuckles against the wall. "Sorry."

"It's okay. All I'm saying is, even if the solution escapes you and this tapestry is never found, it won't change anybody's lives. It'll just be a sad thing that happened."

"That's not much comfort. But it is something." She put her right hand under her left arm and squeezed Dale's hand. "Thanks for the pep talk."

"I'm happy to be your cheerleader."

Ari looked over her shoulder. "Wait. Like... literally...? Like if I got the uniform..."

Dale swatted Ari's butt and shoved her away. "Mind on the game, Willow. Just let your mind rest a little bit. Stop pushing on the door and see if it swings open a little on its own."

"Good advice."

Dale went back out to her desk. When she saw down, she could see Ari stretching out on the couch in her office. They'd spent a lot of time on that couch together. First as boss and employee, then as friends, and finally as lovers. They had slept together for the first time on that couch. It was platonically and accidentally, but it still counted. The first time she'd woken up and felt Ari's weight against her back, had rolled over to see the tangled strands of hair falling across her face.

She smiled at the memory and pushed it aside so she wouldn't be distracted as she went back to her tedious assignments.

Ari wasn't fully asleep. She heard Dale moving around in the office, heard the phone ring. "Bitches Investigations, this is Dale. Yes, I called about a tapestry called Crossing-Over Place... no? Okay, would you know of anyone else who might be contacted about that sort of item? Thank you very much." There were times when she knew she drifted off, but the actual unconsciousness was brief. Sometimes Dale hummed.

Ari kept her mind at rest, refusing to chase her tail or try pushing facts of the case into any particular configuration. Eleanor, the twins, Preston, and Vivian were all phantoms at the edge of her mind. All of them were obscured by fog.

She opened her eyes when she heard movement nearby. She knew from the smell of her body wash that it was Dale, and she had her back to the couch so she could pin photos to the evidence board. Each of the Burroughs kids received their own portrait, as did Vivian. They looked like profile photos taken off websites. Probably Elizabeth's winery, Eleanor's app company... she didn't know where the pictures of Evelyn and Preston would have come from, but they looked professionally done.

There was a picture of the house next, and then a picture of Crossing-Over Place. At the end of the row, Dale added a picture of Ari.

"I thought I was only added to the suspect pool as a joke."

"Can't rule out anyone."

Ari sat up and put her feet on the floor. "You've betrayed my trust. I'm going to have to find a new fiancée. And secretary, assistant, lover, best friend..."

"Maid."

"I'm not that messy."

"*Maid*," Dale said again.

"Fine. Too much hassle. I guess I'll just keep you."

She rested her chin on her fist and looked at the row of portraits. She wondered where Preston had gotten a professional picture taken. And why. Maybe it was something rich people did. Either way, he looked handsome. Next to his picture was Evelyn's... no, Elizabeth. Ari narrowed her eyes and stood up to get a closer look. Dale had hung the twins next to each other, of course, and the pictures made it very hard to tell which one was which. Makeup, hair, clothes, the accoutrements of a professional photo shoot made it very easy for one twin to look like the other.

Dale had gone back out to her desk, but came back with

another picture. "I made a dumb mistake. Those are both pictures of Elizabeth."

"What?"

"Yeah, I got them off this stupid family site they have. Apparently it's a modern version of a Christmas card. Anyway, I got two Elizabeths and no Evelyns." She took down one and tacked the right picture in its place. Evelyn's hair was shorter, her cheeks a little rounder, and her expression was more guarded than Elizabeth's almost seductive glower.

Ari grunted. "You're not the only one making a dumb mistake. I was standing here trying to figure out which was which."

"Is it easier now?"

"Well, yeah," Ari said, "now that I know what I'm looking at. It was different when I..." Her voice trailed off and her eyes drifted down the row of pictures.

"Puppy..."

"Oh my God." She turned and went to the computer and tapped a button to make the screen wake up. Dale had left the browser on the last page she'd searched. Ari grunted and hung her head in disappointment, irritation, and frustration.

"You're worrying me, Ari. What's wrong?"

Ari raised her head to lock eyes with Dale, then looked past her at the board. "This case only seems impossible because someone has been lying from the very beginning."

"Who?"

Ari sighed. "Me."

CHAPTER SIXTEEN

DALE WAITED for the punchline. When it seemed as if there wasn't one coming, she echoed what Ari had said earlier. "I thought you were only on the suspect wall as a joke."

"Hold on," Ari said, lifting one finger and closing her eyes. She had to rethink everything about the case, and everything about her initial meeting with Vivian Burroughs, with what she'd learned from the kids, and the revelation she'd just had. "Okay," she said at last. "Okay. Stay with me here."

"I'll do my best."

Ari came around the desk and pointed at the board. "This case looks impossible because we've been assuming two things from the beginning. First, we've assumed the tapestry was in the room six weeks ago because I was telling everyone I saw it. What if I didn't?"

Dale said, "But... you did."

"I saw a wall-hanging and Vivian *told me* it was Crossing-Over Place. I had no reason to doubt that fact. Which brings us to the second assumption we've been making: that Vivian is innocent."

"That seems like an easy assumption to make, given the circumstances."

"True," Ari admitted. "But looking at the facts, it might not be accurate. Vivian spent thirty grand to hire us. She spent another five grand on hotel rooms and flights for her daughters... that's five grand *each*, so a total of at least fifteen thousand dollars bringing her girls home. Just so they can be there in person when she reveals none of them are getting the tapestry."

Dale said, "Well, there's the official will reading. There may be other things in the house the girls might want to pick up."

"Fair point. But she spent that much money for her daughters, while her son has become homeless. Do you think she wouldn't have known about that? Maybe he would have tried to keep it from her, but I find it much more likely he asked her for another in a long line of loans he would never have to pay back. Maybe that's why she said no this time. Maybe it was just because she knew he would eventually get her house so there was no point in keeping him in his old apartment."

"That makes sense to me," Dale said. "As do the hotel rooms. Yes, she was throwing around a lot of money, but she had it to throw around. And it's not like she could take it with her when she went. I, for one, plan to have a negative balance in my bank account when I finally shuffle off the mortal coil."

"Leaving me with all your debts? Real nice."

"No, I'm taking you down with me."

"Oh, okay, that's fine then." She held a hand up to the board. "Back to this... your way makes a lot of practical sense, but it doesn't take into account what I've learned about Vivian. She's vindictive and petty. Her last conversation with Elizabeth was to shame her for being gay. On top of that, when we met, Vivian apologized for the fact I'd have to interact with her kids. I think her kids are great! They can be buttheads when they're all in a room together, but what family isn't guilty of that?"

Dale said, "Let's say Vivian is a bitch. How do you make the leap that this is all a conspiracy she orchestrated before she died?"

Ari went to back to the computer. She turned the monitor around so Dale could see the screen, and she pointed at the picture.

"That's not what I saw."

"How can you be sure?"

Ari shook her head. "I don't know, I just... this is very close, but there's something off about it. The thing I saw was different somehow."

"The thing you saw six weeks ago."

"I know," Ari said. "I know, but I'm a detective. I can tell when something is off. I realized it with the pictures of the twins. I thought you'd pinned up pictures of two different people, so I was trying to find the differences. I did the same thing when I met with them in person. And the thing is, I almost convinced myself I could tell the difference between the women in the pictures."

"Isn't there a risk you're doing the same thing with the tapestry?"

"No. Well, yes, sure, technically, but I mean... This is the opposite. I saw a tapestry and then, when I saw the picture online, it was close enough that I didn't question it. I didn't look for the differences. When I realized that, I looked at this image, and it-it's *wrong*. The thing I saw was a forgery. A good one, but probably not one that would have fooled any of the kids or an expert who knew what it was supposed to look like. Vivian brought me in to confirm Crossing-Over Place was still in the house. If you owed something that expensive, wouldn't you have it insured?"

Dale's eyes widened. "And when it mysteriously went missing, your private investigator did her due diligence to find it~"

"But the case can't be closed, so eventually insurance is going to pay out."

"To a dead woman," Dale concluded.

Ari straightened. "Yeah, that's admittedly an issue. We've confirmed Vivian actually... I mean, it's a morbid thing to ask..."

"We saw her obituary," Dale said. "She was cremated. I'm sure the lawyer has some kind of death confirmation. I can give him a call if it's too weird for you."

"I would appreciate that. Thanks. Find out where she was cremated, too."

Dale nodded and looked at the board. "So Vivian had somebody create a fake Crossing-Over Place..."

"It wouldn't even have to be very good. It just had to fool me, and that's not very hard." Dale started to protest, and Ari held up her hand. "When it comes to tapestries, I'm a dunce. But thank you for trying to jump in like that, baby. I see you."

Dale winked at her. "I'll call around and see if there's anyone who made something like that in the past few months. But here's another question... why? You just said that Vivian shelled out, uh, well, let's just round it up to a hundred grand to cover our bill, the hotels, flights, making a fake tapestry of that size and quality, everything." Ari nodded. "And she did all that to con the insurance company? She was rich enough to throw around that kind of money, so what's the point?"

"Maybe she's actually broke."

"Our check cleared, no problem."

Ari twisted her lips, brow furrowed with thought. "This case refuses to make sense..."

"You'll get there. You found this, you're going to find something else. The pieces are all there. In fact, I think it's less impossible than it was yesterday. I have faith in you, mutt."

"Whoa," Ari said. "Hey. I told you before, I don't like that. Where's that coming from all of a sudden?"

Dale shrugged. "I don't know. It just slipped out. I must have forgotten you said you don't like it." She sighed. "Anyway. Sorry."

"It's fine. Just... stick with puppy. I love puppy."

"You got it. I'll go get Timothy Dodd on the phone so we can confirm Vivian Burroughs actually did go through with ending things."

"Can you find the name of the clinic where she... where it was... she..."

Dale took pity on her. "Emerald Care. The number is already on your phone."

"Thank you. They probably won't talk to me about a specific patient, but I'll see what I can learn about the whole process. And maybe someone will be willing to talk to a nosy private eye." She gave the evidence board one last look as Dale went back out to the front office. When she came out, she knocked on the corner of the desk. "Dinner tonight? We can go out somewhere. Shake Shack?"

"That sounds good."

"I'll text to let you know when I'm done."

"Okay."

Dale was already scrolling through her phone to find Timothy's number, and Ari had her phone out to get Emerald Care's address as she headed to her car.

The rest of the day was a bust. Emerald Care was a stone wall of patient confidentiality, which would be a huge point in their favor under other circumstances. Ari did get the basic run-through of what a client could expect at the clinic, but no one would even speak hypothetically about anyone who may or may not have come in on Sunday night. Ari was grateful for the information but in the end, none of it was particularly helpful or illuminating to the case.

Dinner wasn't much better. Ari got a chicken dog, and Dale picked at her cheeseburger and barely touched the order of fries they'd gotten for the table. Ari's updates about Emerald Care were met with non-verbal responses, and her eyes were constantly aimed down at the table rather than on Ari. Finally, Ari touched her knee under the table.

"Hey, is everything okay?"

"Yeah. Just fucking tired." She rubbed her eye with the heel of her hand. "Watching security video nonstop, reading those essays... I might wear my glasses tomorrow instead of fucking around with my contacts."

"Well, I think you look pretty sexy in glasses, so I'm all for that plan."

That received a tepid smile, and Dale went back to being mostly non-verbal.

"Was there something in the essays that upset you, or~"

"Can we just drop it? We talk all day at the office, we talk all day at home, some days there's just not much to talk about."

Ari sat up straighter, stunned. "Yeah. Okay. We can just have a meal together."

"Fantastic."

Whatever was bothering Dale would still be there in the morning, Ari decided, and maybe then she would be willing to talk it out. If distance was what she wanted right now, then that's what Ari would give her. They drove home in silence, and Ari felt like an uninvited guest as she followed Dale inside. She went into the kitchen to make tomorrow's lunches while Dale was in the shower. When the water shut off, she went in and knocked on the door.

"I'm going for a run. I shouldn't be out long."

"Mm'ay," Dale said around her toothbrush.

"I love you."

"Mm," Dale responded.

Ari tried not to feel hurt as she undressed in the living room. Tired eyes, a headache from watching monotonous video footage, a lack of progress on their case... it was enough to make anyone grumpy. Dale usually clung to her through those moods, though, and being shut out like this was awful.

She folded her clothes on the couch, opened the door, and let herself out. She paused and listened to the neighborhood sounds. A trashcan being rolled to the curb next door, a car revving its engine on the next block, but no one close enough to spot her. She bent down like a runner on the starting block and let the wolf wrap itself around her.

Her next conscious memory was a blur of streetlights, strange smells, a cacophony of sounds she couldn't hope to categorize, and an ache in her joints. She was back in a runner's position and unfolded herself, stretching sore muscles. Sweat covered her, which meant the wolf had been busy before finally giving back control. She blinked the stinging moisture from her eyes and examined her surroundings. Trees, thickly packed, which was good considering her nudity. She was on a narrow dirt trail and she could smell water. *Colman Park*, she thought, which was good. But there weren't a lot of restaurants, diners, gas stations, or pay phones.

She was near the community garden so, after determining no one was nearby, she pushed through the underbrush and climbed the rise to where her stash was buried. She dug it up and pulled it loose from the mulch and unzipped it. A few minutes later she was dressed in jeans, a T-shirt, and a pair of old tennis shoes, and she had five dollars in her pockets along with some change. There was also a wristwatch in the bag and she checked the time: twelve minutes past one. Not too bad. She wrapped the remaining clothes back up in their plastic sacks, zipped the bag, and returned it to the hole.

There was a shack nearby where the gardeners could keep supplies, and she was able to jimmy the lock without much trouble. There was an old-fashioned rotary phone on a table and she dialed Dale's number. She sniffed and ran her free hand under her nose as it rang, watching the windows for any night watchman or joggers who might come down the trail. The phone buzzed again and she frowned. She was pretty sure she had dialed the right number. She pushed down the switch to disconnect the call and dialed again. This time it rang once and cut off.

Ari furrowed her brow and hung up. Rotary phones were difficult, and she hadn't used one since she was a kid. There was a chance she'd dialed wrong. Or maybe Dale's headache was worse than she'd let on. Either way, she didn't want to try a third time, so she hung up the phone and left the shed. She made sure to lock it again behind her before she started walking.

It was just over two miles home. Not a terrible trek, but also not really worth stripping down and changing back into the wolf. The tennis shoes from her stash were good for jogging, so she set out at a steady pace. Hopefully no one would see her running and get the wrong idea.

When she got home, she was exhausted and sore from running

in both her forms. She let herself inside and went directly into the bedroom. Dale's hair had fallen across her face, and Ari remembered the night not long ago when she had gotten home under her own power and woke Dale to let her know she was safe. It was getting to be a habit with them. But this time, she also wanted to make sure Dale was feeling okay.

She crouched by the bed and placed her hand on Dale's forehead to see if she was feverish. Dale jerked, startled, and Ari shushed her.

"It's just me..."

"M'sleeping," Dale murmured. She raised her arms and tried to push Ari's hand away.

"I know, babe, I just wanted to make sure you were okay."

Dale rolled her head across the pillow. "Stop..."

"You had a headache, you didn't answer your phone~"

Dale lashed out, sitting up and smacking Ari in the chest with both hands. "Get your hands off of me, you goddamn mutt!"

Ari fell back onto her ass, staring up at Dale. Dale stared back, hair in her face, lips puffing out with the force of her breathing. She waited for an apology, either for the shove or the slur, but neither was forthcoming. Ari got to her feet but didn't move closer to the bed.

"I don't know what's going on with you," Ari said, "but you need to take that word out of your vocabulary."

Dale sighed and laid back down. Ari watched her for a long moment and then left the bedroom. She really had no clue what had just happened, but she wasn't willing to spend the night next to whoever Dale had become. They would talk it out in the morning. She was sure Dale would apologize, there would be some explanation, and eventually they would laugh about it. Maybe. She stretched out with her head on the arm of the couch and let her exhaustion take her to sleep.

The next morning, she was woken by the sound of the front door opening. She saw Dale slip out, pulling the door shut behind her.

"Dale..." She got up and chased her out of the house, only to see her car pulling out of the driveway. She watched, completely and utterly confused, as Dale drove away without so much as a look back.

CHAPTER SEVENTEEN

ARI POUNDED on the front door of her mother's house, then stepped back to the edge of the porch. Her mind was so frantic that she almost forgot she had knocked by the time Milo answered. She was in pajama pants and a tank top, and had clearly just gotten out of bed, but Ari ignored all of that and stepped forward to look past her.

"Is Dale here?"

"What? No, was she supposed to be?"

Ari growled at the back of her throat and retreated again. "I don't know. But she's not at the office, and I waited for her to show up, even though she left before me..."

"Whoa, whoa, slow down. Come inside." She hooked her hand around Ari's elbow and pulled her inside. "Go sit down in the living room. Catch your breath. I'll be right back."

Ari did as she was told, because it meant she didn't have to think or make a decision for herself. She perched on the edge of an ottoman and squeezed her hands together, hunched forward, trying to think of what she might have done to prompt this, or where Dale might have gone, or anything that could make sense out of the past few hours. Dale had been mad at her before, but there had never been anything like this. Nothing even close.

Milo returned with Gwen in tow. Gwen was wearing a bright blue robe, her hair wet and swept back out of her face. She sat next to Ari on the ottoman.

"What's going on? What's wrong with Dale?"

"I don't know," Ari said. "Last night she said... she had a headache, she wasn't talking. I thought she was just working too hard. Her eyes were hurting. She's been watching a lot of security videos and reading those Magnusson essays, so it made sense. Then she didn't answer the phone when I called her to come pick me up. So I was worried. I thought maybe she was sicker than she said. So when I got home, I felt to see if she had a fever and she said..." She looked away, feeling the tightness in her throat which indicated she was close to losing control.

Milo, standing awkwardly to one side, said, "Whatever it was, I'm sure it was just a heat of the moment thing. I know I've said awful things when I felt poorly."

"She shoved me and said 'get your hands off me, you goddamn mutt.'"

Gwen and Milo both went very still. Ari was pretty sure that Gwen didn't take a breath for a full minute, reaching for Ari's clenched hands and squeezing them both.

"She wouldn't do that," Milo muttered. "Not Dale."

"Believe me, it echoed," Ari said. "I've been hearing it all night. And... and it wasn't the first time she's called me a mutt. She did it twice before. I told her to stop, but she... I guess... forgot."

Gwen said, "Well... she does throw around the word 'wolf' a lot."

"So do we," Milo said.

"That's different." Her voice was gentle. "How many times have you ripped into someone for calling you a wolf?"

Ari said, "I told her she could do it. She calls me puppy, too." She finally cried then, the tears that couldn't get past her eyelashes breaking free. "She says wolf, but she calls us *canidae* when it matters. And I know that if I told her to stop, she would in a heartbeat. I know her. I *know* Dale Frye, and I know she would never use that word the way she did last night. She threw it at me, Mom. Like it was a dart." Her voice cracked again and she said, "She wanted to hurt me."

Milo said, "Well, and what happened this morning?"

"She woke up, got dressed, and just left. I tried to stop her, but she just got in the car and drove off. I went to the office. I tried calling. Nothing."

"She might have taken herself to the hospital if she was feeling bad enough," Milo said.

Ari shook her head, still staring at a random spot on the carpet. "I don't think she was ever sick. I think she just said that so she wouldn't have to talk to me."

Gwen rubbed Ari's forearm. "Has anything happened between you that might prompt a reaction like this? Any fights?"

"No. We actually..." She glanced sideways at her mother, then at Milo, and away again. "We, uh, we actually... got engaged."

Gwen's hand went still. "Really?"

"Wow," Milo said. "Congratulations."

"It's not a big deal," Ari said. Then, to her mother, "We hadn't told anyone yet."

Gwen said, "I understand. But... maybe it's a big deal to Dale. Maybe bigger than even she realized. People can panic in the face of a big change, and with Dale... she's marrying a *canidae*. That's bound to create cold feet in even the strongest relationship. She may have just needed to go somewhere and be alone to clear her head."

Ari muttered, "Maybe..."

Milo said, "I could call her. Maybe if she's screening her calls, she'd be willing to talk with me." She went out of the room and retrieved her phone from elsewhere in the house.

"What if there's something in the essays?" Ari said. "What if she learned something about *canidae* that would make her not want to be with me?"

Gwen reached up and stroked Ari's hair. "I can't imagine anything like that, Ariadne. The things that girl has gone through, and she still ran to you at the end of the day? The things she's done to save you? I wish you had seen her when you were in prison. I didn't invite her to stay here out of loneliness, I did it because she needed someone to watch over her. She was a wreck without you. I can't imagine a world where she would choose to be without you."

"Well, look around, because we're in it."

Milo came back with her phone. She gave Gwen a quick head-shake, indicating Dale also hadn't answered her call.

"Did you get my phone, too?"

"Yup." She held it out and Gwen stood to take it. "Think she'll answer you?"

Gwen said, "I'm not calling Dale. I'm calling Charlie Otto.

They're an old friend, lives in France. I called them about the essays. They said they'd call me back, but I'll see if they know anything that might ease your mind, Ari." She dialed and walked toward the couch as she waited for an answer. "Charlie. Gwen." She lapsed into French.

Milo leaned closer. "She's asking for anything they might know about the essays. It's urgent. She wants to know if there's anything controversial or upsetting, because someone who was reading it..." Gwen stopped and then spoke again in a different tone of voice. "Oh," Milo said, "Charlie's not happy that someone was reading it, apparently. Gwen said it was a human."

Gwen listened to Charlie and turned to look at Ari. "*Pourquoi?*" Her eyes flashed, and she broke off into a stream of quick French. Ari sat up straighter, her anguish forgotten as she watched her mother rage at someone across an ocean.

"What's she saying?"

"I can't keep up," Milo said. "Something about warning, and, uh, Charlie should have told Gwen when she called the first time..."

Gwen lowered the phone and threw it onto the couch. Ari and Milo both stood, but Gwen paced to the wall with her hand to her temple.

"What's going on?" Ari asked. "What was all of that about?"

"Charlie told me there's a reason no one is allowed to read the essays without being approved. They're poison texts. Apparently whoever reads them gets... their minds get manipulated. It's not exactly brainwashing, but it's bad. Charlie... Charlie said..." She was looking at the floor, hands on her hips, trying to control her breathing.

Milo said, "Gwyneth, please, just tell her."

"In the thirties, before *canidae* got their hands on the essays and prevented them from being published, Magnusson was going to use it to train a new generation of hunters. Wolves who read it got self-destructive, suicidal. Humans who read it... became worse. Ari, there's a chance that reading those essays turned Dale into a hunter."

"Bullshit," Milo said before Ari could find her voice. "No, that is *bullshit*. Dale Frye? Dale, who crawled on her hands and knees to clean wolfsbane from a *canidae* bar? Who ran unarmed into a gunfight to save one of us who had been hit? I'd give that woman a loaded gun and put the barrel on my forehead, and you're telling me she's turning into a hunter? No. No."

Gwen said, "The book is powerful. It's... it's why they have it under such heavy restrictions. Charlie said no one is ever given permission to access it long enough to read more than a page or two. It's too dangerous."

Ari began to respond but was interrupted by her phone ringing. She grabbed it, expecting to see Dale's face on the screen, but it was an unknown number. She answered just in case.

"Dale?"

"Ah. No, I'm afraid this is Timothy Dodd."

For a moment, Ari had no earthly idea who that was. Then she remembered the case, Crossing-Over Place, the Burroughs. "Right. I'm sorry. I'm... i-it's been a morning, Mr. Dodd. How can I help you?"

"Today is the reading of Vivian's will. I thought you would like to be in attendance. The children will be here at ten-thirty."

Ari looked at the clock above the mantle. She had enough time to get downtown, just barely. Part of her wanted to tell Dodd the case was closed, give him the theory about a fake tapestry, and focus all her energy on Dale. But if she was wrong and a priceless piece of art was still out there somewhere, she would regret it. The timing was godawful, but it would get her mind off of it.

"I'll... I'll be there. Thank you for letting me know." He gave her the suite number and she hung up. "I have to go. It's a case."

Milo said, "You're working on a case today? Now?"

"I have to," Ari said quietly. "I can't just sit here. We'll talk about this after I get back. Maybe Dale will have made contact by then."

Gwen said, "Go. We'll see what we can do in the meantime."

Ari felt a swell of emotion for her mother. "Thanks, Mom. And... and about... everything we talked about..."

"That's not part of this," Gwen said. "You can go back to being mad at me when everything is settled. This isn't your forgiveness, I know that. This is family."

Ari crossed the room and hugged Gwen, startling everyone in the room. She buried her face in the plush material of the robe and, after her shock wore off, Gwen returned the hug.

"I love you, Mom."

"I love you, too. And congratulations on your engagement. I'm so happy for you, Ariadne." She pressed a kiss to Ari's cheek and pushed her away. "Go, you have work to do."

Ari went to Milo and touched her face. "You're family, too.

You're like a sister to me."

"Don't make it weird."

Ari laughed, and more tears fell free. She hugged Milo. "I love you, Millicent."

"I love you, too."

She was almost to the door when Gwen called to her. "Ari. When I told Charlie that a human had read the essays, they said to run. Run far, run fast. Whatever tainted those pages, it's incredibly potent. A human who read it should be almost immediately driven to violence. Dale's first instinct was to put distance between the two of you. *She* ran away, Ari. Whatever might be happening in her brain, I think that's pretty solid evidence of where her heart is."

Ari twisted her lips, teeth clenched tight, and nodded once. "Understood. Thanks."

She left the house with her emotions in more turmoil than when she'd arrived, and the answers she'd received about Dale's behavior only made her feel queasier, but she couldn't worry about that now. Going to work would give her something to occupy her brain. She was grateful for the puzzle of Crossing-Over Place, and the whole sordid Burroughs saga.

Anything to keep her mind off the puzzle of her own life.

Dale drove to Myrtle Edwards Park, one of the few parks in Seattle which wasn't hiding a stash of Ari's clothes. It was a jogging park, with lots of flat exposed land where people could picnic or play fetch with their dogs. Just the thought of dogs spiked her headache and twisted her insides. She pressed her fist against her stomach, just above her navel, and tried to stay upright. The park also had three large slabs of stone called *Adjacent, Against, Upon*. She focused on them as she walked, and eventually the nausea faded enough for her to put her hand down.

She had tossed and turned all night. She didn't know what was wrong with her. She didn't know why it took all her willpower to stay in bed and not go into the living room where that damn dirty mutt - *My puppy, Ariadne, my sweet lovely fiancée* - was sleeping. She'd clenched her fists until the fingers cramped, scared of what she might do with them if she didn't. When she got to the park, she climbed onto the platform of the Against stone and sat down facing the water, letting her feet dangle.

"Miss Frye. Or may I call you Dale now?"

She didn't look toward Isaac Hayden, just waited until he was close enough to get into her line of sight. She glared down at him from her perch.

"What did you do to me?"

"I didn't do anything. I just provided you with information that had been withheld from you for too long. You were indoctrinated by the wolves, only heard their side of the story, forced to take sides without all the facts. You deserved to know the truth."

Dale realized how close they were to her car. She was engaged to a detective, she was making herself way too easy to find. She jumped down, stuffed her hands in her pockets, and started walking. Isaac followed, at first lagging behind but then speeding up to walk alongside her.

"I'm glad you called me. You're not the first human who has been seduced by the wolves."

"Don't call them wolves," Dale said.

Isaac looked at her. "What do you call them?" *Mutts, mangy mutts.* "I call them *canidae*," she said. "It's what they are. And even if I did call them wolves, it's not... you don't have the right. I've given a decade of my life to that woman~"

"Not a woman," Isaac interrupted. "She may look female, but she's not. None of them are. They're a different species. Even when they're in human form, they have heightened senses. Their skeletal structure works in ways ours never could. There's a reason a bite from them is fatal. A human can't become a werewolf, no matter what the myths tell you. I believe if it was possible, either Willow or her mother would have turned you a long time ago."

She tried not to think about how many times Ari's teeth had been on her neck, or her fingers had been in Ari's mouth just inviting a bite. She shivered, even though those memories still felt warm and loving. She felt like her mind was wrapped in barbed wire, and thinking one way would tear the memory up while the other way would spare her pain.

"It was the essays, wasn't it? There's something in them."

"Indeed there is," Isaac said. "The truth. And soon the whole world will know what's been living hidden in the shadows."

Dale imagined the news breaking. She saw people spray-painting slurs on the office, on their home. People would harass them in restaurants, clients would refuse to hire her. They'd been lucky to live in a city where that never happened just because they held hands or kissed in public. And there would also be paranoia, witch hunts, caused by the fact you can't spot a *canidae* just by looking at them.

"Ariadne is going to get hurt, isn't she?"

"Probably. She has a habit of sticking her nose where it doesn't belong. Those are the types of dogs who tend to get their snouts hit by the newspaper."

Dale wrinkled her nose and turned away to look out to the bay. The water was choppy, and the waves smacked against the rocks and logs along the shore. A huge tanker was lumbering out toward the sea, and she breathed in deep to cool down the fire in her head. She hated hearing Isaac use such an offensive metaphor about Ari, but she also knew that the comparison paled in comparison to what she'd said the night before. *You goddamn mutt.* She almost sobbed when she remembered it. Ari's face... betrayed, hurt, confused. She would never forget that.

I did that. No matter what else I've done for her, I'm the one who made Ari look like that.

Isaac stood next to her. Two women jogged by behind them.

"Why me?" she asked. "Why'd you come after me?"

"I didn't. I had no idea you existed until a few weeks ago. But sometimes things work out. You're the key to all of this, Miss Frye. I could never just hold up the essays and claim the threat is real, but with you by my side..." He laughed softly. "You're the witness. You are by far the best *canidae* expert I've ever met. You can use everything they've told you over the years and finally expose them. You can give humanity a fighting chance to protect ourselves against this threat. Will you help me, Miss Frye?"

She closed her eyes and smelled the salt water, felt its spray on her face. After a long moment, she turned away from Isaac and started walking again. She was putting more distance between herself and where she had parked, just in case. She looked over her shoulder at Isaac.

"You can call me Dale."

CHAPTER EIGHTEEN

TIMOTHY DODD'S office gave Ari flashbacks to GG&M, even though the aesthetics were actually quite different. Faux-marble floors, pale yellow wallpaper, golden accents on everything, and just enough mirrors to give the illusion of space without turning it into a carnival sideshow. The flowers were real enough to cause Ari to sniffle as she signed into the guest book and was directed down a narrow hall of identical offices with fogged glass doors.

Timothy's office door was open and Ari saw Elizabeth Burroughs inside. It really was easy to tell the twins apart once she'd spent some alone time with each of them. The office was empty except for her, and she was standing at a table near the windows pouring herself a cup of coffee. It had been brewed strong enough that Ari believed it would have been overwhelming even if she wasn't a *canidae*. Elizabeth looked up and smiled when she saw who had arrived.

"The detective. Coffee?"

"No, thank you." The office was empty save for the two of them. "Where is everyone else?"

Elizabeth looked at the clock. "We're a little early. And I assume Preston and Evelyn will both be late. Eleanor is probably in the lobby waiting until the exact moment the appointment was for."

She sipped the coffee and examined Ari. "Are you okay? You look rough, if you don't mind me saying so."

"I'm fine," Ari muttered. "I think your mother was screwing everyone around. Myself included."

"How so?"

"I don't think I saw the real Crossing-Over Place. I think it was a fake just convincing enough to fool me if I glanced at an image of it online."

Elizabeth said, "So the tapestry didn't go missing in the past six weeks..."

"It could have gone missing at any point since the last time someone in your family saw it. I assume that would be Preston, so I'll ask him when he gets here."

"Ask me what?" Preston said as he came into the office. He wore a wrinkled white T-shirt and jeans. When he caught Elizabeth's disdainful look, he sneered. "What, it's not like this is a memorial or anything. We're just here to listen to some guy read the will. She didn't get dressed up, either."

Ari looked down at herself and realized she was still wearing the shirt she'd slept in under a hoodie.

Before she could apologize, Elizabeth said, "Yeah, well, some people can pull off scruffy. You're not one of them. Either grow a beard or invest in a razor."

Ari moved past the compliment. "I wanted to ask you about the last time you saw Crossing-Over Place."

"I have no idea," he said. "I never went into Mom's study. And even if I did, I barely even noticed the tapestry anymore."

"But it was huge," Ari said. "You would have noticed if it was missing, just like if you walked into your apartment and the TV wasn't there."

Preston said, "Missing? You said it was there six weeks ago when Mom gave you the key."

"That's no longer, ah... we're looking into the possibility that I might have been wrong."

"Oh, great, that's fantastic." He walked between them and took a seat in front of Timothy's desk.

Elizabeth said, "Are you still breaking into the house every night and sleeping in your old room?"

He spun to look at her, then glared at Ari. She glared back. She didn't give a damn what this spoiled brat thought of her, and her ability to care was even lower today. When she didn't wither, he blew air out through his nose and faced forward again, arms over his chest.

Elizabeth looked at Ari again. "Let's say you're right. Mom created a fake tapestry just to fool you?"

"She wanted me as proof it was still in the house six weeks ago. When it goes missing, I'm determined to solve the case. If I can't, it remains unsolved."

"And the insurance money goes to a dead woman!" Preston said. "That's a genius plan. Unless she faked her death, but I don't think we're in a soap opera."

"I did check with the funeral home, and they confirmed she was cremated on Monday morning. I didn't get much information from the clinic where she spent her last moments."

Elizabeth said, "Maybe a family member would have more luck."

"I didn't want to ask."

Elizabeth shook her head. "No, we're as invested as you are. I want to know what happened as much as you do."

"God, just bone already," Preston muttered.

"You're a real piece of shit," Elizabeth said without emotion.

Ari walked to the window and looked out. Dale was somewhere out there, alone, probably confused. If what the French person had said about the essays was true, she must be having some insane thoughts. The fact she couldn't go running to wherever she was, hug her, tell her it was going to be all right, made Ari's skin itch. Elizabeth joined her a moment later.

"Don't listen to him," she said, not bothering to lower her voice. "He's a jealous asshole who's always hated that I have a better track record with women than he does. And you *are* my type. But he still shouldn't have said anything."

"It's fine," Ari said.

Eleanor arrived at that moment. "Looks like most of us are here," she said. "What's going on?"

"Elizabeth's going to bang the PI."

"Oh, Lizzie," Eleanor sighed.

"No one is banging anybody," Elizabeth said. "Preston's just being an asshole."

Eleanor looked around as if Evelyn was hiding somewhere in the small office. "Where's Evie?"

"Not here," Elizabeth said.

"I can see that," Eleanor said with the measured patience of an elementary school teacher. "I was hoping you might have some insight."

"Well, congratulations, now you know as much as I do."

Ari closed her eyes. She was starting to understand why Vivian might have wanted to screw these people around.

Eleanor had settled in on the divan near the window when Evelyn finally arrived. She was out of breath and pushed her hair out of her face as she scanned the room.

"Lawyer man isn't even here?"

"You don't have much room to complain about someone being late," Eleanor said.

"Fuck you, Eleanor."

Ari pushed away from the wall and said, "Shut the *fuck* up. All of you. Just shut up, okay? Shut your goddamn mouths and stop acting so fucking superior to each other. You jump down Preston's throat because he took money from your mother, but she gladly gave him that money. Because he was the only one out of all of you who stayed close enough to help her. He might not have had a choice, because the three of you ran as far and fast as you could, but he stepped up. He was there for Vivian when she needed him.

"You look down your nose at Evelyn because she isn't punctual, but she's the only one of you who is working right now." She stepped forward and tugged the receipt which she'd seen poking out of her shirt's breast pocket. "She was delivering breakfast for an app. She just made five bucks this morning. That's why she was late."

Ari pointed at Elizabeth next. "Maybe you think Elizabeth was indifferent to your mother. If I was Elizabeth, I would have put a continent between myself and my mother. The things she said to Elizabeth were cruel, unwarranted, and she planned her death with no intention to ever apologize for them. She was comfortable with the fact she made her daughter feel wrong, and there is no way I could ever forgive that."

Elizabeth was hugging herself, head down and turned away so none of them could see her face.

"And Eleanor..." She faltered. "You're... Well, you're just kind of bitchy and superior. No one likes that."

The office fell silent. Ari caught her breath, already regretting what she'd said, when Eleanor snorted. She brought a hand up to her mouth, covering the lower half of her face, and bent forward. Preston watched her, eyebrows raised in surprise, and then began to laugh with her. Evelyn was the next to start, and she walked over to sit next to Evelyn on the couch. Elizabeth wasn't laughing, but she did lift her head, shake the hair out of her eyes, and smile appreciatively at Ari.

Timothy finally arrived and stopped cold on the threshold, staring at the gathered Burroughs children who actually seemed to be enjoying each other's company.

"The secretary told me you'd all arrived. I apologize for my tardiness."

"A few minutes," Eleanor said. "Who's counting."

Evelyn laughed and bumped her shoulder. Timothy looked confused but unwilling to argue. He crossed to his desk, nodding hello to Ari, and took a seat.

"Perhaps we should get this business out of the way while everyone is so... chipper. This won't be a formal recitation of the will. It's simply an itemized list of what each person is entitled to. I'm only providing the information along with any deeds, proofs of ownership, or provenance that may be required. The will can be contested, but this is not the time nor the place for those grievances. Am I understood?"

The group nodded. Timothy nodded as well and opened the file in front of him.

"We'll begin with communal property. Each Burroughs child will receive two hundred and fifty thousand dollars. The remainder of Vivian's liquid assets shall be split evenly among the charities she's outlined elsewhere. I can provide a list of those if anyone wishes to see them." Eleanor lifted her hand. Timothy acknowledged that and moved on.

"To Preston McBride Burroughs, Vivian leaves the house and all its furnishings save for items listed elsewhere in this document."

Ari expected some kind of outcry to that, but none of the girls reacted at all. Preston brought a hand up and wiped it over his face. He had just gone from homeless to being worth at least three quarters of a million dollars in the space of five minutes. It was enough to make anyone emotional.

"To Evelyn Hannah Burroughs, Vivian leaves her vehicles. There's an itemized list here. Two cars, and a boat."

"And a wheelchair," Preston said under his breath.

"Preston," Eleanor scolded, but she was smiling. Her sisters were as well, and even Timothy looked like he was on the verge of a grin.

"To Elizabeth Garrison Burroughs, my wine collection, including the bottle of Cheval Blanc 1947 which is being stored~"

Elizabeth made a choking noise and clapped a hand over her mouth, eyes wide. Everyone, including Timothy, looked at her. She finally blinked again and realized she was the center of attention. Ari noticed her fingers were shaking when she lowered her hand.

"It's... it's the best wine of the twentieth century. It's worth..." She shook her head. "It's worth a lot of money."

Timothy cleared his throat. "Yes, well. There's another list of the wines, vintages and value, and where they're stored. I'll get that to you."

"Thanks, thank you," Elizabeth whispered.

"And finally, to Eleanor Ashton Burroughs." He tapped his thumbs on the desk and stared at the page. He worked his jaw back and forth, tapped his thumbs again.

Elizabeth said, "Is everything all right?"

Timothy looked at her, then at Eleanor. "Yes." He cleared his throat and worked his neck as if suddenly his collar was too tight. "To Eleanor Ashton Burroughs, Vivian leaves nothing."

Preston sat up straighter. "Turn the page over, it's probably on the back."

"No, no," Timothy said. "It actually... it says the words."

He held up the page and Eleanor stood, took the paper, and stared at the entry. Ari watched a parade of emotions cross her face. Confusion, sadness, anger, disappointment. She pressed her lips together so tightly that they turned white. Color also faded from the rest of her face.

Preston leaned forward. "Hey, look, any jewelry she had..."

"If she wanted me to have it, she would have left it to me."

"Yeah, but come on, what am I going to do with it?"

Eleanor dropped the paper back on the desk. "Fuck it. Fuck this and fuck her." She looked at her sisters, then at Ari. "Do you want to know where Crossing-Over Place is? The bitch probably burned it. She probably hired you, then burned the damn thing so you would spin your wheels looking for it. That's what she does. Did. Damn it, it's..." She huffed and swiveled her head to look at everyone. "We were the bad kids. We were monsters who couldn't be left alone in a room together. Because that's what she made us. We were her projects, her little games, her toys. She turned Ellie and Evie into twins who live six hours apart because even they don't like seeing each other very often. She turned Preston into her errand boy and kept his dependent on her until the very end. And what was I? Who was I? No one. Nothing. Not even worth an afterthought in her will."

"Eleanor..."

"Save it, Elizabeth. You know better than any of us what she was capable of. Don't try to defend her just because you got some fancy booze."

"I think all our emotions and moods are all on edge right now," Timothy said. He stood and hurriedly headed for the door. "Why don't we take five? There's coffee in the break room, just at the end of the hallway... If you'll follow me."

Eleanor left the office and went the opposite direction of the executor. Preston slowly rose from his chair and looked at his sisters. Evelyn motioned for him to come with her, and she put an arm across his shoulders as they left as well. Elizabeth started to follow, but Ari put a hand out to stop her.

"Your mother left Evelyn cars and a boat. Those weren't at the house."

"No, they were at the storage unit downtown. Shit... we should have told you about that on Wednesday."

Ari waved off the apology. "No, it wouldn't have been pertinent until I came up with the fake tapestry theory. But now, yeah, I definitely want to go take a look at it."

"Mr. Dodd probably has the key and the address."

She nodded and went to find him so she could ask. As worried as she was about Dale, she knew it wasn't a problem she could beat into submission until she found an answer. The missing tapestry, though... she felt like she was close to a breakthrough. Even if it was just uncovering the fact that Vivian was an awful person, it would be some kind of closure.

CHAPTER NINETEEN

ISAAC TRIED several times to strike up a conversation, but Dale ignored him and just looked out at the water, trying to guess how long it would take the tanker to disappear from sight. It didn't take as long as she expected. When she got tired of walking, Isaac suggested an early lunch. She suggested a place called Li'l Woody's, mainly because she and Ari never went there and she wouldn't have to worry about her showing up. Isaac drove in silence, and Dale looked out the window, blindly watching traffic and pedestrians. Part of her wanted to spot Ari in the crowd, and another part dreaded it.

She dropped her hand to the bracelet around her wrist. Her first instinct was to tear it off, throw it out the window, and scrub the spot it had been resting until the skin was pink and raw. But there was another part, something which felt hidden behind a brick wall at the back of her mind, that knew she couldn't do that any more than she could tear her own heart out and drop it on the street. She remembered the first night she'd shown it to Ari.

They were at the cabin where they first made love, taking a vacation after the war. It was a surprise, hair from Ari and fur from the wolf, twined together. She'd asked Ari to put it on her. Had it been raining that night? Yes... maybe? She was annoyed she couldn't remember. But then again, who cared what was happening outside the car? She was focused entirely on the woman with her. No, the thing with her, not a woman or a person.

She flinched at that, pressed her fist against the side of her head. Isaac looked over but didn't comment.

When they arrived at the restaurant, she followed him up the stairs and inside as if she was on a leash (*like those mutts ought to be, every one of them*) and shook her head to clear it of rotten thoughts. She went to a table by the window while Isaac ordered, keeping her head down on her arms until he arrived with two salmon burgers, French fries, and two milkshakes.

"I got vanilla and chocolate both, because I didn't know which you'd prefer. I'm good with either. And just in case you didn't know, you can dip your fries in the milkshake, and~"

"This isn't a date," she said.

He stared across the table at her. "I know."

"Then spare me the milkshake hacks and start talking. Who are you really?"

"I'm exactly who I said I was. My name is Isaac Hayden. My job is investigating the mythical. Creatures that most people don't believe actually exist. They're out there, as you well know. Bigfoot. Vampires. Werewolves."

"Mermaids," Dale said.

He nodded. "I've heard rumors, but I've never taken the time to really explore it. When I was younger, I was fascinated by werewolves. They weren't like vampires, who could never really hide among humanity. Weakened by the sun, garlic, drinking blood. They look human but they're still monsters. Wolves, though. Wolves lie, wolves can hide."

He sat up straighter and scanned the restaurant, so Dale looked as well. A trio of college guys, two girls in pastel blue and pink workout clothes, an elderly couple.

"Anyone in this room could be a wolf, and we would never know unless they wanted us to know. I found that fascinating and disturbing at the same time. I became obsessed with finding out as much as possible about them."

"So you could kill them?"

"No." He looked down at his food, but she knew he was seeing something farther away. "No, at first it was purely academic. I've investigated countless creatures like this over the years. But because of their nature, because of their... brutality... their ability to hide.

They weren't just another species. They were invasive. You've spent a lot of time with them. You've seen how they spread. What do you think the wolf population of Seattle is?"

Dale said, "It's a fraction of..."

He held up a finger. "You heard the howl. Hell, you were probably part of making it happen. That was a call to action. That was every *canidae* in the city announcing itself to the world. How any human could hear that noise and not flee immediately is beyond me."

"What happened to you?" Dale asked. "Something must have happened to turn you into this."

"I simply had my eyes opened. In the seventeenth century, a village in Estonia was besieged by wolves. They were killing livestock. Only one family's farm was left untouched. Pretty damning evidence. So the villagers marched on this family, surrounded the house. They killed the father in front of his children, strung him up, gutted him."

Dale said, "And the wolf turned out to be his wife."

"The wolf turned out to be some asshole who had specifically skipped that farm so everyone would suspect that man. When the witch hunt began, the real wolf grabbed whatever he could carry and headed off into the forest. This is just one of a dozen stories I've found along the same lines. Wolves who only cared about themselves, who sacrificed humans so that they could survive. This is what they do. Do you think Ariadne Willow kept you around so much because she loved you? A wolf can't love a human. They never have. It's simple biology. She wanted you nearby as a decoy. To look normal. And if that failed, so you could be her sacrifice."

"Ari... wouldn't..."

"It hadn't been an issue yet. I've spent the past few weeks reading up on Miss Willow. She's very good at weaseling her way out of tight spots. But if it came down to life or death..."

"It has," Dale said. "A couple of times. She never tried to sacrifice me."

Isaac held his hands up. "Maybe she's different. Maybe she's the one wolf who can care, who sees beyond her species. But I truly believe you just got lucky. You got away before she was cornered."

Dale didn't want to believe him. She didn't want to believe any of the trash coming out of his mouth. There were dozens of instances where Ari had risked life and limb to save her. She touched her hair, pushing aside the strands to feel the scar tissue where a bullet had skimmed the side of her head. She remembered how hard Ari pushed herself after that. She'd gone feral, transformed so terribly that she'd hurt for days afterward. Dale slid her hand to the back of her head and made a fist, like she could grab the conflicting thoughts and yank them free.

"I'm just so confused."

"That's to be expected. You've been indoctrinated for so long that the truth sounds like a lie. When did you last spend any amount of time with humans?"

Dale didn't even have to think. "Three weeks ago. Dinner with Diana and Lucy. They're our friends, they know everything about Ari."

Isaac looked worried. "That's not good. If Willow has been grooming other people~"

"Don't use that word."

"What word?"

"Grooming. That's a pedophile term, using it to describe Ari's relationship with people is disgusting."

He shrugged. "But is it inaccurate? Witches have their familiars. Wolves have their humans."

Dale closed her eyes. "I've never felt this way about Ari or her family or her people..."

"Never?" he said.

She looked at him.

"Come on, Miss Frye. Dale. You never had the slightest trepidation about dating someone who was a completely different species? You never once weighed the pros and cons?"

Dale rubbed her upper arms and looked away from him. Their burgers were getting cold and the milkshakes were melting. Isaac picked up his burger and took a bite.

"Mm. Salmon. I'm from inland, so salmon burgers aren't really an option. I've been eating a lot of seafood since I've been here. It's fantastic, but I'm sure after a while you're just... you're in the mood for a nice steak or a regular USDA beef~"

"I won't hurt her."

Isaac stared at her. "Miss Willow...? No, I understand why you might have qualms about that. Don't worry. I have no intention of harming her. At least not directly. Once the ball is rolling, I have the feeling the Willows and Miss Duncan will get up to their usual antics. Things may happen then, things I have no control over and things in which I would never ask you to participate. You deserve a quiet life, Dale, normalcy."

When have I ever asked for normalcy? Dale wondered. *God, save me from a quiet life.*

"You're going to expose the *canidae*, aren't you?"

"That's my plan, yes. I'm going to release the book to the public, and I need you by my side to prove it's true. There will be turmoil at first, obviously. The information is going to change the world. People will react with hate and fear. Lives will be lost. But once things settle down, everything will be better. People will accept the new world, and peace will settle. Everything will be as it should be."

Dale laughed and shook her head. "We can't even accept people whose skin is a different color or who pray differently than we do. You really think we'll find common ground with dirty fucking mutts?"

Her stomach twisted at the words and tears pricked at the corners of her eyes. Her head was hurting again.

"I believe in time. But even if we can't, even if there are horrible losses, it will all be for the greater good. Because people deserve to know. They deserve to know if their neighbors are a threat."

"How?"

"Like I said. I'm going to finish the work Karl Magnusson started. I'm going to publish those essays. I think enough people know the truth, or suspect it, that I will be taken seriously. And even if I'm not, maybe that's better. People will bring me on their talk shows to laugh at the werewolf freak. But I'll have undeniable proof. I'll have a video of my own, of an actual werewolf transformation. It will spread on social media, people will share it on social media, and before long, people will back it up with their own stories. And I'll have you, the woman who lived among wolves for a decade. You have the information, you won't be tripped up by journalists. You'll confirm it isn't just a publicity stunt. Eventually it will be impossible to ignore or dismiss."

Dale said, "People will just claim the video is special effects."

Isaac said, "You've most likely seen dozens if not hundreds of wolf transformations up close and personal. Even with the magic they can do in Hollywood, have you ever seen anything close to what a real change looks like? I know you haven't, because I've seen one, and the movies don't even come close."

"No," she admitted.

She swallowed the lump in her throat as she remembered what it was like to see Ari go away and a wolf unfold in her place. Even when she and Ari were deeply in love, she found something unsettling about the shift. It was wrong. But then she remembered when Ari transformed on top of her, how the muscles had felt under her hands. It felt intimate. Like something divine that no one else could ever claim. She closed her hands into fists and put them in her lap.

"I need some time to think about this."

"Of course. I want you to feel comfortable."

She said, "What will happen if I decide to join you? You said you won't make me hurt Ariadne. That includes deceiving her in any way." She was disgusted by the idea of faking a romance with a mutt, but also disgusted by that thought. It felt like mold at the front of her mind, always growing and reaching into every corner of her mind. "I won't pretend to go back to her just to get more evidence."

"You're already the best evidence I could hope for. A human who has spent years in close proximity with wolves. Living with them, sleeping with one of them. You've been accepted by the *canidae* of Seattle in a way no human has ever been. When the book gets published, I want your insights. Your experiences. I want a new essay for the book, written by you, to be included as the foreword. You will help convince everyone that what I'm telling them is true."

Dale said, "They'll call me the wolf fucker."

"They'll probably call you worse than that. There's a good chance authorities will try to charge you with bestiality."

"Oh, come on, that's absolutely bullshit. Ari's..."

"A wolf half the time," Isaac said.

"She's a sentient being. She's not a wolf, she's... she's..." The fog almost cleared then. She felt something approaching relief, like breaking the surface before being dragged back underwater. "She's... I'm not... I wasn't..." She looked at her hands, which had become unfolded. "I was in love with her."

Isaac said, "And now?"

"Now I'm not."

He smiled sadly. "I know this is difficult for you. Your feelings were real, even if they were manufactured. But Dale, I want you to know, you're on the right path now."

"It doesn't feel like the right path. I don't even know where I'm going to sleep tonight."

Isaac held up a finger. "I thought about that. I'm going to get you a hotel room~"

Dale laughed. "No. Sorry, but there's no way. Wherever I end up tonight, it won't be anywhere near your hotel room."

"Okay. You're right, that makes sense." He took out his wallet and put five hundred dollar bills on the table between them. "Get a room wherever you want. You don't even have to tell me where it is. The important thing is that you separate yourself from outside influences. That includes both the Willows and me. You need to make your own decision."

He opened his bag and again produced the original book of essays. He held it out to her.

"I also want you to have this. Knowledge is power, especially in this case. There are things in here you won't find online, things wolves will want to keep quiet. Take it with you to wherever you end up, read it, and make an educated choice."

Dale took the essays. "You're going to let me take the real thing?"

"I'm asking you to put a lot of trust in me. I want to show it's going both ways."

She had to admit, that did make her feel better. She looked down at her bracelet. *I don't love you, Ariadne. I don't love a mutt. I don't want this disgusting thing on me anymore.* She pinched it between her fingers.

But she didn't break it and she didn't unfasten it. She left it where it was.

Just for right now.

CHAPTER TWENTY

VIVIAN'S STORAGE unit was in Queen Anne, though Ari didn't know why she bothered to pay for a fancy neighborhood when every storage facility she'd ever been in was exactly the same. She supposed it had something to do with extra security for the large items in the fenced-in area, alarms, and better-trained guards. But when it came down to it, they were all big concrete blocks filled with claustrophobic corridors and identical blue doors with padlocks on them.

Timothy had provided Ari with the keys and address, and both twins volunteered to accompany her to the storage unit. Preston wanted to talk with Timothy more about his new responsibilities as the owner of the house, while Eleanor hadn't been seen since she stormed out of the office. When they arrived at the facility, Evelyn went to find someone to let her into the auto lot while Elizabeth led Ari to Vivian's unit. Both girls had spent the ride in their own heads, looking out the window, and Ari was grateful she didn't have to force her way through a conversation. But now, navigating the storage labyrinth, she could tell that Elizabeth wanted to say something but didn't want to break the silence.

"So how are you dealing with everything?" she asked. "I got the impression that wine she left you was pretty special."

"It's *the* wine. There are only about a hundred thousand of them. It's ridiculously expensive. I don't even know where I'm going to store the thing."

"How ridiculous are we talking?"

Elizabeth sighed and shook her head. "Everyone is talking about how much the tapestry is worth, but this wine...? You could buy a winter house on an island, or you could buy this bottle of wine."

"Damn."

"I know."

"When I came up with the fake tapestry theory, I was thinking maybe Vivian was secretly broke. But today kind of blew that out of the water."

Elizabeth glanced down one row, checked the numbers, and kept moving. "We haven't cashed the checks yet. It could all just be for show."

"True. But I feel like the reading of the will would have been the ideal time to come clean. Right now I'm hoping the storage unit has something that will point me in the right direction."

"What will you do if it's a dead end?"

"Quit." Ari didn't know she was going to say it until it was said, but she knew it was the truth. "Vivian showed her true colors today with what she did to Eleanor. That was maybe the cruelest thing I've ever seen a mother do, and that means a lot coming from me. If I can't find a lead here, I'm going throw in the towel and accept I got screwed."

Elizabeth looked surprised and disappointed. "Sorry to hear that. But I get it. Unsolved mysteries happen all the time. A tapestry goes missing from a locked room... there will probably be a podcast about it someday." She turned a corner and Ari followed. Now she was paying closer attention to the numbers on each door. "I guess I can't feel too bad about you dropping the case since I'm going home soon anyway. My flight leaves Monday night."

"It'll probably be nice to get back to normal."

"You have no idea." She stopped in front of Vivian's locker and took out the key. "So... did you talk to your girl about the threesome idea?"

Ari was surprised by the change in topic. "Uh. Yeah. She wasn't very interested. Sorry. It had nothing to do with you. She thinks you're very attractive. It... it might have more to do with me."

Elizabeth looked at her. "Everything okay there?"

"No idea. Go ahead and open the door."

"Don't want to talk about it. Gotcha." She slipped the padlock off and pushed up the door. She went in, groping in the dark for a light.

Ari's hope that they could just walk in and scan the contents collapsed as she saw just how full it was. The space was large, ten by twenty, and it was filled with furniture and stacks of boxes. She'd seen apartments that were smaller. Elizabeth stepped around a stack of boxes and touched a lampshade, slowly passing her attention over everything.

"This is a real blast from the past," she said. "This is the furniture that was in the house when we were little. I had my first kiss on that divan. Mom liked to keep things fresh." She stopped next to a wardrobe and opened it, examining the clothes inside. "Oh wow, I remember this dress. Every few years, she changed everything up."

"It's going to take ages to go through all of this," Ari muttered. She opened a box at random and saw books carefully stacked inside. The tapestry was relatively huge, but it could very easily be hidden anywhere in this space. "I don't even have a solid lead that she actually hid anything in here."

Elizabeth said, "You're sounding awfully defeatist over there."

"Maybe because I don't see how I could possibly win this. Hell, at this point, I'm not even sure what would count as winning. I don't think anyone stole the stupid thing anymore, I think Vivian took it herself, and put up a copy in its place, and then sent us on this wild good chase just... just so..." She gestured, then flipped her hands up. "Fuck, I don't even know that much! This case doesn't make any sense. Why would she spend all of this money for a game she wouldn't even get to watch play out? And why bring me into it?"

She moved a box off the nearest chair and dropped into it. Elizabeth found a path through everything and stood in front of Ari.

"What would you normally do if you hit a wall like this?"

"I'd go talk to Dale. But we're... she's... I think we're in a fight right now."

Elizabeth tensed. "I hope not because of the threesome thing."

"No, she liked the idea in principle. It's a long story, and really hard to explain without getting really personal with you."

"Ah, I understand. Well, I might not be Dale, but I'm here. Talk to me. Lay it out."

Ari sighed and slapped her hands down on her knees. "Okay. At some point before Vivian hired me, she replaced Crossing-Over Place with a fake for reasons unknown. That was at least six weeks ago. A week ago, you and the rest of your siblings start arriving for your final goodbyes because Vivian had decided it was time to end her life. You each had separate meetings, except for Eleanor and Evelyn, who... shared the last meal."

Elizabeth said, "Why did you pause?"

"Everyone got a solo meal with Vivian except for Eleanor and Evelyn. Everyone was bequeathed something very valuable in the will, except for Eleanor. Is there any reason your mother would have been shunning Eleanor?"

"I don't think so."

"Out of all the kids, she moved the farthest away. She was also the most disdainful of the family money. Maybe there was a falling out between her and your mother."

Elizabeth shrugged. "It's hard to say. Eleanor rarely comes home. Like you said, it was farther for her to travel."

Ari stood up and went to a stack of boxes. "Okay, so we'll put a pin in that. Vivian decides to end her life. She wants everyone gathered to reveal the tapestry is going to a museum. But she's still giving you all a small fortune anyway."

"Except for Eleanor."

"Right, except for her." Ari raised an eyebrow. "Maybe it wasn't important for *everybody* to be here for the tapestry reveal. Maybe it was only important that Eleanor show up, and she could only ensure that would happen if she demanded you all show up."

Elizabeth said, "That's possible. If Mom had just asked Eleanor, she could have begged off for any number of reasons. Work, couldn't get a flight. But if saying no would screw things up for the rest of us, she would have made more of an effort."

Ari said, "Okay, let's back up. Your mother was diagnosed with an inoperable brain tumor. She decided she would end her life, so she began putting her affairs in order. She started putting together her will. That's when she decided to cut Eleanor out completely. That's probably also when she decided to pull this stunt with the tapestry. She tells you all to come, but it's possible Eleanor is the only one she wants here. She asks you all to have private meals together, but again... maybe she only wanted Eleanor here for that."

"And Eleanor sidestepped it by inviting Evelyn along."

"Yeah. I wonder if she asked Evelyn to arrive on the same day.

It may have been a last-minute plan to avoid whatever Vivian wanted to say."

"But Mom knew where we were staying. If she wanted to talk to Eleanor, she could have just gone to the hotel and cornered her."

"Possibly. The streets are level enough for a wheelchair, and the hotel itself seems accessible." She was pacing now. "But there's no car at the house, and judging from the security footage we saw, Vivian rarely if ever left the house. Maybe she couldn't leave the house unless someone came to her."

Elizabeth said, "That sounds right. When I came to pick her up, I had to put down those little track thingies so she could get off the porch. I don't know if she would be able to do that herself."

"Eleanor apologized to me for how fancy the hotel was. But when she found out she wasn't getting anything in the will... well, beyond the quarter of a million dollars... she got angry and stormed out. Because it wasn't about money. She didn't care about the money. When Timothy asked about the charities Vivian had left the rest of her fortune to, Eleanor was the only one who wanted the list. I think she wanted to be sure the money was spread out evenly. She might have even been planning to donate her check as well, and wanted to be sure she wouldn't give to someone who had already gotten a lot of money from the estate."

"It's a bit of a leap," Elizabeth said. "But it does sound like Eleanor. So why the tantrum?"

"Because it's not money she wants. It's something in the house. She wants something in the house."

"She could have taken it at any time during the past week," Elizabeth said.

"That would have been stealing it," Ari said. "She expected to get it legitimately." She remembered having a similar conversation with Eleanor about the tapestry. She'd asked why any of the children would have stolen Crossing-Over Place before they knew they wouldn't get it in the will. "Is there anything in the house Eleanor would have wanted? Anything with some special significance?"

Elizabeth pursed her lips and thought hard. "I can't think of anything... She liked the parlor. But that's because the computer used to be in there. She liked doing computer things on it. I'm not very tech savvy. But it couldn't be that thing. It was an old desktop. We probably gave it away years ago. And if she did anything on it worth saving, she would have taken it with her when she left."

"And none of this has anything to do with Crossing-Over Place." Ari stood and headed for the door. "But for now, it's the best lead I have. Come on."

"We're not going to go through all of this shit?"

"Not right now. I think Eleanor went back to your mother's house to get whatever she hoped to receive from the will. But we need to hurry. She had a good head start on us, so she might already be gone." She took out her phone and dialed Dale's number. It was habit, an urge to share the potential break in the case, and she realized a moment too late what she'd done. She looked down at the screen, her finger hovering above the 'end call' button when the screen changed and she heard a tinny voice coming from the speakers.

"Hello?"

Ari looked back and saw Elizabeth had pulled down the door and secured the padlock. She brought the phone up. "Dale?"

"I don't think we should talk."

"I know. I..." She was very aware of Elizabeth lingering nearby. She wasn't eavesdropping, but the tight corridor didn't give her much choice but to listen in. "Dale, you don't know the whole story. We should talk in person. The essays~"

Dale said, "I know you don't want me to read them. But don't I deserve to hear both sides of the story? All these years I've just heard what you've told me about the wolves."

Ari closed her eyes. God, it was painful to hear such flatness in Dale's voice. "Right. But you know I'd never lie to you. I would never mislead you. I've been upfront with you about everything from the very beginning."

Silence from the other end. "I know. I just need time. I need to think."

"Dale, the essays are messing with your head. Don't read any more of them until we've had a chance to talk in person. Okay?"

"I shouldn't have answered. Goodbye, Ariadne."

"Wait. Dale, wait..."

She looked at the phone and saw the call had been disconnected. She lowered it and stared at the blank screen before remembering Elizabeth, who was standing a few feet away and awkwardly staring at the wall.

"Sorry."

"It's fine. It's whatever." She shoved the phone back into her pocket. "Let's go get Evelyn. Hopefully Eleanor will still be at your house by the time we show up."

She started walking. A moment later, she heard Elizabeth follow.

CHAPTER TWENTY-ONE

A CAR was parked in front of the Burroughs house, but Eleanor was nowhere in sight. Ari and the twins all had keys, but the door was already unlocked. Elizabeth entered first and called for Eleanor without receiving a response. The house felt empty to Ari. The thing about these huge expensive houses was that they tended to be much smaller on the inside. They were a bunch of "cozy" rooms all bundled together without much room to hide. While the sisters went inside to look for Eleanor, Ari walked to the end of the porch and went around the side of the house to the backyard.

Eleanor was sitting in the swing, one leg tucked under her while the other pushed back and forth on the porch. She was looking at her hands but snapped her head up when Ari appeared. She smiled and nodded.

"Detective. I should have expected that."

Ari stepped onto the porch and took a seat next to Eleanor on the swing. "I assume you already got what you were looking for."

"No." She shook her head and looked out at the street. There were tears in her eyes. "I went inside planning to take it. I found it, too. But I stood there and just stared at it for the longest time trying to make my hand move. Couldn't do it. I couldn't just grab it and leave."

"I'm assuming this doesn't have anything to do with the tapestry."

She smiled. "Sorry. Can't solve that for you. It's a locket. A gold locket with a picture of her and my grandmother. It's been passed down since our family came here from Cornwall. Two hundred years. They worked their way up in New York, and my great-whatever grandfather decided to try making a new start in a city that was also just starting. Seattle. The settlement was originally called New York Alki. That meant it would one day be a new New York, and he wanted to be in on the ground floor instead of just holding on to a city which was already thriving. He came out here, bought a house, started a company. The only thing he could afford for my grandmother's anniversary was a cheap little locket. She loved it. She gave it to her oldest daughter. Who gave it to *her* oldest daughter. And you're a detective..."

"Yeah, I see the pattern. It was supposed to be yours. I really don't think your sisters or brother would contest it if you wanted to take it."

"No, we're... it's supposed to be passed down on our twenty-third birthday, because that's how old many-great-grandmother was when she received it."

"Why didn't Vivian give it to you then?"

Eleanor took a deep breath and let it out slowly. "Because when I was nineteen, I had an abortion. I was just starting college. I got stupid and lazy, woke up one morning with bad news from the doctor. So I weighed my options. I decided there was no way I'd be raising a child with the father, and trying to be a single mother meant I could continue with school. So I made the decision. It isn't something I'm proud of, but I also don't regret it. Maybe I would have made a good mother. I don't think so, but who knows. Mom... Mom was furious. She's all about the lineage, the Burroughs line."

Ari said, "That came up with Elizabeth."

"Yeah. I always wanted to tell her I understood how she felt. But Mom never mentioned it to the other kids, and I... I didn't want... them to know. I wanted them to think Mom still liked me."

Ari didn't know how to respond to that, so she moved to a different topic. "Preston offered you the jewelry..."

"They didn't know. They all assumed I got the locket when I was supposed to. Took it with me to Philly. If I asked for it, they would have known. It wouldn't have been so bad if they found out through the will, because at least then she would still be giving it to me. Just a little late. I hoped... part of me hoped... maybe she would have forgiven me. Finally passed it on." She blinked the moisture from her eyes and wiped at her cheeks even though none of her tears had fallen. "I guess she decided the line was finally over."

Elizabeth came around the corner of the house. By her slow approach, Ari assumed she had been standing just out of sight long enough to hear most of what had just been said. Eleanor wiped at her face again and ducked her chin as her sister stepped onto the porch. Ari got up to lean against one of the support beams while Elizabeth took her place and slipped her hand into Eleanor's.

"I wish you'd told us," Elizabeth said.

"I liked you not knowing. It was better if you thought I was a bitch who didn't care about her mother rather than... vice versa."

Evelyn appeared then, hurrying around the corner and joining them on the porch. She was slightly out of breath when she dropped onto the bench on Eleanor's other side and presented a satin jewelry box.

"I found it."

Eleanor stared at it. "No. I... I can't, it's not..."

Elizabeth took the box and placed it in Eleanor's hand, folding her fingers around it. "Even if the line ends with us, it ends with *us*. Not Mom. One of us might still have a kid someday. It's not outside the realm of possibility. Whether or not that happens, this belongs with you."

"Thank you," Eleanor whispered, finally accepting the box.

Ari's mind caught on something Elizabeth had said, "It's definitely not outside the realm of possibility... Elizabeth, you and Evelyn are... thirty-five?"

"Thirty-six."

"Thanks, Evelyn," Elizabeth said.

Ari said, "And Eleanor...?"

"Thirty-eight." Eleanor sniffled, holding the locket with both hands. "What does that have to do with anything?"

"All three of you could still have children for years. The 'never after forty' thing is bullshit, but even so, it's definitely possible. And Preston, hell, he could knock someone up when he's eighty. I know Vivian was facing a terminal illness, but she still had time left. She could have waited a few months, maybe even a year. She was willing to exile two of her children because they won't continue the family name. She could have lived another year or two. Plenty of time for anything to happen. Why would she be so quick to end her life when there was a chance of seeing a grandchild?"

Elizabeth said, "I don't know about everyone else, but I made it pretty clear to her that children were never going to be in my plan. And it's not exactly like I have to worry about it happening accidentally."

Eleanor said, "I suppose it was possible with me. Unlikely, but stranger things have happened."

"Yeah," Evelyn said, then cleared her throat. "It's probably a fifty-fifty shot."

Elizabeth snapped, "Evie!"

"Hey, I do my best, but you know how things can happen."

"The point is," Ari said, "Vivian was desperate to the point of cruelty for the family name to live on. She just gave up? She didn't seem like the type to just give up."

Eleanor said, "Well, she did commit suicide in the end."

Elizabeth lightly slapped her older sister's forearm. "That's not giving up. Considering the tumor, I think it was a valid option. She chose to go out on her terms. That isn't surrender."

Eleanor shrugged. "Okay. Well, I don't see what any of this has to do with Crossing-Over Place."

Ari was staring at the porch, brow furrowed. "I don't know. But learning more about how Vivian's mind works is the surest way of figuring out what she was up to."

"Maybe this is what Mom wanted all along," Evelyn said. "All of us in the same place, actually talking to each other. I mean, look at the three of us. Sitting here on the swing like... like friends. Would you have ever thought that would happen when we first got to town?"

"No," Eleanor said, "but I also don't think Mom would have been able to plan everything going like this. And I don't think she could have planned for Miss Willow to jump through so many hoops. It's a nice thought, and I'm grateful for the outcome, but I don't think we can give Mom that much credit."

Elizabeth said, "Also, she doesn't give a shit if we get along or not."

Eleanor laughed and nodded. "Miss Willow, if you're only staying on this case for our sake, you shouldn't feel obligated. It's terrible about the museum, but we stopped caring about the tapestry when we were kids. Priceless or not, it just doesn't matter."

"It's a piece of history," Ari said. "It belongs in a museum."

Elizabeth laughed and everyone looked at her. She prompted

Ari with her eyebrows and, when Ari seemed as confused as everyone else, she said, "Indiana Jones. Oh come on, Evie, you're the one who told me to watch it!"

"I just thought he was sexy in *Star Wars*. If I had known you would just get all gaga over Marion..."

Elizabeth rolled her eyes.

"I'm going to keep investigating, if it's okay with you. Elizabeth, could I have the key to the storage unit? I'll get it back to Mr. Dodd when I'm finished."

"Sure." She stood and fished it out of her pocket. She held it out, but didn't let go when Ari took it. "There's every chance the tapestry doesn't exist anymore."

"I don't believe that. Vivian was an awful person, but I don't think she would destroy something that valuable and then send everyone on a wild goose chase. It's out there somewhere. I'll find it."

"Good luck," Elizabeth said.

"Thanks. Do you need a ride back to your cars?"

Eleanor said, "No, I'll take them. We can call Preston and have him meet us somewhere. I think it's well past time we had a family dinner."

Ari wished them well and headed back to her car. Vivian had kept a locket she had no intention of ever giving to Eleanor. She'd also gone to the trouble of having a fake Crossing-Over Place made to trick Ari. Someone who went to those lengths wouldn't just destroy the actual tapestry. It was out there somewhere, and she was going to find it if it was the last thing she did.

"Ariadne?"

She opened her eyes and, for a moment, thought that maybe the past few days had been a nightmare. She was sitting on a couch with a tall bureau in front of her, two lamps on either side, and a wall of boxes stretching out in both directions. At first she thought maybe she was on a stage but then remembered she was in Vivian Burroughs' storage unit. An open cardboard box in front of her was full of photo albums and encyclopedias, two things which had gone extinct within Ari's lifetime. She pushed the box away with her foot and rubbed her face.

"Ari?" The voice was closer now but it still echoed off the other unit doors.

"In here, Mom."

It took close to a minute before Gwen appeared. She wore a simple black dress and slip-on shoes, the type of outfit she wore when she expected to transform at some point. She sighed with relief and inside. "This place is a maze. If I hadn't been following your scent, I never would have found you."

"That's disgusting, Mom."

"What are you doing in here?" Gwen asked.

Ari stood and went to a random box. "I'm looking for clues. Or a fake tapestry. Or a real tapestry. Or a videotape of Vivian Burroughs that starts with 'if you're watching this, then I'm dead.' I don't know. I'm open to the possibilities."

"Do you know what time it is?"

"Not a clue," Ari said. "Judging by the fact I just fell asleep on the couch, I assume it's after one in the morning, but that's really just a guess."

Gwen said, "All this will still be here in the morning. Why don't you go home?"

"Because Dale isn't there. And because I don't know where Dale is, or when she's coming back, or *if* she's coming back, and it's the first time in years that I've been able to say that, and I fucking hate it." She picked up the box and hurled it at the wall with a shout that echoed out of the unit and down the corridors. It crashed and spilled its contents - just clothes - onto the ground.

Gwen said, "Wow."

"If this was a movie, that would have broken open a secret compartment and the tapestry would be inside. Along with the real Dale, who has been held captive this whole time, and she'd make fun of me for taking so long to find her."

"Apparently it isn't a movie."

"No." Ari fell onto the couch and put her hands over her face. She was too exhausted to stop herself from crying, so she just let the tears come.

Gwen moved closer. "I want to help you, Ariadne. But I don't know how. It's breaking my heart. I hate to see you cry. You cried when you found out what I'd done to you as an infant, right before you left. So I guess we know the emotional threshold for tears." She crouched and put a hand on Ari's shoulder. "Come home with me."

"I have to stay here. I have to... there's something here. It's not at the house, it's not... it's nowhere. The tapestry is as tall as a person when it's rolled up, and it can't just vanish." She stood up and walked deeper into the unit. "It has to be somewhere. And if I find it, then this case can end, and everything goes back to normal, and Dale comes back to me, because the case is over."

Gwen said, "What happens if you find the tapestry and Dale doesn't come back?"

Ari took a deep breath. "Then... I don't need to be Ariadne Willow anymore."

"What? Honey..."

"Vivian refused to live with a death sentence. I don't want to get used to not having Dale. So if she's really gone for good, I'll let the wolf take over and head out into the woods. Change into a person every week or so. *Canidae* have done it before."

Gwen said, "Yes, but eventually they became more animal than people, even when they were in human form. They lost everything about themselves."

Ari smiled ruefully. "Yeah, we don't have to worry about that, Ma. If Dale is really gone, then I've already lost everything."

CHAPTER TWENTY-TWO

THE MONEY from Hayden would get her a hotel room, but Dale wasn't going to go much longer without some clean clothes, toiletries, and other necessary items from home. She waited until night and then called Neka to see if Ari's car was in the driveway. Neka said it wasn't, and that Ari had been gone since early that morning. Hopefully that meant she was at Gwen's, or the office, but either way she wouldn't be at home. Dale arrived and immediately went to the bedroom, opened the suitcase on the bed, and began transferring her things into it.

The house felt cold and abandoned. She didn't know where Ari was or what she was doing and, despite everything that had happened in the past few days, that caused her a pang of sorrow. She tried to keep her head down, tried not to think about memories or focus on anything that could send her brain off on a tangent. But she saw her navy blue shirt and remembered Ari knotting a tie for her on a day she had to testify in court about a case.

"Do I look professional?"

"You do. You look very..." Ari put her hands on Dale's shoulders, lips pressed together as she pondered the next word. "Would you prefer handsome or pretty?"

Dale smiled and tucked her hair behind her ears. "I'm good with pretty handsome."

Ari kissed her nose and then both cheeks. "It works."

She shook the memory out of her head. She didn't look at the sheets, or the pillows. She didn't think about the times she'd crawled into bed and kissed Ari's hair before going to sleep. How many times had she woken up with the wolf next to her? She'd been comforted by that, loved knowing that both sides of Ari were comfortable enough to sleep around her. The wolf sometimes had a wild, feral mentality so the fact it stayed beside her was...

Terrifying. All those nights she could have woken up with her hand in its mouth, its jaws closing around her face, and she'd just stayed there.

The front door opened and Dale froze. She'd left the lights off in the front room even though it faced into the backyard, but the bedroom lamp was on.

"Dale? You here?"

Milo. Dale closed her suitcase and zipped it shut. Milo, drawn by the sound, appeared in the bedroom doorway.

"Hey. There you are. Where you goin'?"

"Past you, out that door. Anything more than that is none of your business."

Milo said, "Maybe not mine, but it's definitely Ari's business. She's worried sick about you. Gwen just went out looking for her."

An image of Gwen being hit by a car flashed through Dale's mind, so vivid that it made her flinch. She wanted to throw up at the image but she kept her face neutral.

"I need time to think."

"That's fair. Everyone needs time to think, and you deserve your space. But Dale, those essays you've been reading? They're messing with your head. That's why no one is allowed to read them. There's something in them, some... subliminal message or something. People have been using it to make hunters since the forties, okay? It's like a spike in your brain telling you all these horrible things."

Dale said, "Or I've been listening to you for so long that I can barely recognize the truth when it's staring me in the face."

"This is truth?" Milo said. "You running away from Ari, using slurs against her, that's true? That's not the Dale Frye I know."

"What's the Dale Frye you know? A puppet? A toy? Some prey y'all tamed and lead around on a leash?"

Milo laughed. "You? Led around on a leash? Girl, you

remember how we met? Gwen had this big ol' master plan set up. You and Ari completely blew it all to hell and did your own thing, just like you always do. No one could lead you, and the path you take always leads you back to Ariadne."

"I'm done running to that mutt."

Milo stepped closer and got in Dale's face. "Don't you dare use that word on her, okay? Not because she doesn't like it, but because I know you. And I know eventually you'll come to your senses and you're going to remember every single time you used that word to describe the woman you love, and it's gonna hurt. So you're gonna want to keep that shit to a minimum."

Dale grimaced and stepped around her. "I'm done with all this wolf shit."

"Are you?" Milo stepped into Dale's path, but Dale just corrected her course and kept going. "Because you're still wearing that bracelet. I know that means something to you. It means the *world* to you. Don't throw that away."

Dale paused at the door, with her back to Milo. "Would you be with a human?"

"What?"

"You heard me. Would you ever be with a human."

"I've slept with a few~"

Dale turned around. "That's not what I asked. I asked if you, personally, would ever be in a relationship with a human. Because for the past ten years or so, all I've been hearing is that Ari is one of the only wolves in history to have a relationship with a non-*canidae*. But I've never asked you. Would you, Millicent Duncan, ever marry a human?"

Milo glanced away and lowered her head. "That's... No, Dale, I wouldn't." Dale nodded and started to leave, but Milo closed the distance and grabbed her arm. "But a few years ago, Gwen might have said she'd never be with a woman. When I first met Gwen, I thought she was a stone-cold bitch. Hot, sure, but I didn't like her. I flinched when she put her hand on my shoulder. People can change their minds, Dale, and nothing changes a mind faster than falling in love. Ariadne didn't go out looking for a human to fall in love with. She met a human who accidentally got all tangle-tied in her heart."

"Take your hand off me."

Milo complied and stepped back. "Don't read any more of those essays, Dale, I'm begging you."

"They're the closest thing I've ever gotten to the truth about all of this nonsense."

"They're a weapon," Milo said. "You want to know how your new buddy Isaac got his hands on the book? 'Cause me and Gwen, we've been looking into it all day. He broke into the place where it was being held and killed the *canidae* who had been assigned to guard it. Just killed them. Four *canidae* killed in cold blood."

"Four less wolves in the world," Dale muttered.

"I'm not kidding, Dale. Sooner or later, you'll get your sense back, and you're going to hate yourself for this, and there's not going to be any way to take it back."

Dale opened the door and stepped outside. "Lock up on your way out. Or don't, I couldn't care less. Nothing worthwhile left in there to steal anyway."

Ari didn't feel comfortable sleeping in the storage unit surrounded by someone else's memories, and she also didn't want to go home and sleep in their bed without Dale. That just left the office.

The building was creepy at night. Music played in the antiques shop next door, a place neither she nor Dale had ever seen anyone - customer or employee - enter. She paused in front of their cluttered window and peered inside, but she could only see the faint glow of a lamp burning far at the back of the shop. She thought about knocking, or just barging in, finally solving the mystery of their neighbors, but she didn't trust herself to solve any mysteries these days. Besides, without Dale there to delight in the answer, what would be the point?

What was the point of anything, really? Tomorrow would be Sunday, and most of the Burroughs kids were going home in a few days. None of them cared about the tapestry. She could just let it stay lost. So one museum would have one less tapestry. Would the world really suffer?

She stretched out on the couch in her office and kicked off her shoes. She was reminded of her days as a solo operation. Willow Investigative Services. She'd once considered adding "Detection, Observation, Mysteries" then shortening it to WISDOM Agency, but she decided against it. It was Dale who suggested the change to Bitches. Another slur, now that she thought about it, but that wasn't Dale's intention. Same with calling them wolves. It wasn't hateful. It wasn't meant to be cruel or dismissive. There was a huge difference between how Dale used those words and the way she had spit 'mutt' out.

Dale's ghost was all over the office. Crawling between the desk and the wall to plug in the new phones, bringing in countless cups of coffee and bags of lunch, straddling Ari on the couch to massage the kinks out of her weary muscles. Ari reached up and rubbed her shoulder. Before Dale, she just resigned herself to the pain. Other *canidae* didn't suffer as badly, but Ari couldn't see any other option. She had to transform. So she lived with it. Until Dale offered her a massage on a particularly bad day. There had been nothing sexual about it, nothing but one friend helping out another, but it had most likely set them down an inevitable path to falling in love.

She also saw Dale's ghost at the window behind her desk, sitting on the little ledge, head against the glass and tilted up to watch the rain cascading down. They were still getting used to being a romantic couple, still navigating the waters between personal and professional. Ari had come in from getting lunch and watched her for a long moment before announcing herself.

"Everything okay?"

"Mm-hmm," Dale said. *"My head hurts a little bit. The glass is cold. It makes it feel better."*

Ari came around the desk. "Do you need anything? I can get you an ice pack or a painkiller... do you have any painkillers left...?"

"No, it's fine. This is helping."

Ari moved her hand up to the base of Dale's skull, under her hair, and massaged. Dale cooed and pressed back into the touch.

"You got shot in the head because of me."

Dale chuckled. "That's not how I look at it."

"I'd love to hear another interpretation."

"I'm doing a job I love, with a woman I love, in a city I love. Being shot in the head means I don't have to wait for the other shoe to drop. I get everything I want in life, but in exchange I have to get grazed by a bullet and thrown into a hedge. It evens out."

Ari bent down and kissed Dale's hair. "You're the most amazing thing that's ever happened to me, Dale Frye."

"The feeling is mutual."

Ari wiped at her eyes as the memory faded. She knew that if she went to sleep, the ghosts would attack en masse and infect her dreams. She couldn't risk that. Instead, she went out into the front room and grabbed the chair from Dale's desk and pushed it into the office. She positioned it in front of her evidence board.

"Okay, Dale. Time for you to figure out the case for me. I

know it's late, but I'm not going to sleep, so we might as well do this now." She clapped her hands together and faced the board. "Vivian Burroughs, nice to strangers but an absolute monster to her kids. She's only concerned about keeping the family name alive, so she shunned the daughter who is gay and the other daughter who had an abortion. Oh, right, that's new information."

She stepped forward and added Eleanor's abortion to the wall.

"Vivian probably kept Preston close because he was the most likely to have a kid by accident. He was her best bet at the Burroughs line continuing. Then she gets diagnosed with a brain tumor. It's terminal. She decides she's not going to waste away, she'll end things on her terms. So she sits down to start getting her affairs in order, and she comes up with a plan... a crazy plan, a complicated plan, a plan with no end game that I can figure out."

She stared at the board and tapped the end of the marker against her chin.

"Come on, Dale. Work with me here, babe." She paused and then nodded. "You're right. We don't need to know what the end result was, because we can work through the actions she took to achieve it. So... okay. First she came up with a way to get Eleanor in town, probably so she could have a shitty conversation with her, like she had with Elizabeth. 'You kept me from having a grandchild, you killed the Burroughs line,' that nonsense. She told all the kids to be in town for the big reveal about who would get Crossing-Over Place. Once she'd..."

Ari stopped as suddenly as if Dale had actually interrupted her.

"Why was that a reveal?" she whispered. "None of them cared about the tapestry. The locket was the heirloom, the tapestry was just decoration. They all told me they didn't want it, so why was *that* the draw to get them in town? They came because... Vivian told them it was required, and they would have to be here for the reading of the will anyway, so why not just come a little early. And of course that made them think about it, and realize how valuable it was, and they thought, 'hey, one of us is getting an extra bonus with our inheritance. Cool.' So they showed up, suddenly caring, and she pulled the rug out from under them. As it were."

She began to pace.

"Because... because why? Dale, come on, babe, you're really not pulling your weight on this one. I need your insight here."

Silence from the empty chair.

"No one in the family cared about Crossing-Over Place until

Vivian made a big deal about it. She fabricated this whole thing to... to..." She slapped the board hard, which made her palm sting. "To what! Why! How! I don't even know how she got it out of the house. I assume she used the housekeeper's key to get in. Vivian stole her own fake tapestry, which she had hung up at some unknown point in the past. We don't know what happened to the original or the fake. We don't even know where the fake came from. Or why she made one."

It's like magic, she imagined Dale saying. *Misdirection. Look at this, poof, that thing over there disappeared. Voila!*

"I think they actually say 'ta-da,'" Ari muttered. "But you're right, Dale, it's a magic trick. Vivian brought me into the house, walked me to the tapestry, and explained what it was. And she made sure I was there for the big unveiling to reveal it was gone. I was the only proof it had ever been there in the first place. The whole big drama was just to drum up excitement, because Eleanor's the only person who would care if the locket vanished. She wanted drama. She wanted everyone here looking for the tapestry, because she didn't want them focused on something else. But what?"

Dale had fallen silent again.

"Fat lot of help you are. There's something she didn't want her family to know about. So she spent what would be a fortune to anyone else to make sure everyone was looking at Crossing-Over Place. The fake tapestry and the disappearance is all just part of the ruse. I'm part of the misdirect, too. So what is it that Vivian was so desperate to hide?"

She looked at Dale's empty chair.

"You're much more help when you're actually here, you know. But whatever Vivian wanted to hide, there's one person who probably knows everything about her final days. I think tomorrow morning I'm going to finally sit down with Mr. Dodd."

CHAPTER TWENTY-THREE

DALE WAS on the ground in the dream, not tied down or restrained but unable to move. Ari, Gwen, and Milo stood over her, with other shadowy figures moving in the darkness behind them. They were all human, but their mouths were stretched in grotesque grins to accommodate wolf fangs. Dale tried to get away from them, but other wolves surrounded her. She watched their hands deform into claws, huge dinosaur talons which glistened in whatever light was allowing them to be visible to her.

She woke herself up by flailing, one hand shoving the book of essays onto the floor. She was covered with sweat and out of breath, as if she'd been running, and she lay on the bed for a moment to let her brain catch up with reality. Eventually she got up to retrieve the book and placed it on the desk. She had gotten a water-view room at Motif, because if she was going to stay in a local hotel on Isaac Hayden's dime, she might as well live it up.

The curtains were open and the Sound looked like a vast emptiness beyond the lights of the city. It felt like she was on the edge of a chasm and the slightest breeze might knock them all in.

She shook off that dread and stripped as she went into the bathroom to shower off her sweat. She always took off her bracelet when she showered, but this time she truly wasn't sure if she would put it back on afterward. She closed her eyes, turned off her brain, and let the water hit her in the face. She'd read most of the essays in the book by now. Magnusson talked about the way wolves hunted, how they could remain hidden among 'normal humans' while using them as cattle. "Wolves are only cannibals if one views them as human," Magnusson wrote, "so one must make a decision regarding their classification. Whatever decision is ultimately made, however, they must be considered as less than human."

The woman she loved wasn't human. She was a descendent of a long line of beasts, cannibals, monsters.

"Ow ow ow..." Dale leaned hard against the fridge, face contorted in pain.

Ari hurried into the kitchen. "What's wrong, what happened?"

"Cramp. Leg cramp..."

"Poor thing." Ari crouched and pushed up Dale's pants, kneading the tight muscle. Dale grunted and put one hand on the counter for balance. "Any better?"

"Lots better. Thank you."

Ari smiled up at her. "I think this makes us even."

Dale laughed and tapped the top of Ari's head with her fingers. "If you're talking about massages, I think the score stands at five thousand to, hm, three?"

"I've given you more than three massages!"

"Hm, must not have been very memorable..."

Ari stood and wrapped her arms around Dale. "C'mere, I'll show you memorable..."

Dale laughed and let herself be hauled into the bedroom.

She cupped her hands under the water and brought them up to her face, ran her hands through her hair, threading it through her fingers. The essays were a gross generalization of an entire species, but it was based on facts. She knew wolves sometimes attacked humans. She knew there were bad wolves, evil wolves, but Ari and Milo and Gwen, the British pack, they were all good. Right? Did she know that for a fact? Could she swear that Milo and her packmates had never killed a person?

But speciesism wasn't the same as racism. She would run away from any lion she happened to see, even if someone claimed it was a "good" lion.

On top of it all, she still loved Ari. She'd had an ache in her chest all day that she knew could be eradicated by a single hug, or touching Ari's hand. She knew she was causing Ari pain, and that pained her in turn. It would be so much easier if her newfound hate had also drowned the love she felt for Ari, because now she had all these conflicting feelings spilling in her gut like a whirlpool.

She turned off the shower and pushed the fogged glass door open. She retrieved her towel with one hand while she gripped the handrail with the other as she stepped over the lip of the stall. She paused and looked down at the steel bar. It was a safety feature, but it was also an aid for handicapped visitors to get in and out of the tub. A thought occurred to her, just a spark, a question rising up from the back of her mind that related to Ari's case.

Dale wrapped the towel around herself and hurried, still dripping, into the bedroom. She grabbed her phone and hesitated with her finger over the screen. Her idea might be nothing. It might not help the case at all, and if it was just a dumb passing thought, she didn't want to give Ari false hope by starting a conversation with her. She remembered earlier, Ari's accidental call. She'd been so torn about answering. Part of her had thought about sending it to voicemail and blocking the number, but she'd eventually answered. And now, here she was again, considering another call.

She pressed her lips together, fingers curled to prevent any of them from flicking out to hit the screen.

Ari jumped when her phone rang, its screen brightening up the whole office. She fumbled with it, then stared in confusion and wary hope at Dale's picture. She swept her thumb across the smiling portrait and closed her eyes.

"Dale?"

"Stairlift."

The call disconnected. Ari blinked in confusion. "Dale...? Hello?" She looked at the screen even though she'd heard the click. "Stairlift? What the hell does that mean?"

She wiped her face and squeezed her eyes shut. She was still groggy and half-asleep. Maybe she'd misheard. Airlift? Stare... She shook her head and stood up. The office was dark but she could see the outline of the case board. She put it together then.

"Oh, stairlift."

Vivian had a stairlift. But why bring it up now? She'd only seen it when she visited the first time, and it was gone the next time she~

Ari stiffened and blinked. "Oh. *Stairlift.*"

She ran to the light switch and slapped it on, then looked at the board again. She felt wide awake now, and furious at herself for not thinking about it earlier. Vivian had a stairlift installed in her house. It was a large model, big and sturdy enough to carry her entire chair up to the second story. It had been gone when she arrived to the will reading. She just assumed it had been removed by Timothy or the kids, or maybe Vivian had returned it to whatever medical company she'd gotten it from since she wouldn't need it anymore.

The point was that Crossing-Over Place wasn't the only thing that had vanished from the house following Vivian's death. The stairlift was also missing. It was big and bulky enough that whatever was used to take it from the house would also be able to conceal a tapestry if it was folded right.

Ari grinned, though her eyes were wet with tears. "I love you, Dale. I really freaking love you."

She went to the computer and booted it up. She knew Dale would have said something if she'd seen the medical company removing the stairlift, but she wanted to look for herself. If didn't mean anything if Fitz's cameras hadn't seen anything because of how piecemeal his coverage was. But if the stairlift's removal wasn't on Vivian's cameras, then it could only mean one of two things: Vivian had it removed before she died, or it was taken out afterward and the footage was deleted.

Either way, answering the question would solve a very big piece of the mystery.

"I hope you don't mind me saying this," Timothy said as he took a seat behind his desk, "but you're looking very tired today, Miss Willow."

Ari smiled. "Normally I would assume that was sexist, but I only got an hour of sleep last night and you actually seem concerned. So for that, plus the fact you were willing to come in on a Sunday, I'll give you the benefit of the doubt."

"I hope you're not losing sleep over this case. The family has made it clear that they aren't overly concerned about the tapestry's whereabouts. The museum will be a little disappointed, I'm sure, but in the end it seems like a mystery that might never be solved."

"Maybe," Ari said. "But I like to be absolutely sure before I throw in the towel. Especially with something this historic. Not to mention the money involved."

"Mm," Timothy said.

"I was wondering if you could clarify the timeline for me.

Vivian decided to end her life on Sunday night. Exactly a week ago, actually. She called a service who came to pick her up. She left the house and went to Emerald Care."

He held up a finger. "Yes, about that. Elizabeth Burroughs left me a message last night. She called the clinic and received confirmation that Vivian passed away peacefully at seven-seventeen last Sunday. She has all the documentation from the clinic and the crematorium if you would like to see them."

"I would, thanks. I'll give her a call when I leave. But that's not why I'm here right now. I want to know more about the time between Vivian's death and the reading of the will on Wednesday morning."

"Okay. I will help out however I can."

Ari said, "The stairlift at the house. What happened to it?"

"Vivian bought that from a medical equipment company. She donated it to a charity in case there was anyone who might be in need but couldn't afford it new. The company was..." He furrowed his brow and turned to the computer, tapping a few keys until he found the appropriate part of the file. "Ah, here it is. Columbia Care. This says they sent out an associate on Monday evening. They dismantled the stairlift and removed it from the home."

"Here's the thing, Mr. Dodd," Ari said. "I have security camera footage from Vivian's house. The front door camera. I looked at the footage from Monday night. Actually I've looked at the footage from Sunday to Wednesday. I really wish I had asked you to narrow it down before I did that, but like you pointed out, I'm sleep deprived. There's no footage of the stairlift being removed."

Timothy said, "That is rather odd. Perhaps Vivian's camera suffered the same glitch as the cameras on Mr. Anstartz's property."

She shook her head. "I thought the same thing, so I kept an eye on the time code. It recorded the whole day, no gaps. Definitely nothing long enough for a medical service to park, uninstall a stairlift, and get it out of the house. Well, I misspoke. It recorded without gaps for most days. Monday was the only one missing a two hour window."

"That's an unusual error."

"Very unusual," Ari said. "So I got to thinking... what are the odds that Vivian's camera would crap out for just long enough to miss the medical company's visit? And what are the odds that Fitz Anstartz would have the exact same blind spot on his footage? I'm not going to say it's impossible, but it's definitely very unlikely. It would have to have been done deliberately by someone who wanted to conceal the lift being taken out of the house."

Timothy said, "So someone would either have to know when Mr. Anstartz's camera wasn't recording, or ask him to delete the relevant portion of the tape. That's dangerously close to a conspiracy theory, Miss Willow."

She nodded. "I know, right? I actually thought the same thing when I first came up with it. But you know... Elizabeth told me that Fitz was extremely eager to please. And he's a gamer. So I think if someone approached him the right way, if they told him it was part of a game, he might go along with it. He might delete the footage, and lie to a private investigator about it. Because, see, I thought it was odd that he knew his security footage was sketchy but he still offered it up to me. He didn't mention a thing about missing time, he just gave me a file and wished me the best. Why would he do that? He knew what was at risk, because of the slip-and-fall case he fouled up."

"Perhaps he thought the system had... corrected itself."

Ari smiled. "Or he was told to. Come on, Mr. Dodd. He described you pretty well when I ran all this by him this morning."

Timothy lowered his head and then pivoted to look out the window. Ari waited. Finally, he started talking.

"She didn't know you nearly as well as she knew her kids. She expected you to focus on the people and ignore the tapestry. She knew her children didn't care about it. But she also knew that she'd burned many bridges with them over the years, too many to mend in the time she had left. She had alienated Eleanor and Elizabeth so completely that she doubted they would ever find it in their hearts to forgive her. And if they did, would it mean anything now? At the end of her life? It would be forgiveness for the sake of closure. So she brought them together. She reiterated every awful thing she'd ever said to Elizabeth about her sexuality, and she withheld the locket heirloom from Eleanor. She did it to bring them together, to unite them."

"Vivian destroyed her relationship with two of her daughters?"

Timothy said, "Vivian had spent a lifetime destroying those relationships. She was merely acknowledging that it could never be repaired. She brought the girls together so they would have each other. Elizabeth and Eleanor had so much in common, and yet hadn't spoken in years. They're closer now."

"That's pretty cold," Ari said.

He shrugged. "It was Vivian's idea of making amends. It was the best she could hope for in the time she had left."

"How'd she make amends with Preston and Evelyn?"

"With Preston, she made amends by telling his landlord to evict him. Mr. Favaloro was willing to give him a little extra time, like always, but Vivian knew when her house would be empty and she knew Preston would break in. He would have a roof over his head but he would also see the consequences of how he'd been living these past few years. And, of course, a week later she knew he would have the house. She wanted him to suffer just enough to change his ways. Hopefully. Whether that was successful remains to be seen, but I am hopeful."

Ari said, "And Evelyn?"

He raised an eyebrow and held his hands up. "Actually, Vivian had no regrets when it came to Evelyn. She was intelligent, she knew the value of a dollar, and she was happy with her life. Vivian thought Evelyn's only real problem was being estranged from her family. She hoped by bringing them all together for this spectacle would take care of that problem."

"Okay." Ari furrowed her brow. "So this whole thing was a plot Vivian concocted to bring her kids closer together."

"She believed much of their unhappiness was due to her interference. She also believed that by being gone, they could be a family again. She paid me handsomely to sit back and watch it all unfold without interfering unless someone went off the rails. If Evelyn went home early, or if Eleanor abandoned the locket. There were contingency plans in place, but thankfully we didn't have to use any of them. The Burroughs children acted precisely as she expected them to."

Ari said, "Okay. Fine. So the fake tapestry, the disappearance, it was just to keep me asking questions? Force the kids together?"

"Not exactly." He drummed his fingers on the desk. "I'm not supposed to tell you this next bit until Tuesday..."

She closed her eyes and counted to ten. Finally she opened her eyes, looked out his window, and saw the water reflected off the building next door.

"Mr. Dodd, with all due respect to Vivian's wishes, I don't give a damn. My personal life is exploding, and I would much rather be dealing with that instead of letting a dead woman lead me around on some wild goose chase. I don't want to go digging through storage units or wait for you to dole out some piece of information.

I'm not in the mood for a treasure hunt. So why don't we just pretend I have a time machine?"

He smiled apologetically. "You've already figured out the fake tapestry was smuggled out of the house in the stairlift. Vivian concealed it in the packaging of the lift. You were also correct about your purpose in this scenario. You provided testimony that Crossing-Over Place was hanging in the Burroughs house on a certain date, safe behind a locked door. In truth, it was removed from the house two weeks after Vivian's diagnosis."

"And it's... where? The storage unit? Already at the museum?"

"No, not yet. On Tuesday, I was going to contact you with a file I had allegedly just discovered. A file with the name of someone who was to be added to Vivian's will."

Ari raised an eyebrow. "Well, don't leave me in suspense, Mr. Dodd. What's the name?"

"Megan Garfield. She's a schoolteacher in Pigeon Point. You were going to track her down and ask her some questions to determine why Vivian would leave her anything. You would discover that Megan Garfield was found abandoned outside a fire department as an infant. A little more digging, and you would find evidence that Megan was Vivian's first child. Born of an affair, abandoned to prevent scandal or divorce. Vivian believed that the woman who wouldn't let Laura Gavin die with a bad reputation would also do everything in her power to ensure Megan received her birthright."

"Vivian had a secret child?"

"No."

Ari narrowed her eyes, then sank back into the chair as she realized. "Vivian *faked* having a secret child."

"Vivian had a regret. Just like her regrets about Elizabeth and Eleanor and Preston. Megan Garfield was her attempt to correct that."

Ari said, "The family name."

Timothy nodded so slowly it was almost a bow. "Megan Garfield has two daughters. When all was said and done, she would officially change her name to Burroughs. The line would continue."

"Okay," Ari said. "And Crossing-Over Place... I assume the fake would eventually be found."

"You were on the right track. And very close. It's in the storage unit."

"Damn," Ari hissed. "I was right there."

Timothy shrugged. "Don't feel too bad. She made sure she hid it well."

Ari said, "So I find the tapestry. Take it to the museum. They verify it's fake. And Megan reveals she has a tapestry that looks a lot like it."

"It's verified as real, thus solidifying Megan's claim as a member of the Burroughs family."

Ari took a deep breath and let it out slowly. She leaned forward and rested her arms on her elbows. "And how would you explain the fake vanishing from the house?"

"We would say Vivian knew it would be discovered as a fake and hid it, ashamed."

"How did Megan get the original?"

Timothy started to answer, then tilted his head. "In actuality, or the story we would give?"

"Either or."

"In the story, Megan tracked Vivian down when she was eighteen. Vivian gave it to her to keep her quiet. In actuality, Vivian gave it to her as a down payment when she came up with this plan. Recompense and payment for going along with the lie. Megan would surrender Crossing-Over Place to the museum, she would be verified as a Burroughs, and she would receive her part of the inheritance. Two-hundred and fifty thousand dollars, just like every other Burroughs child."

Ari shook her head. "That's a long way to go to keep a name alive."

Timothy said, "Vivian felt it was worthwhile. All the money she spent and the trouble she was going through, it was the cost of keeping the Burroughs name alive."

"What about DNA?" Ari said. "Surely someone, somewhere along the line would suggest confirming Megan was Vivian's daughter."

"We have that. Doctored, of course. We actually tested a sample from Eleanor."

Ari leaned back and looked out the window. Timothy tapped his fingers against the desk and let the silence build between them. Finally, he gave in.

"So how shall we proceed?"

"What do you mean?"

He showed her his palms. "Do you plan to reveal Vivian's plot? Her lies, her... machinations?"

"I was hired to find Crossing-Over Place," Ari said. "I basically did that. I haven't seen it, but I trust you enough to say I know where it is. And it's going to be 'rediscovered' soon anyway. Right? You're still going through with the discovery of the fake and revelation about Megan's existence? You don't really need me for all of that."

"Well... no. I suppose not."

Ari stood up. "Then I consider this case closed. If it's all the same to you, I have bigger issues right now than Vivian manipulating her whole family and this poor Megan Garfield girl. So... best of luck to everyone. So long and good riddance."

She headed for the door, waving goodbye to Timothy over her shoulder.

"Long live the Burroughs name."

CHAPTER TWENTY-FOUR

ARI ENTERED her mother's home without knocking, moving through the foyer to the living room. Milo was on the edge of the couch with a laptop open on the table in front of her. She looked up without surprise as Ari stormed in, sitting up straighter with her hands still poised over the laptop keys.

"Where's Mom?"

"Upstairs, on the phone."

Ari went to the foot of the stairs and thought about yelling up, but she didn't want to interrupt the call if it was important. Instead, she went back into the living room and sat down in the armchair.

"I just closed my biggest outstanding case. As of right now, I only have one job: getting Dale back."

Milo smiled, but her eyes were worried. "Happy to have the help. Gwen and I have been looking into it ever since Dale went all barmy. We might have a hell of a fight ahead of us."

Ari said, "Tell me what you have. How can a bunch of essays change someone so completely? How could it change Dale of all people?"

"We don't think it's the essays themselves. I mean, yes, a biased report can change someone's mind, but this goes way beyond that. And the book has taken down bigger targets than Dale. It's turned *canidae* into self-loathing time bombs. Killed pack members, killed loved ones, killed themselves. Most of what we know about the book comes from the Kirsch pack, German wolves who realized what was happening when the first essays leaked out in 1932. Anyone who read them went ballistic. Adam Kirsch tracked down Magnusson and tried to convince him not to publish the essays. Magnusson refused, so Kirsch stole the book. Magnusson made a few attempts to get it back and was eventually killed by the pack. Since then, they took it upon themselves to protect it."

"You said the book had been used to create hunters before."

Milo nodded. "Yeah, in the forties. Protection of the book fell by the wayside for whatever reason. I guess there was something big going on in Germany around that time. Anyway, the book was stolen from the library where the Kirsch pack had hidden it. By that point, the book had become legendary, so a bunch of hunters decided to test its powers. For about ten or twelve years they passed it around to new recruits."

Ari rubbed her temples. "I still don't understand how reading them can make Dale into a bigot."

"It's more than just a book. It's a grimoire. It's... it's the *Necronomicon*, Ari. Magnusson may have had pure intentions when he wrote the essays, but the Kirsches didn't think he was operating under his own power. The essays were written in a very particular way. Magdalena Kirsch believed that just looking at the words was enough to feel their power. Reading them would be the same as reciting the words of a spell."

"So if this thing gets published..."

"Then everyone who reads it, even as a lark, will get tainted. They'll be on the road to becoming hunters."

"So Dale is a hunter now?" Her voice broke, but she tried to cover it with a cough.

Milo said, "I don't know. I hope not. I've been trying to find anything about reversing the effects, but there's not much. It basically just says never, ever read the essays for any reason."

"Great."

"We'll figure it out, Ari. You stopped the war, this can be our contribution."

Ari stood up and walked toward the back door. "She called me this morning. Middle of the night, called me, said one word. One word. And it cracked the case for me. It was the piece I needed to go after the co-conspirator and make him spill his guts."

Milo sat up straighter. "That's actually great news. It means she was thinking about you. She wanted to help you. The essays may have changed her brain, but not who she is. Right now, Dale's essentially a hostage. She's fighting for you."

"Who's fighting for..." Gwen appeared on the stairs and spotted Ari. "Oh. Ariadne." She came the rest of the way downstairs. "Have you told her what we discovered?"

"Just background stuff. Not the worse bits."

Ari turned around. "Wait, there are worse bits?"

Milo cleared her throat. "The Kirsches retrieved the book in the late fifties, early sixties. Since then, they've been watching over it. Until about four months ago."

Gwen said, "My contacts in France hadn't heard from them in a while, so they went to check things out. All members of the Kirsch pack were dead. Slaughtered."

"Hayden," Ari said.

"That's the theory they're going with, yes," Gwen said. "That's the only way he could be in possession of the original book. We don't believe he has any reason to harm Dale if she is actually working with him. But he's an extremely dangerous man, Ariadne."

"Then we have to get her away from him. The people who have been... infected... by the book, are there any stories about how they could be fixed? You said you were looking into that."

Milo and Gwen exchanged a look, but neither said anything for a moment. The silence hung between them until finally, Gwen took the bullet.

"There are some stories," she said. "But you have to understand, Ari, there's never been a situation like what you have with Dale. There's never been a case where a human infected by the book has been in a romantic relationship with a *canidae*."

Ari picked up on the phrasing. "But there have been cases where *canidae* was infected. What happened there?"

Milo spoke while staring at the floor. "A man read the essays, unaware of what it was. He turned against his friends, his family. Went on a rampage. They eventually cornered him. Convinced him the essays were lies, that he was under the influence of powerful magic. He went home. Locked all the doors and windows and set the place on fire with himself and his kids inside. Killed 'em all."

"Well, we'll just have to find another way."

Milo and Gwen looked at each other again.

"I need the optimism, ladies."

"Right," Milo said without conviction. "Another way."

Gwen smiled.

"First, I need coffee. Then we're going to go through everything you've found and look for some answer you've missed."

"What if there isn't one?" Gwen asked softly.

Ari said, "Then we fucking make one up."

Dale was exhausted. She'd slept, but gotten no rest. Her brain was full of spiders. No, wolves. Monstrous wolves, waiting in the dark to tear her to pieces when she let her guard down. But even if she ignored her relationship with Ari, she knew for a fact that fear was a lie. She'd seen *canidae* (wolves, mutts) being tender. Loving. Hannah with Mia. Gwen with Milo. They'd sacrificed for her, fought for her. How could she see them as monsters? How could she see Ari as a monster, given everything they'd been through together? If anything, Ari needed her protection. Without Dale, Ari's business would have failed years ago. She would have been trapped in kennels for untold days and weeks. She would likely still be in prison, if everything with Cecily Parrish had still happened the same way.

She was at a window seat in Specialty's across from her hotel. An untouched pastrami sandwich was on the plate in front of her. She saw Isaac hurry across the street and sat up straighter, taking a long drink of her coffee so she would be as buzzed as possible when he joined her. Today he was in a tan suit and a pale blue shirt, looking like a Miami-based spy on a TV show she used to watch.

He sat across from her and eyed the sandwich. "Mm, that looks good."

She pushed it across to him.

"Oh, no. I couldn't. I'll just order my own."

"Take it. I don't even know why I ordered it."

Isaac hesitated but then repositioned the plate and picked up the sandwich with both hands. "Thank you. I skipped breakfast this morning." He took a bite and they sat in silence as he chewed. "So... you look like you had a late night. Read something interesting...?"

"I have questions."

"I would be shocked if you didn't. I hope I'm able to answer them."

Dale thought about how best to begin. "Okay. You came to Seattle following the hunters."

He held up a finger. "I came because of the attempt to restart wolf manoth. Hunters are far easier to track than wolves, for obvious reasons. I had a suspicion there would be a large wolf population here because of the wilderness all around. It really was just dumb luck that I found a connection between the hunters' finances and Gwyneth Willow. That led me to Ariadne, and... again, dumb luck."

"Okay. So you didn't know about Ariadne before coming here?"

Isaac shook his head. "Meeting her was like crashing through a doorway. I started digging into anything I could find about her. She's a remarkable specimen, as I'm sure you realize. The first wolf to have a successful relationship with a human."

Dale's stomach twisted, and she was grateful she hadn't eaten anything.

"She also negotiated a peace with the hunters." He widened his eyes and made an expression of shock. "That's... that's unheard of. That's like the cockroaches convincing the exterminator to let them stay in the house. I almost respect her. And, you know, to be entirely honest? With her looks, she might be an excellent representative of her people. I'm sure those liberal talk shows would love to have her on to talk about mutt rights. You could be the counterpoint. Former lovers, now bitter rivals. It's a hell of a story."

"It's a sad story," Dale said softly. She put her hand on top of the bracelet.

Isaac nodded as if he was sympathetic, but didn't quite understand. "Do you mind if I ask a personal question?"

"Yeah," Dale said, "if you thought about it just now after mentioning my love life with Ari, I definitely mind. I'm not answering any sick questions about that."

"Okay. Okay. I was just curious. A lot of people will be. You can probably expect a lot of speculation and discussion on this topic. I don't want that to dissuade you from coming forward but I do want you to be prepared for that."

I'll go down in history as the Werewolf Fucker, she thought. *My Lover, the Wolfgirl.*

"When this goes public, a lot of wolves are going to get hurt. Killed."

"Then they'll be the prey for a change." His voice was suddenly hard, bitter. He ducked his chin, his eyes shadowed. Dale watched his shoulders rise and fall as he collected himself. "The hunters have existed for a thousand years. They were created because wolves were beginning to overrun England. And they were successful! They ran those beasts into hiding. But the hunters have become lazy. Complacent. And the wolves can sense that. We have no way of knowing how many of them are in this city, Dale, and that is terrifying. Because they aren't just in this city, they're in New York and the Canadian wilderness and cities across the globe. We forced them to learn how to hide, and now we're never going to see them coming. You and I can give our species a fighting chance to beat them."

Dale said, "Because even if a few hundred die... it's just population control."

Isaac smiled. "Exactly. And listen, hey, maybe one day when they have more... tolerable numbers... maybe they can even integrate into society."

Dale felt cold. She felt physically ill, but her brain still burned when she tried to focus too hard on it. She brought her fingers up to her temples and massaged gently.

"When will my head stop hurting?"

"That does happen occasionally. It's a side effect of having your world shifted so much in such a short amount of time. Don't worry, it usually goes away quickly."

She put her hands down and focused on him. "So what's the next step?"

"Ah. Well... I was willing to let you take a few days, read some more of the essays. You're making a very large change here, Dale. You're turning your back on the woman you love. I don't expect you to make that decision lightly."

"The more I read of that book," she said, "the sicker I feel. Every time I walk outside, I worry I'm going to run into Ariadne on the street, and I don't know if I'll be strong enough to walk the other way. I am afraid... I'm just afraid. I think the sooner we can get started, the better I'll feel."

He gave her a sincere smile and bobbed his head. "I feel the same way. And in that case, our next step is to get ourselves to New York. I have a publisher who is interested in the book, but she'd really love to meet someone who has the inside scoop. Someone like you. I'll make sure she doesn't lean too heavily on the former-lover angle. We want this to be a scientific discovery, not some prurient website clickbait. Facts. Historical data."

"Right," she said. "How soon can we leave?"

"Uh. Well, I have a private plane waiting for me at Clay Lacy.

All I have to do is give them a call and they'll gas it up, have it ready. If you're absolutely certain you want to go now."

Dale looked out the window. Seattle was her home. Pennsylvania was where she was born and where her parents chose to raise her, but Seattle was where she'd chosen to make her own life. And she'd succeeded, damn it. She'd made a great damn life here. And now she was just going to throw it away. Her career. Her life.

Her partner.

"Dale?" Isaac's voice was gentle. "Look, this is a huge step. We don't have to do anything right now. I'll give you more cash for a hotel. I want to move at a pace you're comfortable with."

"Call the airport and have them get the plane ready. I'll get my things from the hotel room." She nodded across the street. "You wait here. We can leave right away."

"You're sure?" He was very clearly trying to rein in his excitement.

She nodded. "I have to get out of this town. I'll feel better once I put some distance between me and Ariadne."

He finally allowed himself to smile. "Okay, then. Fantastic. Thank you, Dale. Thank you so much, this... this is the culmination of years of my work."

She nodded, unsure how else to react. "I'll be right back."

"I'll, uh, I'll call the airport and finish your sandwich."

Dale left him at the table and went across the street to the hotel. She was basically sleepwalking, her mind completely oblivious to what her body was doing. This was her final day in Seattle. The sun would set on her in New York. She might never see the Space Needle again, or have another burger from Dick's Drive-In. She would never see their apartment again. Never sit behind her desk at Bitches, or cover Ari with the afghan when she fell asleep on the couch in the office. She would start to regularly sleep through the night.

She used the keycard to get into her room and put the suitcase on the bed. She knew she was crying, but didn't know when she'd started. The tears were just there, rolling down her cheeks. It was ten years. Ten years of indoctrination, Stockholm syndrome, lies, manipulation. She wiped at her face and closed her bag. She checked to make sure she had her chargers and picked up her phone. She stared at it, then swiped a finger across the screen.

Ten years. She couldn't just vanish. *That* would be cruel and inhuman.

She sat on the foot of the bed and dialed Ari's number. There was a click and she held her breath, but then sighed with relief when she realized it was the voicemail message. Just hearing Ari's voice was like a rubber band twisting around her heart.

"This is Ariadne Willow. Leave a message."

"It's m-- Th-This is Dale. I wanted to let you know that... I'm not going to be around anymore. I'm leaving town. Today, in... not very long from now. Isaac has a plane waiting at Clay Lacy. I didn't want you to worry about running into me in the street or a-at home. The apartment is yours now, and... and the office." Her voice broke and she sagged forward, choking from holding back the sob.

"Puppy," she managed.

She sat up, sniffled, and wiped at her eyes with her free hand. "Don't try to follow me. I know how you are. You're like a... like a d-dog with a bone." She laughed under her breath. "It's what made you so good at your job. But you'll be wasting your time. Trust me. Just forget about me. I'm going to try to forget about you, too. It'll be the best. And I'm... I'm..."

She looked out the window.

"I'm sorry for what's going to happen next. I'm sorry that it's going to be me doing it to you. I know that I've changed a lot in the past few days, but you're still the same person. So this must hurt you terribly. I'm sorry for that. But everything you've done over the past ten years has been... cruel. And it's been wrong."

She closed her eyes.

"Good-bye, Ariadne."

She hung up and stood, then tossed her phone onto the bed. She didn't trust herself not to answer if Ari tried to call back, and it belonged to the agency anyway. She took the suitcase to the window and looked outside at the city, her city, for the last time as a resident.

She took the time to make sure she had stopped crying, checked the mirror to make sure her eyes weren't too puffy, then picked up the book of essays off the table. This phase of her life was over.

It was time to start her new life.

CHAPTER TWENTY-FIVE

ARI CAME down the stairs at full speed, practically leaping to every third step while her hand only skimmed the railing. Her phone was in her other hand, gripped tightly enough to stress the case. Milo and Gwen both looked up at the thunderous sound.

"Why did you let me go to sleep?" she demanded.

"Because you needed it," Gwen said, rising to her feet. "What's going on?"

Ari stopped by the couch, her hand shaking as she pushed her hair out of her face. "Dale called. I missed a call from Dale. She called five minutes ago. Isaac is taking her to an airport, he's... they're going somewhere. He's taking her away, Mama."

Gwen's eyes widened at the last word, a term Ari rarely used even when she was a child. "Just take a breath, Ari..."

"I don't have time to take a breath!" Her eyes were shining with tears. "I don't know where they w-were, and they have a five minute head start... He's taking Dale away."

Milo said, "Just slow down. Five minutes isn't much of a head start, especially not when a flight is involved. SeaTac?"

"No, she said another place. Clay... Clay something."

"Clay Lacy," Gwen said. "I know where it is. It's about four miles away from here. It's a private airport, which means he might not have to worry about security and pre-flight and... I'm saying they could be getting the plane ready right now."

Ari whimpered.

"Don't worry, pup, we'll get you there. We can take my bike."

"My car is going to be faster than a bicycle," Ari snapped.

Milo grinned. "No one said it was a bicycle." She turned to Gwen and cupped her cheek. "You wanna call the cops? Get them out there, arrest him for killing the Kirsches?"

Gwen hesitated, then shook her head. "As much as I despise it, we can't do that. We can't risk him telling the police why he was arrested."

Ari said, "The Werewolf Murderer of Frankfurt. It would be trending on Twitter by dinner. Milo, come on, we have to go. Now."

Milo put her hands on Gwen's hips and leaned into her. "We're going to go get our girl back."

"Be safe."

"Always. I love you."

"I love you, too."

They kissed, and Milo pulled away, motioning for Ari to follow. "C'mon. I plan to make up some time on the road, but we better get a move on."

Gwen hugged herself as she watched her lover hurry from the house, her daughter in hot pursuit. She was terrified, both for Dale and for what might happen when they got to the airport. Three of the people she loved most in the world, the only three people she'd ever really considered her pack, were about to jump feet first into the fire, and all she could do was sit and wait to hear how it had gone.

"Please don't get hurt," she whispered, praying for all of them in equal measure, knowing it would be a disaster if even one of them didn't come back. "Please be okay..."

Dale ignored Isaac on the drive to the airport, but she could tell he was about to burst from excitement. He flexed his fingers on the steering wheel, turned on the radio just to turn it back off again, and checked his phone at stoplights. Traffic was mostly okay, and they seemed to be making good time. She felt like she usually did right before becoming sick, and her emotions were as unsettled as the man behind the wheel. Excitement at her escape, fear at what might come next, despair... she was really feeling the despair. She told herself it was just a side effect of leaving her old life behind, but what if it was more?

She put her head against the window and closed her eyes. She tried to remember things she'd read in the essay. *No one knows where the first wolf appeared. The classic chicken-egg argument is especially hazy in this circumstance. Were they beasts who learned to wear a man's clothing, or a man who surrendered to his darker instincts?*

"Is everything okay?"

Dale nodded. "I'm just a little queasy."

"Oh. I think there's some airsickness medication on the plane if you feel like you'll need it. And there are airsick bags if the meds don't work."

They followed the train tracks south through an industrial small-town neighborhood south of Seattle. There were funky little stores, strip malls, tattoo shops, and so much wide open sky that it was hard to believe downtown was just a few miles away. Isaac drove until they arrived at what appeared to be a typical office park. He pulled into a spot and sat back, staring out the windshield for a long moment before he finally looked at her.

"This trip really has turned into a remarkable success, Dale. I want to thank you for giving me a chance to open your eyes. For... allowing me to save you."

She rolled her eyes and got out of the car. She retrieved her bag from the backseat and waited while Isaac retrieved his own bags. She had started to turn away when she saw a flash of metal, looking in time to see him drape his coat over a gun tucked into the back of his belt.

"What the hell is that?"

"Insurance," he said, as casually as if she'd asked the brand of his suitcase. "Don't worry, we don't have to go through security or anything like that."

Dale said, "Insurance for me?"

He looked stricken. "God, no. Dale, you've spent ten years with these wolves. I can't just hope they let you go quietly. If any of them found out where you were, I have to be prepared to protect you from them."

She wasn't certain she believed him, but at the moment her brain and stomach were twisted up in knots, and her heart felt like it was three beats away from giving up entirely. So instead of arguing, she closed the car door and followed him across the parking lot. A private plane waited on the tarmac, gleaming gray and almost unreal against the overcast sky. Isaac picked up the pace, not quite running but moving quickly that Dale had a hard time keeping up with him.

The hatch opened from the top, stretching down to the ground to create a flight of steps leading up into the plane. A pilot was standing in the opening with his hand raised in greeting. Isaac waved back, and the pilot disappeared into the plane.

"That was Joe. He's a good guy."

"How do you know he's not secretly a wolf?"

He smiled back at her as he climbed the steps. "I've gotten pretty good at telling them apart from real people."

Dale still felt a twinge at language like that, but it was getting easier to tolerate. She didn't know how she felt about that. Once they were aboard, Joe pulled the door shut and secured it before turning to her and offering his hand.

"Good afternoon. My name is Joe. The co-pilot up there is Brian. Flight time to New York is going to be just about five and a half hours. Let us know if you need anything during the flight and we'll do our best to get you settled."

Isaac had stowed his bag and then did the same for hers. "I know five hours seems like a long time, but it'll fly by. Pardon the pun. They have iPads with movies on them, or you can sleep... the seats at the back pull out into a bed."

Dale said, "I think I'll be fine."

She took her seat and buckled in. Isaac sat on the other side of the plane, one row up to give her privacy. She closed her eyes and relaxed against the headrest. She planned to sleep, shut her mind off for a few hours, maybe wake up in New York as a new woman. She hummed a few bars of the *Hamilton* song and actually felt a little better. The plane began to taxi, and she laced her fingers over her stomach to prepare for takeoff.

A minute or so after they began to taxi, Joe the Pilot called back, "Uh, sir? We might have an issue up here."

Isaac leaned to one side to see through the door. "Is it something with the plane?"

"Not exactly," Joe said. "You should come take a look at this."

"I thought people only said that in movies." He unfastened his seatbelt and stood up, moving carefully toward the cockpit. He braced himself in the doorway and leaned forward to see out the front of the plane. "What the hell..."

Dale's curiosity got the better of her. She got up as well and joined Isaac at the cockpit to look over his shoulder.

"They just came out of nowhere," Brian said. "Zipped in from toward the parking lot... probably got in through an open gate or something?"

"Yeah, mechanics are always leaving those gates open," Joe said under his breath.

A motorcycle was speeding on the runway directly ahead of the plane. Even if she hadn't recognized it as Milo's new bike, she would have recognized the slender woman clinging to Milo's back despite the fact they were both wearing helmets. Milo weaved the bike in a serpentine path before straightening out and putting on an extra burst of speed. A moment later, she slowed way down and almost disappeared under the nose of the plane.

"Damn!" Joe said. "She keeps doing that. If we can't get up enough speed, we're never going to lift off. And the longer she plays chicken with us, the more fuel we burn."

"Just go around her," Isaac said.

Brian shook his head. "We can't just go skimming across the whole runway. Besides, that one on the back seems to be signaling her. If we change direction, she'll just move with us."

Isaac turned and looked at Dale. There was betrayal in his eyes. "How did they know where to find us?"

Dale considered lying, but she shook her head. "Ariadne Willow was almost a decade of my life. I couldn't just disappear on her."

"Damn it," he said, slapping the wall. "I understand, believe me, but you've completely screwed this up. If you wanted to say goodbye, I could have arranged it! Safe, monitored."

The plane started to slow. Brian said, "We can't just let them lead us around like this. We're almost out of tarmac anyway. Get out and talk to whoever that is and we'll try again."

Isaac pushed away from the wall and stalked back into the cabin. "I'm going. You stay here, Miss Frye. I can't risk one of them tricking you or grabbing you and making a run for it."

"The gun stays here," Dale said.

"Miss Frye..."

"It stays *here*."

He sighed and took the gun from his belt. He put it down on the first seat next to the door and faced her again. "You stay on the plane. No matter what." Dale nodded, and he twisted to look into the cabin. "If anything happens to me out there, you leave. Follow the original flight plan."

Joe and Brian looked at each other. "What exactly do you think might happen to you?"

"Hopefully nothing," Isaac said.

He lowered the stairs, gave Dale a reassuring nod, and descended.

Ari felt like she was going to throw up. Milo had broken every speed limit and every street law known to man to get them to the airport in time, only to see Dale and Isaac boarding a plane from the wrong side of a chain-link fence. Finding the open gate was pure dumb luck, the first time it felt like luck had worked in her favor this week, and Ari had nearly broken Milo in half when she realized what the plan was.

Milo put them in front of the plane before it got up to full speed, and then adjusted accordingly to maintain a steady distance between them. Every time Ari looked back, she was positive the plane was seconds away from rolling over them, leaving them as a stain on the asphalt. She guided Milo by patting her shoulders, moving her left and right to keep the plane from getting around them.

Finally, miraculously, the plane began to slow to a stop. Milo circled just in case it was a trick, but then Ari pointed at the door opening, and stairs unfolding onto the tarmac. Milo nodded and brought the bike to a stop. Ari climbed off the seat and wobbled a little, steeling herself as she advanced. Isaac came down the steps and held out his hands to show he was unarmed.

"Miss Willow. Miss Duncan. Were the theatrics really necessary?"

"You're kidnapping my fiancée," Ari said, "and you brainwashed her."

"I didn't brainwash anybody. I only gave her access to the facts you denied her. I educated her about what she was actually dealing with, and she made up her own mind. Just like everyone who will read those essays when I have them published. You wolves have been hiding far too long. It's time to step into the light and face the consequences of what you are."

Milo was standing a few feet away from Ari, arms crossed over her chest. "And what's that, mate? Monsters? You're the one who killed the Kirsch pack just to get a damn book. Humans are the ones who hunted us to near extinction. Turned it into a sport. You skinned us, hung our hides on your walls, beheaded us."

"While you overran our settlements, devoured children, tried to change us into beasts like you. Every wolf we killed meant a greater chance of survival."

Ari held up her hands. "Okay, let's just admit both sides were awful to each other in the past. But Mr. Hayden, you have to understand what exposing *canidae* in this day and age could do. People are more afraid of differences now than ever. Do you really think we'd be greeted with open arms, or would be rounded up and stuck in cages, cut up in labs?"

"You would prefer to hide?"

"No! Not really, but when the alternative is slaughter, we don't really have a choice. At least there's peace."

Isaac said, "People deserve to know what might be living next door to them."

"Maybe in some cases, it's none of their business. Wolves aren't inherently dangerous. We're not bombs waiting to go off."

He raised his eyebrows. "Aren't you, though?"

"Isn't everybody?" Milo said. "When provoked, or pushed, or threatened, we all could be the worst kinds of weapon. You publish that book, you make every human who reads it into an enemy of *canidae*. Some of us will take that as an invitation to fight back. Preemptive strikes. You're not setting up a genocide, you're starting a war."

Isaac remained focused on Ari. "You know Miss Frye is not here under duress, right? I didn't kidnap her, Miss Willow. She chose to come with me. It was her idea to leave today. So what's your plan? Follow us to New York? Drag her back here kicking and screaming? In that scenario, *you* are the kidnapper. You are the one ignoring what she wants."

Ari looked away.

Milo said, "Pup, don't listen to him..."

"He's right, though. We saw her. She was carrying her own bag."

Isaac lowered his hands. "Go. Go aboard the plane. Ask her to leave with you. I won't stop you."

Ari looked at Milo, who shook her head. "If she's that far gone..."

"I have to try."

Milo looked uncertain, but shrugged and looked back at Isaac. "I'll keep an eye on this'n."

Ari walked forward, giving Isaac a wide berth. He held his hands out to the side, still looking like a kindly older man. He was even sort of smiling, the smile of a man who knew she was just going through the motions and that he was about to be proven right. Ari passed him and walked faster, almost running by the time she got to the stairs. She climbed up, terrified of what she was going to find inside. When she got to the top, she saw two pilots standing at the cockpit entrance and motioned for them to go back and shut the door.

"Dale?"

"Stay back."

Dale was pressed against the far wall, keeping as much distance between her and Ari as possible. Ari almost cried. It had been so long since she and Dale had been in the same room together, and just seeing her made Ari crave a hug, a kiss, the scent of her hair. The frantic look in Dale's eyes, like a caged animal, was almost too much for Ari to bear. She showed her hands.

"I'm not going to hurt you."

"I can't make that same promise."

Ari smiled. "I don't believe that. I'm not scared of you, Dale."

Dale closed her eyes. "You should be. You don't know what my head is like. I've learned things, Ari." She opened her eyes and saw Ari had come closer. "No! Back up! Get away. I promise. I'll h-hurt you."

Ari retreated past the first row of seats. "I know what the essays can do to a person, Dale. They're poison. But I also know what they did to you. They made you run away from me when I was vulnerable. They made you call and tell me exactly where you were. And I know they couldn't stop you from helping with my case when you figured it out. You may feel like a hunter but you're acting like the woman I fell in love with."

Tears were shining in Dale's eyes. "Mutt. You're a mutt."

Ari said, "No. Don't listen to that side of you. You're stronger than it is." She glanced down and saw the gun on the seat next to her. She didn't think about what she was about to do, she just reached out and picked it up.

Dale tensed, tried to retreat further. "No!"

"I know what the book can do," Ari said, "and I know who you are, and I have faith in you. Every time, Dale, I'll choose you every time."

She turned the gun around so she was gripping it by the barrel.

She walked down the aisle, ignoring Dale's pleas for her to back up, go away. When she was within arm's reach, Dale punched Ari, once on the shoulder and once in the chin, but Ari took both blows without reacting. She took one of Dale's hands, brought it down, wrapped it around the grip of the gun.

"What are you doing, don't. Stop! Ari, stop!"

Ari pressed forward. The barrel of the gun dug into her stomach just below her ribs. Dale went very still, her eyes wide, the lashes trembling under the weight of tears they hadn't let go yet.

"If I'm a monster, then the last ten years have been a lie. A long con. A manipulation. If that's true, I never loved you. Every time I held you when you were sick or comforted you when you were sad, it was all bullshit and it meant nothing. I'm a mutt, I was pretending, I was laughing behind your back. If you believe that, then pull the trigger."

Dale parted her lips, but no sound came out. Ari didn't blink, didn't say anything else.

"Puppy," Dale whispered, and the gun swung to the side, and her whole body seemed to go limp. She sobbed the word again, "Puppy," and fell forward. Ari caught her, held her, closed her eyes as she breathed in Dale's scent. "What did I do? Oh god, I could have shot you."

"No. You couldn't have." Ari kissed her hair and squeezed her tighter. "I love you, Dale."

Dale was crying openly now, sobbing against Ari's shoulder. "I love you, Ariadne. I love you, Ariadne. I love you, Ariadne..."

Ari eventually lost count of how many times Dale said it, but she was willing to listen to as many repetitions as necessary until Dale felt heard.

CHAPTER TWENTY-SIX

AS GOOD as it felt to put her arm around Dale to guide her out of the plane, Ari's mood was improved even more when Isaac turned around and she saw the smug grin melt off his face. By the time they reached the ground and were walking toward him, he looked positively ill. He looked at Dale, almost betrayed, and then turned to Ari with an angry scowl.

"What the hell did you do to her?"

"She talked to me," Dale said. "She reminded me who I am."

Isaac said, "Miss Frye... Dale... please. You read the essays. You know what they are. You know what wolves have done!"

"Yeah. And I know what humanity has done. To *canidae*, to each other, to anyone who is different. If you want to be scared of anyone, be scared of us. Maybe wolves started the war. Maybe they were just defending themselves against humans. I don't know and honestly, I don't care. I'm not interested in trying to classify an entire species as good or bad. I know this wolf. And that one. Hey, Milo." She nodded at Milo. "And I've known bad *canidae*. I've known bad humans, and I don't think you're one of them. I think you're confused, like I was. I think you saw something that looked like the truth and you let that poison you. It made you scared."

"We should be scared! When these wolves rise up~"

"*If*," Dale said. "And right now, they have no reason to fight. But if you publish that book, you'll give them an enemy, and you can be damn sure they'll defend themselves. You said you researched Ari, but there's one thing you didn't pay close enough attention to. Ariadne doesn't start wars. She ends them."

Ari tightened her hand on Dale's hip, her eyes still locked on Isaac. "Stay away from the people I love, Mr. Hayden."

They walked away from him. Ari stopped, let go of Dale, and walked back to where he was standing. He lifted his chin and raised his eyebrows, anticipating more conversation. Instead, Ari punched him. It was a solid blow, completely unrestrained, the kind of punch she'd rarely thrown. Isaac went down hard, flailing in a futile attempt to break his fall, ending up flat on his ass with one hand covering the lower half of his face. He stared up at her with a shocked expression.

"That's for giving her the damn book in the first place."

She turned and walked away from him. Dale out her hand, and Ari took it even though her knuckles throbbed when Dale squeezed them. It was a good pain.

Milo fell into step next to them. "I don't want to be a spoilsport, but I'm not sure all three of us will fit on the bike. I could take Dale, come back..."

"Actually," Dale said, "I could really use some air. I saw a bus stop down the road. The walk will help clear my head."

"Do you want company?"

Dale started to answer, then gripped Ari's hand. "I need to think. Just think. Talking won't help, so I would just be completely in my head."

"I understand."

Ari started to pull her hand away, but Dale gripped it tighter. "No, I'm... I'm saying that I won't talk, and I don't want to have a conversation, but if you're okay with that, then I'd really like for you to walk with me."

"I can do that. Absolutely." She held out her hand to Milo. "Thanks for the ride."

"Any time. See you back at Gwen's? She's going to want to make sure little foxy here is okay."

Dale raised an eyebrow. "Foxy...?"

"Cause of the red," Milo said, winking and then wincing. "Trying to be cute. Too soon?"

Ari took her helmet so Milo wouldn't have to figure out what to do with it, then turned to see Isaac was still sitting where she had dropped him. She turned her back to him, slipped her arm around Dale's waist, and Dale put her head on Ari's shoulder as they walked away from the plane.

Gwen shot to her feet as soon as the front door opened, her expression hopeful but guarded. Dale entered cautiously, twisting her fingers together as she looked at Gwen and Milo. Dale had spent the entire bus ride wondering what she would say, what she could possibly tell them to explain her actions over the past few days. Ari told her about the book while they were walking, how reading the essays was like reciting a magic spell. She insisted Dale wasn't to blame for the hatred she'd been spewing, but it had to come from somewhere, right? There had to be some part of her, maybe hidden deep inside, that thought *canidae* were mutts who deserved to be put down.

"Hi, Mom," she said, and unexpectedly began to cry.

Gwen crossed the room in two long strides and gathered Dale in a hug. "It's okay, sweetheart. It wasn't you. It wasn't your heart."

Dale sniffled and stepped back. "The things I said..."

Milo put a hand on Dale's shoulder. "If you want forgiveness, we'll give it to you. But no one in this room feels like it's necessary. People have killed because of that book. You managed to keep it to a couple of slurs. I think in the grand scheme of things, we can overlook a few bad days."

Dale swallowed the lump in her throat and turned to look at Ari. "The things I said to you."

Ari shook her head. "It wasn't you."

"But it was."

Gwen cupped Dale's cheek. "Listen to me, Dale. We all tend to be fearful of the unknown. Our genes tend to see differences as a threat. I'm not saying we're all born racist, I'm saying that the fear is an easy response. It's an ignorant response, and it's one that can be unlearned and ignored. Those essays made it harder for you to ignore that part of your brain. It shut a door. Ari opened it again."

Dale looked at Ari and smiled. The barbed wire around her brain was gone. Every time she touched Ari on the bus ride, her heart had swelled and then caved in on itself when she remembered some of the awful things she'd said after reading the essays.

Gwen said, "I'm sure that when Ari gets you home, you'll find your center again. You'll–"

"I-I'm not going home with Ari."

Everyone in the room went still. Ari squared her shoulders and seemed braced for a killing blow.

"Not right away," Dale said. "I can't. She got through to me on the plane, and I feel like myself for the first time in days, but that doesn't change the fact that when I woke up this morning, I was disgusted by the idea of being in the same room with her. I wanted to hurt her. I wanted to hurt all of you, I didn't care if all of you died because of me. I don't know if that's a switch that can be flipped, or if it's going to stay flipped, or..."

"I get it," Ari said, though she sounded on the verge of tears. "We need to be sure. I understand. We can call Diana and Lucy, see if you can stay with them. Or I could stay here and you could go home..."

"No, I think I need neutral territory. Puppy, please don't think this is about you, or us, or~"

"I don't. I know. It's smart. I... I've just... missed you."

Dale released Gwen and went to Ari. "I'm back, puppy. I just need to make sure I'm all the way back before I trust myself. I hope it won't be long, I want to get back to normal, but I had some dark, awful thoughts..."

Ari laid two fingers across Dale's lips. "I don't care how long it takes for you to get back to me, as long as you're walking in my direction."

Dale hugged Ari, who tightened the embrace. "I'm going to marry you, Ariadne. I've never wanted anything more than I want that."

"I know." She moved her lips so that only Dale would hear her when she said, "I love you, Dale. I never stopped loving you, no matter what happened. I want you to know that."

Dale could only nod, worried anything else would make her start crying again.

When they eventually broke the embrace, Dale saw that Gwen and Milo had vanished at some point, no doubt silently vacating the room to give them some privacy.

"You can come out now," Ari called.

Milo came out of the garage. "I thought I heard someone trying to steal my bike. Gwen was gonna scare 'em off."

"Sure," Ari said. "I'm going to take Dale home. Let her pack, call Diana to make sure she's okay with having a houseguest for an indefinite amount of time. And you can figure out what to do with this."

She reached under her shirt and pulled out the book of essays, tossing it onto the kitchen counter. Dale hissed, and backed up a step. Ari looked at her, confused.

"You knew I had that."

"I know. I saw you take it. But I... I don't want to be anywhere near it."

Gwen pulled a hand towel hanging off the front of the oven and wrapped it around the book. "We'll figure out something to do with it. Get her out of here."

Ari nodded and ushered Dale out of the house. Once the door was closed behind them, Dale stopped and took a deep breath.

"There are copies of the essays in my desk at work."

"I'll burn them," Ari said.

Dale nodded and put her arm around Ari's shoulders. "Thank you, puppy." They started for the car. "Did you solve the case? The tapestry, did you find it?"

"Sort of. I figured out where it is. That's enough for me." She kissed Dale's temple. "You gave me the key. You showed me who I needed to talk to, and he spilled everything."

"Way to go, puppy. I want to hear the whole story. Maybe not right now, but... I really am curious."

"It'll be waiting to be told as soon as you're ready to hear it."

She got Dale into the passenger seat and walked around the back. They might not be out of the woods yet, but she was confident she had Dale back. *Her* Dale, the real Dale, the woman who gave her strength and helped her through even the darkest woods. Together they could fight against anything the world wanted to throw at them next.

A few days later, on Wednesday, Ari was back at the W outside Elizabeth Burroughs' room. Elizabeth had called the night before asking for a meeting before she checked out. The whole mystery around Crossing-Over Place seemed like a thousand years ago, but Ari was willing to answer any questions she might have. Dale was welcomed at the Macallan home with open arms. Both Diana and Lucy insisted she was welcome to stay as long as necessary even before Ari explained their circumstances. She and Dale hadn't seen each other in person since, though they talked frequently on the phone.

Ari spent Monday and Tuesday at home, staring at the TV

while random Netflix shows streamed across the screen. She didn't want to take any new cases without Dale there to help her, doubted she would be able to focus on anything long enough to make a difference, so she was using Vivian's check to take an indefinite vacation.

Elizabeth answered the door in a pinstripe black suit with a low-cut silk blouse underneath, her hair pinned back. She smiled and motioned Ari inside, returning to the closet to remove another outfit.

"Thank you for dropping by, Miss Willow."

"I'm happy to help you get any closure I can. The rest of the family?"

Elizabeth said, "Eleanor and Evie went home. We're planning to get together again soon. Just to try it out. We can certainly afford the plane tickets. Preston has been pretty busy figuring out what to keep and what to sell in the house. He's going to sell the whole thing when it's been cleared out. He'll get something a little more practical to live in."

"Probably the smart thing to do," Ari said.

"We all agree. It's sad that the house won't be in the family anymore, but... well, you got to know us pretty well. None of us are really the sentimental sort."

"Right." There was a lull in conversation. "So I hear Crossing-Over Place turned up."

Elizabeth paused in folding her clothes and looked at Ari. "Yes. Very fascinating story about how that happened. Turns out we had another sister we never knew about. Mom gave her the tapestry to keep her quiet, made the fake so none of us would notice it was missing, but then she felt guilty about trying to freeze Megan out of her inheritance. And, surprise surprise, Megan has two kids. The Burroughs name gets to live on after all."

Ari walked to the window and looked down at the street below. "That sounds crazy."

"Yeah." Elizabeth said. "The only thing crazier would be if Mom tracked down an orphan, someone who had tried to track down her birth mother through many different agencies. Someone who was the right age, who looked like us, who had the right blood type, and would be willing to change her name in exchange for a quarter-million dollars. But that would be really insane, wouldn't it?"

"Seems like the easiest answer is probably right. Your mother had a child no one knew about and wanted to make amends. Everyone gets what they want in the end."

Elizabeth nodded, still packing. "A lot of work. It would be a shame if there was a tiny little flaw in her plan. Something small and stupid that might come out after a few drinks with someone who is better at holding her liquor. I drink a lot of wine, Miss Willow. I can hold my liquor."

"Uh-huh," Ari said, not willing to commit one way or the other to what Elizabeth was saying.

"Megan Garfield was born when Mom was six weeks pregnant with me and Evelyn."

Ari couldn't help but laugh. Elizabeth laughed, too. Ari said, "I guess Megan was a nine out of ten in everything else, so they decided to fudge the numbers a little. Smooth trick, getting her drunk."

Elizabeth shrugged. "I didn't even really have to get her drunk. She was eager to get to know us all. I don't think it was really about the money. I honestly think she's excited to have sisters. We're a family. That's something she's never had, something she's spent a long time trying to find."

"It doesn't bother you that she took your mother's money?"

"Where else should it have gone? Charity? Okay, so in that case it goes to help someone have a better life. It's helping Megan have a better life. So where's the harm? I mainly called you to see if I was right."

Ari said, "So you're not going to throw a wrench in your mother's plan?"

"Why bother? She went to a lot of trouble to make this happen. No one is going to look too closely. Eleanor would only be upset if Megan was older than her, which would mean giving up the locket, but at least Mom was kind enough to let her stay the oldest. So now we're five instead of four. Worse things could have happened."

"That's an excellent way of looking at it. A happy ending for everyone."

Elizabeth said, "I do love happy endings." She zipped up her suitcase. "How about you? Happy ending? Everything work out with that girl of yours?"

"It's in the process of working out, yeah."

"That's great. I wish I'd gotten a chance to meet her."

Ari said, "You mean... meet her, or..." She glanced at the bed.

"*Meet* her?"

Elizabeth grinned suggestively. "Either one works. But if you're worried that this was a wasted vacation, you can rest easy."

"Good to know. Are you ready to go?"

"Yep, on my way out."

Ari nodded at the door. "I'll escort you."

"So chivalrous."

They walked together to the elevator and stepped into the empty car when it arrived. Once the doors were closed, she turned to look at Ari.

"Did you know it wasn't really about the tapestry?"

"No," Ari admitted. "It was a good mystery. It almost drove me crazy, but I couldn't walk away."

Elizabeth said, "Okay. But you knew none of us cared about it. We would have been willing to let you drop the case. You stuck with it because... you were bored?"

They arrived at the lobby and stepped out of the elevator. Ari thought about her answer before she spoke. "I spent a long time hating my mother for something she did to me when I was young. Recently I discovered something else about her, something I disagree with, but I'm trying very hard not to let it ruin our relationship. Your mother told me you were all monsters. You all told me your mother was hateful. You were all exaggerating, and you were all telling the truth. I guess I wanted to get the middle ground. I wanted to prove there could be a middle ground, because I need it in my own life if I want to maintain the relationship I've created with my mother."

"Did you find it?"

"I don't know. I know it felt good to see you and your sisters hugging on that porch swing. I know that recent events in my life would have gone a lot worse if my mother wasn't there. I'm definitely going to try."

"That's great. I'm glad our family helped you get to that decision."

Ari said, "It's not such a bad family, you know."

"Yeah, sure, Megan had to be paid a quarter of a million dollars just to say she was part of it."

"Don't go by her. I would call myself a Burroughs for half that."

Elizabeth laughed. She called an Uber for the airport and Ari waited with her at the curb until the car arrived and took her away.

Ari rolled her shoulders and breathed in the breeze coming up Seneca Street from Elliott Bay. She started walking west with no destination in mind. No open cases to worry about, no Dale waiting for her at home, nothing to stop her from just wandering her city. She wasn't far from Pike Place. She could find somewhere, call Dale, see if she wanted to meet up for lunch. It would be like a good old-fashioned date, the only silver lining to their current situation. The late night conversations, the dates, the making out in the car. She knew Dale was back, knew whatever the book had done to her was faded and forgotten, but she was willing to wait as long as it took until Dale was equally convinced.

For now, though, she would enjoy not having responsibilities or commitments. She stuck her hands in her pockets and adopted a casual, leisurely pace toward the water.

EPILOGUE

ARI DROPPED the balled-up sock, used her foot to bump it into position, then eyed her shot. Her hockey stick was a roll of unopened wrapping paper she'd found in the front closet when she decided it needed to be organized. The goal was a trash can she had laid on its side. She swung the "stick" and knocked the socks into the front of the entertainment unit, sending them bouncing toward the "goal." They hit the lip of the can and rolled away.

"Ahh, damn it."

Milo's voice came over the phone pinned between Ari's shoulder and ear. "What are you doing?"

"It's supposed to be hockey," Ari said, "but I think it's more mini-golf than anything else. But I'm in a hockey jersey so I think it counts. Keep talking, I was listening. You're at the airport?"

"Yeah, Gwen's checking us in. She's worried about having the book in our carry-on, but I'm more comfortable having it where we can keep an eye on it."

Ari said, "Probably smart." She lined up another pair of socks. They were on their way to Germany to meet up with a pack who occasionally worked with the Kirsches. They planned to secure the book, keep it away from prying eyes and anyone else like Isaac Hayden who might use it for evil. Gwen was concerned about the fact he still had copies, but Dale was confident he wouldn't be able to get them published. "He needed the original for authenticity," she'd said last time they met for coffee. "But I think the publisher was still hesitant without a personal testimony. That's where I was supposed to come in. Now he's lost me and the original, they're not going to publish it based on his word alone."

For the time being, they could only hope she was right. Isaac had vanished after the airport. They had no idea if he was still in Seattle or if he had fled but, either way, they had all upped their security just in case. Gwen was confident that taking the book back to Germany would remove any reason he had for sticking around and causing more trouble for them.

Ari's next shot also missed the trash. "Damn it!"

Milo laughed. "Maybe you ought to try shuffleboard or something."

"Yeah, maybe."

"You're going a bit nutso, eh?"

"It's been over a month." Ari used the tube to pull the socks back into position. "I know Dale needs her space, and I want her to take as long as it takes. But I don't want to go back to work if Dale's not there, don't want to be at home because Dale isn't here, either. So I basically just don't want to be anywhere or do anything."

Someone knocked on the door and Ari thwapped the socks against the wall. "Someone's here, so I'll let you go. Good luck with security."

"Yeah, thanks. We'll call when we've landed."

Ari hung up and tossed the phone onto the couch. She was almost to the door when whoever it was knocked again. "Hang on a sec." She opened the door and was so stunned to see Dale on the other side that she couldn't think of what to say.

"Hi," Dale said. She held up a newspaper. "I'm here about the ad."

"The..." Ari blinked. "You're what?"

"The ad you put in the paper? You're looking for a roommate?"

Ari stared at her. She had a twinge of panic that Dale's brain had been broken by the essays, that whatever recovery she'd made had now taken a bizarre left turn. But then she saw the look in Dale's eyes, the expression that she knew meant 'come on, puppy, figure it out.' And then she remembered.

"*There's some appeal to the situation,*" Dale had said weeks earlier, at the very beginning of the Burroughs case. "*...in an established* *relationship. One person is at the bar, their significant other comes up and pretends to be a stranger, they flirt, they make up outrageous lies about who they really are, and it ends in wild sex in a hotel room."*

"Is the room still available?"

"The room," Ari said. "Uh, yeah, I... sorry. Please come in." She stepped aside, staring at Dale as she entered the apartment like a stranger. She closed the door and tried to think of what to say next. "So... so you, um, are you new to Seattle?"

"No, I've lived here a while. I went through some stuff recently. Almost lost everything. But I've been getting back on my feet, and I think it's time to put down some roots."

Ari's emotions swirled, but she tried to keep a straight face. "Oh. Well, that's good. I'm glad to hear that. So... this is the apartment. Living room and dining room here, kitchen through there. Laundry room at the top of the stairs. We share that with the landlady. She's cool, you'll like her."

Dale nodded and then pointed at the open bedroom door. "It looks like there might only be one bedroom...?"

"Oh. Yeah, that's the bedroom. We'd be sharing a bed. I hope that's not awkward."

"You'd think that's something you would mention in the ad," Dale said. "But it's not a deal breaker. Are you a snuggler?"

Ari swallowed a lump in her throat. "Yeah, usually."

"Noted." Dale turned to scan the apartment. "This is a great place."

"Thanks. Someone really special chose it for me."

Dale looked at her again. There were tears in her eyes. "You know, um... in the, um, thirties or whenever, Yellowstone wiped out wolves from the park. The whole thing crashed. The elk population blew up, they overgrazed, beavers and birds started dying out. It was bad. They finally reintroduced wolves in the nineties, and it was like a rebirth. The ecosystem might never be exactly the way it used to be, but it's alive. It's thriving. I want my wolf back, puppy."

Ari smiled.

"I don't want to start over, though."

Ari nodded, lips pressed together. "Neither do I." She was trying to keep her cool, but it was increasingly difficult.

"That would mean forgetting the past ten years happened. And I would rather throw myself into Puget Sound than do that. I've spent the last week aching for you, but also still so scared I was going to relapse. I haven't had a bad thought or a nightmare in that entire time. If... if you're nervous about having me nearby or~"

Ari interrupted, "I was never scared. Or worried. I'm the one who put the loaded gun in your hand, Dale. I only agreed to let you stay with Diana and Lucy because it's what you wanted. You're the woman who fought to protect a wolf, then gave it the only food you had. And when the wolf turned into a person, you let her buy you a coffee and listened to her insane story. Why would I ever doubt that person?"

Dale lowered her head and Ari stepped forward, wrapped her up in her arms, and held her. They started with phone conversations, which eventually evolved into actual dates. Conversations over dinner, getting coffee together, going for walks by the water. They had touched during those encounters, held each other and even kissed, but something about this time felt more real, more normal. She cupped the back of Dale's head and pulled back just enough to find her lips. They kissed, and Dale moaned a surrender into Ari's mouth. It wasn't a single kiss, but a series of smaller kisses and pecks. It felt almost like they were making up for every kiss they hadn't shared in the past few days, leaving her breathless and flushed.

Eventually they ended up with their foreheads touching, Dale's eyes closed and Ari examining her features.

"I'm Ari, by the way."

Dale opened her eyes. It was her turn to be confused. "What?"

"Ariadne. People call me Ari. What's your name?"

"Oh. Right, uh. Dale. I'm Dale."

"That might be the most beautiful name I've ever heard."

Dale grinned and closed her eyes again.

"Do you want to test out the bed?"

"Yes."

They went into the bedroom and Dale toed off her shoes as Ari crawled onto her side of the bed. She pulled back the blanket and let Dale settle in, cozying into the slight dip her body had made in the mattress. Ari drew the blanket up over her, tucked it around her shoulders, and left her hand resting lightly on Dale's upper arm. Dale sighed and pressed her cheek into the pillow. Her hands found Ari's waist under the blanket and pulled her closer.

"C'mere."

"It's a little early to go to sleep," Ari said, although she sounded like she was just pointing out a fact rather than complaining.

Dale said, "So we'll just lay here for a while."

Ari nodded. "I like that plan. I wasn't doing anything anyway."

Dale kissed the corners of Ari's mouth, her cheeks, her nose, and chin.

"Tell me a story."

Ari searched her memory for something, anything, but it was a blank. She couldn't even think of a movie or TV show she could recount. Then she realized the perfect story.

"Once upon a time, there was a woman named Vivian Burroughs. Her goal in life was to continue her family legacy. She had four children~"

"Wait," Dale said, touching Ari's cheek with two fingers. "Does this have a happy ending?"

Ari smiled. "Yeah, Dale. This story has a very happy ending."

"Okay," Dale said, relaxing again. "Carry on."

"Vivian Burroughs had four children... and a tapestry called Crossing-Over Place..."

ABOUT THE AUTHOR

Geonn Cannon lives in Oklahoma. He is the author of several novels, including the Riley Parra series which is currently being produced as a webseries for Tello Films, and two official Stargate SG-1 tie-in novels. Information about his other novels and an archive of free stories can be found online at geonncannon.com.

"Riley Parra is a strong, badass heroine for those that like their coffee and their cop fiction bitter." - P Industry

No Man's Land isn't the kind of place you go after dark, even if you have a badge. But Detective Riley Parra was born there, and she refuses to surrender it to the drug dealers, killers and criminals who have made it there home. The case of a body stuffed into a drainage pipe leads her to discover that there is far more at stake than she ever imagined.

~ **Riley Parra, Season One.**

"Cannon's prose is beautiful. This isn't the most plot-filled of his novels but highlights the splendour of everyday life that it's so easy to take for granted. It's there to remind us that love can sometimes happen, not at first sight, but through the captivation and enmeshment that comes from truly listening and being heard by someone out of reach." - Jo at **Goodreads**

For the next two years, Colonel Noa Laurie - the sole survivor of a disaster which destroyed the International Space Station - will be orbiting Earth in an experimental craft called ODIE. Her mission: to clear away the treacherous minefield of space junk that has accumulated around the planet and endangers future missions. Her only lifeline during this mission will be the radio connecting her to the command center and whoever happens to be assigned to the communications desk.

Or so she thinks.

Because tucked away and almost forgotten in an Indiana woodshop is an antique radio. Its owner, Jamie Faris, occasionally uses it for eavesdropping on the truckers passing by on the highway. One day in the third month of Noa's mission, Jamie uses the radio to vent her frustrations by screaming into the ether. She screams and rages and curses into the thick static knowing it won't matter because no one will hear, but she's wrong... someone is definitely listening.

And she's about to say hello.

~ **Can You Hear Me**